"What are we doing?"* Sarah asked. *Her voice was barely a whisper.

Evan's hand paused at her elbow, palm curling around it.

Her nerves tightened.

He looked at her. "Something I've wanted to do for a long time," Evan murmured.

And he lowered his head, covering her mouth with his. His lips grazed hers, barely a whisper. One that sounded through her like a full-bodied orchestra.

Her mouth opened under his, her hands dragging through his hair. She couldn't get enough, couldn't get close enough, and he must have felt the same for his hands dragged down her spine, caught her waist, and she felt her feet leave the ground as he lifted her higher.

She gasped, and still he kissed her. Deeper. Hotter. Her mind spun.

Evan had kissed her once. A long time ago.

This was nothing like it.

This was not like an

Dear Reader,

Children have a way of growing up, don't they?

I know this personally because my youngest began college this year. I know this professionally because readers are often asking me what is going on in Weaver, Wyoming, with that Clay clan.

Evidently, it is time for us all to find out!

While writing *Just Friends?* there were days I wasn't sure which was more difficult to accept—that my own college-bound baby wasn't quite a baby any longer, or that the child of my very first hero and heroine was even more grown-up.

Jefferson Clay and Emily Nichols hold a special place in my heart. They were the beginning of a fantastic journey for the MEN OF THE DOUBLE-C RANCH. And as with my own family, I've nurtured, fretted and rejoiced with nearly equal measure over each member of that family. Facing Jefferson and Emily's adult daughter seemed, at times, a daunting task. But like all things "family" in my life, the task has been more than worth the effort.

Now I hope you'll embrace this new generation of Double-C women and men as wonderfully as you did their parents.

All my best,

Allison

JUST FRIENDS?

ALLISON LEIGH

SPECIAL EDITION®

Published by Silhouette Books

America's Publisher of Contemporary Romance

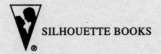 SILHOUETTE BOOKS

ISBN-13: 978-0-373-24810-0
ISBN-10:   0-373-24810-5

JUST FRIENDS?

Printed in U.S.A.

Books by Allison Leigh

Silhouette Special Edition

*Stay... #1170
*The Rancher and the
   Redhead #1212
*A Wedding for Maggie #1241
*A Child for Christmas #1290
Millionaire's Instant Baby #1312
*Married to a Stranger #1336
Mother in a Moment #1367
Her Unforgettable Fiancé #1381
The Princess and the Duke #1465
Montana Lawman #1497
Hard Choices #1561
Secretly Married #1591

Home on the Ranch #1633
The Truth About the Tycoon #1651
All He Ever Wanted #1664
The Tycoon's Marriage Bid #1707
A Montana Homecoming #1718
Mergers & Matrimony #1761
*Just Friends? #1810

*Return to the Double-C Ranch

ALLISON LEIGH

started early by writing a Halloween play that her grade-school class performed. Since then, though her tastes have changed, her love for reading has not. And her writing appetite simply grows more voracious by the day.

She has been a finalist in the RITA® Award and the Holt Medallion contests. But the true highlights of her day as a writer are when she receives word from a reader that they laughed, cried or lost a night of sleep while reading one of her books.

Born in Southern California, Allison has lived in several different cities in four different states. She has been, at one time or another, a cosmetologist, a computer programmer and a secretary. She currently makes her home in Arizona with her family. She loves to hear from her readers, who can write to her at P.O. Box 40772, Mesa, AZ 85274-0772.

For my family.

Prologue

It didn't turn out at all the way Evan had intended.

When it started out, it was just supposed to be a quick trip home during a break between classes. He'd known she'd be home, too, because he'd made a point of finding out. Subtly, of course. It had never paid to show one's cards too easily where Leandra Clay was concerned. She was too quick. Too smart.

Too…everything.

Fool that he was, though, in his determination to appear *any*thing but obvious, he'd invited his dorm-mate.

Jake sure in hell hadn't worried about being subtle.

One look at Leandra and he'd been a goner.

Evan's fault. If he'd told Jake he'd already staked out that territory, his buddy wouldn't have trespassed.

Problem was, Leandra hadn't been Evan's territory. *Never* had been.

So what had Evan done?

Nothing.

And now what was Evan doing?

Nothing.

Nothing except stand there in his suit and a tie that felt like it was strangling him, and lift his champagne glass the way all the other wedding guests were lifting theirs.

"To the bride and groom," he managed to say. "We wish them a lifetime of happiness."

Jake wore a tux, too, and Leandra looked like some princess out of a storybook in filmy white stuff from head to toe. Their arms were slung around each other, giddy grins on their faces.

They'd hardly let go of each other in the year since Evan had introduced them.

The couple drank to the toast, and to the others that followed, kissed softly, sweetly, and Evan turned away, downing the rest of his champagne. But no amount of alcohol was going to deaden the pain inside him.

He hadn't spoken his piece when he should have.

"Hey, you." Leandra had untangled herself from Jake and touched Evan's arm. "Don't go running off now. You've got to promise me a dance after Jake and I do our thing."

He had to steel himself against flinching. "I was just going to find more of your dad's fine bubbly."

Her gaze, as rich as the fudge pudding Evan's mom had made since his childhood, was sparkling and that sparkle was all for her brand-spanking-new husband. "I'm not sure I ever said thank you. You know. For introducing Jake and me. If it hadn't been for you, we'd have never met."

"What are friends for?"

She missed the dark note in his voice. Nothing in her world right now was dark.

She was Leandra Clay and she'd just married the man of her dreams.

She suddenly reached out and hugged him. A quick dip into sweet perfume and soft, rustling white gown. "Thanks." Then she was moving away again, heading back to Jake, never knowing that she was taking Evan's heart along with her.

No, things definitely hadn't turned out at all the way he'd planned.

Chapter One

He woke to the sight of a strange man standing in his bedroom.

"Son of a—" Evan Taggart sat bolt upright, grabbing the bedding around his waist even as realization hit that the young guy with the lumberjack's build wasn't *entirely* a stranger. Nor was the red eye of the television camera the guy held entirely a surprise, either.

He stifled the ripe curse on his lips just in time to keep it from being captured for all eternity—or at least the viewing life of a certain cable television reality show. "I've never been video-taped in bed, with a woman or without, Ted," he said grimly, "and I'll be damned if we're going to start here and now."

Ted Richard's grin was visible thanks to the annoying light he'd erected on a metal stand next to the bed, but he still didn't lower the camera. "The producer would be a lot happier if you *did* have a woman under those sheets. Marian would figure it'd be good for ratings."

Evan wasn't amused. "How did you get in here?"

"Leandra always says Weaver is so safe that nobody ever locks anything. Guess she was right."

Leandra.

Evan should have known. He squelched another oath, this time directed at Leandra Clay and her part in the farce his life seemed to have become over the past week. "Shut that thing off," he warned. If he hadn't been out nearly all night tending a sick bull, he would never have slept through an intrusion like Ted's.

Not that this particular situation had ever arisen before.

Ted still didn't lower the heavy camera from his shoulder. The distinctive red light on top of the thing stayed vividly bright. "Don't shoot the messenger, dude," he said easily. "I'm just doing my job."

Ted's *job* was to follow Evan Taggart around for six weeks for *Walk in the Shoes,* or *WITS,* the cable television show of which Leandra was an associate producer. "Nobody told me your job was to invade *all* of my privacy."

Ted still didn't seem fazed. Nor did the young guy seem inclined to turn off the camera. But he did turn his shaggy blond head when they heard the sound of footsteps on the stairs outside Evan's bedroom.

A moment later, the woman responsible for Evan's headaches of late practically skidded into the room. He got a glimpse of chocolate-brown eyes before Leandra turned her attention to her cameraman.

"Ted, turn off the camera. You shouldn't even be here." She hefted the enormous satchel that hung from her shoulder a little higher and raced a slender hand over her short, messy hair.

Evan grimaced when the cameraman obediently lowered the camera.

"I'll just go back to the motel and catch a few more *z's,*" Ted said cheerfully. "Any changes to today's schedule?"

Evan caught Leandra's gaze skittering over him before she shook her head and stepped out of Ted's way. "Not yet. I'll see you later."

Ted nodded and took the heavy camera, his steps pounding far more loudly on the stairs than had Leandra's. A moment later, they heard the sound of a door slamming.

Evan raked his hands through his hair, wishing he'd gotten more than the two measly hours of sleep he'd snagged. He needed all of his wits about him when it came to dealing with Leandra.

Leandra, who was still standing there in his bedroom, twisted her hands together at her waist. "Sorry about that," she murmured.

For what? Bringing chaos to what was ordinarily a pretty peaceful life? Peaceful, just the way he liked it.

"I didn't send him." Apology turned down the corners of her soft lips. "And I came as soon as I knew he was here," she added. As if that made up for everything.

Peaceful, he thought. Whatever had happened to it?

He'd grown up around Leandra. *And* her siblings. *And* her cousins, and there were plenty of 'em. But what on God's green earth had he done wrong that every time he laid eyes on this particular Clay he felt a jolt?

Bad enough she'd once been married to one of his best friends.

Bad enough she'd chosen Jake over Evan in the first place.

"Well?" Her chin had come up. "Aren't you going to say something?"

She wore loose flannel pants covered in cartoon chickens and a pink long-sleeved T-shirt with *WITS* printed over her breasts. The shirt did nothing to hide the fact that the woman was graced with all the appropriate curves. A woman who looked as if she'd bolted from her bed almost as precipitously as Evan. If she hadn't, she'd have grabbed a jacket, at the very least.

He didn't need the evidence staring him in the face to know it was pretty damn chilly outside.

It was September. It was Wyoming. It was four bloody o'clock in the morning, and he had Leandra Clay's sexy body smiling at him through her shirt.

"I've never seen chickens wearing bunny slippers," he finally drawled. "That the style out in California these days?"

Her lips pressed together. "That's not what I meant."

He was sure it hadn't been.

And he was pleased with the tinge of red he could see in her cheeks as she turned off the blazing lamp that Ted had left behind.

Made him feel a little better at least.

Now he just needed to get her out of his bedroom.

Because it *was* 4:00 a.m. and she *was* Leandra Clay.

He grabbed the sheet and started to slide off the bed.

At the first sight of his bare legs, Leandra frowned and abruptly headed for the doorway. "I'll, um, I'll put on some coffee."

He grunted. At least that would be something useful.

She glanced back at him and he dragged the sheet around himself, managing not to bare his butt to her eyes.

She fled, her footsteps racing down the staircase.

If he'd needed any hint that Leandra wasn't the least bit interested in seeing his butt, he supposed he had it now.

He dropped the sheet back on the messy bed and went into the bathroom, slamming the door shut.

How in the hell had his life come to this?

The question required no searching thought when the simple answer was right downstairs putting on the brew.

He rummaged in the small pile of laundry he'd kicked into

the bathroom the other day to keep the mess from being caught on tape. His clothes smelled of God-knew-what, but he pulled them on anyway, then went downstairs to face Leandra and her coffee.

But when he got there, the coffeepot still sat piteously empty.

"Thought you were putting on the java."

"I was. Am." She closed the refrigerator door with a soft rattle of bottles. "I can't find the coffee."

He opened the cupboard above the maker and pulled out the can. "Suppose you're used to some fancy brand you grind yourself."

She made a face but didn't answer. Which probably was her answer.

Evan knew good and well that Jake—his good buddy Jake—liked his coffee expensive and ground only moments before it was brewed.

Why would Jake's wife be any different?

Ex-wife, an internal voice reminded him. For all the good it did.

Evan was a fool. That's what he was. Pure and simple.

And God didn't protect fools by the name of Evan Taggart.

Punishment was the course, there. Punishment in the form of a golden-haired wisp whom he still didn't have the good sense to say no to.

Now that sprite in question was eyeing him through the brown eyes that had always seemed too large for her heart-shaped face.

He dumped his simple, grocery-bought coffee into a fresh filter and shoved it into the coffeemaker. "You going to drink some of this?"

"If you're offering."

He pulled out the filter, added another scoop of ground coffee, and pushed it back in place. Before he could reach for the empty coffee carafe, she'd plucked it out of the sink and was rinsing and refilling it with water.

Their fingers brushed when she handed it to him.

He sloshed the water into the machine and hit the power button, not looking at her. A reassuring gurgle answered him. "I'm grabbing a shower before that peeping Tom comes back."

"Ted's not a pervert," she called after him as he practically bolted from the room. "He's doing what Marian told him to do."

"Then maybe Marian's the one who's twisted," Evan called back, heading up the stairs.

What had he been thinking when he'd agreed to be part of that stupid show?

What had she been thinking to approach Evan Taggart about *WITS*?

Leandra pushed her fingers through her hair, pressing the tips against her skull as if the pressure could relieve the throbbing ache inside. She'd figured that following the life of a good-looking veterinarian would be just the ticket for the show that had been her home for the past eighteen months. She'd *figured* that veterinarian would be her ex-husband, Jake Stallings, who, despite their divorced status, was usually willing to do most anything that Leandra asked of him.

Jake was everything that her boss, Marian Hughes, loved. Charismatic. Handsome. A veterinarian to a whole host of pampered celebrity pets.

But for reasons known only to Jake, he'd refused her request and reminded her instead about his friend from college.

Evan Taggart.

Evan, who wasn't *only* Jake's old friend, considering Leandra had known him since they were tots. He'd been as much a thorn in Leandra's youth as he had been a friend, and he was the one who'd introduced Leandra to Jake when he'd brought his college mate home one weekend.

Huffing out a breath, remembering that she hadn't even brushed her teeth when she'd made her mad dash over to Evan's, she went to her purse and rummaged inside for her cosmetic case.

She could hear water rumbling in the old horse's pipes and tried not to think too much about Evan upstairs in his shower.

It was bad enough to have seen him upstairs covered to the waist in a rumpled sheet.

She'd found herself wondering just what he'd had *under* that sheet. That, in itself was pretty darned disturbing.

She shook her head, trying to eradicate the image and yanked open the little case. She found her travel toothbrush and squirted toothpaste on it, then brushed her teeth at the kitchen sink, washed her face and streaked some water through her hair.

She had a pair of jeans and a shirt inside her bag, too, but she wasn't going to change into them until she'd had her *own* shower.

Which she would have back at her cousin Sarah's place, where she was staying for the duration of the *WITS* shoot.

She certainly wasn't going to ask Evan if she could cop a soak in his bathroom. The man had made it more than plain that he considered every moment they spent together an intrusion in his life.

She still wasn't certain what had made him agree to participate in the first place. Sure, they were friends from way back, and he and Jake were still buddies, but Evan's consent had been a surprise to her. A pleasant surprise, even. That is, until she'd arrived with her crew the week before and came face-to-face with how disagreeable Evan could be—disagreeable and disturbing.

But she was pretty desperate to have this shoot go well. If

it did—no, *once* it did—she'd finally get out from under Marian's thumb and produce her *own* projects. And they wouldn't involve any shirtless hometown veterinarians, either.

The pipes overhead gave an ominous groan. Leandra looked up at the ceiling, half expecting the pipes to burst right then and there. But the ceiling—plain white with not a speck of dirt or a cobweb in sight—remained intact until the demand ceased and the pipes went silent. Rather than be caught gawking at Evan's spotlessly clean white walls, she hurriedly rummaged around in his refrigerator and cupboards and had the makings of breakfast well underway when he came back downstairs a while later.

"Smells good." He walked across to the waiting coffee.

She wasn't sure if he meant his coffee or the bacon and eggs. "Mmm." She flipped the omelet with a toss of the pan and picked up her own mug of coffee, watching him over the rim.

At least he'd put on a shirt, even if it was just a white T-shirt that hugged every muscle from which good genes and an active lifestyle had graced him.

His jeans looked the same as the other pair he'd just had on. Except this pair was clean.

When it came down to it, all of Evan Taggart's jeans looked pretty much the same.

Well-worn and sexy as hell on him.

Drat it all.

She buried her nose a little deeper in her coffee mug and reached for the spatula again.

Now was not the time for her libido to kick back to life after years of lying unconscious.

As far as Leandra was concerned, she preferred the unconscious state. Life was a lot less complicated that way.

She tipped the omelet onto a plate, drizzled hollandaise over it, then added toast and several slices of bacon and held it out to him.

He stared at the plate as if he'd never before focused those brilliant blue eyes of his on such a thing. "Jake always said you weren't much one for cooking."

"Is that going to keep you from eating it?" She gently waggled the plate. "It's only bacon and eggs."

"Fancy eggs." He lifted the plate out of her hand and set it on the square oak table that he'd shoved against one wall of the kitchen. Presumably to make room for the modern playpen that took up a good portion of the center of the kitchen. The playpen was currently empty, but Leandra knew it was for babies that weren't of the human variety. A few days earlier, it had contained a lamb. "You made enough for yourself, I hope," he added when she just stood there like a bump.

Spurred, she began dishing up her own plate. "Girl's gotta eat." She settled herself across the table from him. "Hope you don't mind that I made myself at home."

The corner of his lips twitched. He angled a look at her from beneath long eyelashes that were practically pornographic. "I'm eating, aren't I?"

He certainly was.

She watched him bite off a corner of toast and looked down at her own plate. Who needed a jacket in September when she was steaming from the inside out? She gulped down a mouthful of coffee and coughed at the intense heat.

"You okay?"

"Fine," she lied a little hoarsely. "And I *am* sorry about Ted busting in on you this morning. If that had been on Marian's schedule, I'd have talked her out of it."

"Marian's *your* boss. How would you plan to do that?"

"The same way I've talked her out of a few other ideas. How long was Ted here filming you?"

"Long enough to be satisfied when he left."

Leandra couldn't deny the truth of that. The guy had been

perfectly agreeable about leaving. Which could mean that he'd gotten whatever shots Marian had been after. "At least you were alone."

He gave her a measuring look. "Oh?"

She was appalled at the way her stomach dropped. She hadn't stopped to consider the fact that Ted had clearly been filming for more than a few seconds. Had Evan had company who'd absented herself before Leandra came riding to her supposed rescue? "*Weren't* you?"

His expression didn't change and her nerves tightened even more. "Yes," he finally said. "The only ones upstairs who didn't belong there were you and your cameraman. And a helluva sight he was to wake up to. So how *did* you know he was here?"

Relief loosened her tongue. "Marian told me when we were speaking this morning."

"You talk to your boss before four every morning?" He made it sound like an accusation.

"I do when she's calling from the East Coast, where she's filming another project, and is a few hours ahead of me."

"That why you're still in your pajamas? You jump out of bed to come rescue me, Leandra?"

Her cheeks went hot again. The truth of it was, once she'd heard that Marian had set Ted, unscheduled, upon Evan, she had pictured just that. Which was ridiculous. "You're the least rescue-needing man I know," she said truthfully. "And this outfit doesn't have to be pajamas. It's pants and a shirt."

"Right."

She decided not to argue the point. After all, she *was* sitting there in her pj's.

"So, where *did* you learn to cook? I know it wasn't at your mother's knee. I remember Emily moaning about the fact that you were always too antsy to stand still long enough to listen to anything that concerned the kitchen."

"There's the problem working with someone you knew while growing up." She wasn't exactly thrilled with the notion that Evan knew so much about her.

"Well, if I hadn't known you growing up, do you think I'd have agreed to this damn situation?" He raked his hair back with long fingers. The short strands were still damp from his shower, and they stood out in gleaming blue-black spikes. "Tell me again why this show is so important to you?"

"All of the stories we've done for *WITS* are important to me."

His sharp focus didn't budge from her face.

"Well, okay, the series focusing on you is a little more important. Do you have to debate every single thing I say?"

"Not *every* thing. The breakfast was good."

"Small mercies," she murmured.

"Which you didn't explain, by the way."

"Nuking bacon and tossing together an omelet doesn't require an advanced degree."

He dragged his toast through the hollandaise sauce. "This sauce stuff didn't come out of a mix."

She shrugged. "Just more butter and eggs and a little lemon juice. No big deal. What's with all the lemons you have in your fridge, anyway?"

"My folks shipped them back while on vacation in Florida. And no changing the subject."

"I learned a few tricks when I was in France."

He went still for a moment.

France. Where she and Jake had gone on their honeymoon. And where Leandra had returned four years ago after their divorce. After they'd lost Emi.

Fortunately, Evan broke the tight silence when Leandra found herself unable to do so.

"Guess if you're going to finally learn to cook, France is one place to do it."

"I didn't take a class. I just picked up a few things from Eduard."

Evan's eyebrows rose. "Ed-wa-ahrd?"

"Don't give me that look."

"What look? You're a grown woman, Leandra. Free to take up with some French guy if you so please."

She rose, gathering their plates to take to the sink. She wished she'd never brought up the topic of France.

"Does Jake know you met some guy over there?"

The plates clattered against the sink as she set them down. She flipped on the water and it splashed hard against the dishes, spattering the front of her T-shirt. "There's nothing for Jake to know. We're divorced, remember? We have been for several years now."

"Yet you still went to him about doing this show before you came to me."

Her nerves felt like a match had been lit against them. It'd never been a secret that Evan hadn't been her first choice where *WITS* was concerned. "What's the matter, Evan? Feeling second-best?"

It didn't matter that Evan's one-time crush on her felt about a million years ago; not when it had been inspired just because he'd been fighting with his girlfriend—who'd happened to be her cousin, Lucy. Leandra still felt catty the moment the words left her lips.

He didn't look fazed, though, when he leaned his hip against the wood cabinet about a foot closer to her than was comfortable. "I guess if either one of us were worried about that, we wouldn't be here, now would we." His deep voice was smooth. Friendly. Easy.

Yet…not.

She frowned, feeling off-kilter. And she didn't know why. Evan had never been serious about her despite that one time when he'd claimed otherwise. He'd been too busy being in love with her cousin. Only Lucy had gone on to New York after high school for a career in dance, and Evan had never been serious about anyone since.

Particularly in college when, according to Jake, Evan had become a complete love-'em-and-leave-'em kind of man.

"I'll take your silence as agreement with me," he said after a moment. He reached past her and shut off the water, his arm brushing her shoulder as he did so.

She barely managed to keep from jumping out of her skin. "I'm not worried about a single thing," she assured him.

His lashes drooped for a moment, as if he were studying something. "Good. Thanks for breakfast."

Then he handed her the dishtowel that was folded over a knob, and walked out of the kitchen.

Leandra squeezed the towel between her hands and tried to ignore the unfathomable shivers that were sliding down her spine.

What *had* she been thinking?

Chapter Two

The sun had still not quite risen when Leandra returned to Sarah's place. The little house was located in the center of Weaver, across from a park and the high school. The bungalow had been home to Leandra's various aunts, and now Leandra's cousin called it hers.

Not until now, though, had Leandra ever appreciated the charm in the little place.

No, she'd been too busy wanting to get *out* of Weaver to understand some of the nicer aspects of her hometown.

She parked behind the house near the garage and let herself in the back door. Like Evan's place, it opened right into the kitchen and again, like Evan's, it was as unlocked as it had been when Leandra had bolted out of it earlier.

She tried to be quiet as she dumped her purse in the second bedroom and padded into the single bathroom, where she flipped on the shower and waited for the hot water to steam up the small room. She felt cold to the bone.

She hadn't exactly dressed for a cold morning trek over to Evan's, after all. *That* was why she still felt haphazard shivers attacking her.

No way were they caused by Evan Taggart himself.

She stepped under the streaming water, nearly groaning with relief as the hot needles stung her skin.

"I thought I heard you leave already." Sarah's voice rose above the rush of water, breaking through Leandra's dazed heat-giddiness.

Leandra looked around the tastefully striped shower curtain to see her cousin peeking around the corner of the door. "I did. I'll just be a sec. I know you need to get ready for school."

Sarah pushed the door open farther and entered. "Sorry," she said as she flipped on the faucet and reached for her toothbrush. "Have a parent meeting before school this morning. Time's tighter than usual."

Leandra ducked back under the shower, which ran even hotter now that Sarah was using some cold water, and rinsed the shampoo out of her hair. "I'm the one who should be sorry. I could have stayed at the motel with the rest of the crew and not put you out."

"You are *not* putting me out." Sarah's voice was muffled by the toothbrush. "Idiot."

Leandra made a face and hurried through the motions. When she turned off the shower, Sarah tossed her a thick towel over the shower curtain. Leandra quickly toweled off and wrapped it around herself, then stepped out so her cousin could take over occupancy. "All yours."

"Where *were* you earlier, anyway?" Sarah reached beyond the curtain and turned the water back on.

"Evan's." She dragged her fingers through her hair.

"In the middle of the night?" Sarah looked amused. "Anything you need to confess to Auntie Sarah?"

Leandra just shook her head as she left the bathroom. "I'll put coffee on if you've got the time to drink it."

"I always have time for coffee." Sarah's voice followed her down the short hall.

Sarah was a Clay, too. For the most part, the Clays were all inveterate coffee drinkers.

Leandra quickly dressed and started the coffee. The grind-your-own-beans kind that she'd sent Sarah the Christmas before. There was a half pot brewed by the time Sarah entered the kitchen. Her long, strawberry-blond hair was twisted into a thick wet braid that roped down to the middle of her back. She wore a loose-fitting knitted beige sweater over an ankle-length red skirt and looked exactly like what she was—a somewhat prim elementary school teacher.

Only Leandra knew her cousin wasn't *all* prim and proper. They'd been thick as thieves while growing up, after all. "Here." She handed Sarah a tall travel mug filled with black coffee.

"Thanks." She took a sip, winced a little, and set the mug on the small kitchen table. "So, what was the deal with Evan? He trying to back out of the show?"

"He might hate every minute, but I'm not worried about him doing that. It's been a long time since I moved away from Weaver, but I doubt Evan has changed in *that* regard. Particularly when the first episode airs in a few days."

"True. He's generally a reliable guy. But in what other regard is he supposed to have changed?"

Leandra shrugged. "None."

Sarah looked skeptical, but she didn't pursue the point. "So, you're still going to be free tonight for supper, right? Family is all meeting at Colbys to talk about Squire's surprise party."

Squire Clay was their grandfather. "Friday night at Colbys. Wouldn't miss it for the world."

"Good. You've been so busy with the shoot since you arrived that hardly any of us have had a chance to sit down for long and visit with you." She grinned as she tossed a jacket around her shoulders and grabbed up her satchel. "Everyone's been bugging me to fill them in on all your latest, and I had to break their hearts by telling them there *has* been no latest, even for me."

Leandra felt a quick knot in her stomach. Not even with Sarah had Leandra been able to share everything over the past several years.

Not since Emi had died.

How could she? Sarah—nobody—could ever understand just what Leandra had endured.

Endured because of her own failings.

"I'll be there," she promised. "After spending a day shooting with Evan and my crew, I'll be *more* than ready to sit back and chill for a while."

"Well, I promise we won't make it too late of a night."

Leandra smiled faintly. "There was a time when late nights didn't stop us."

Sarah's light blue eyes twinkled. "True. But right now, you look like you need about twenty hours of sleep, my friend. And those days when we could play all night have passed me by. Too old, I'm afraid."

"Old? Please. We're only twenty-eight. I can still hold my own, even against Axel and Derek."

"I seriously doubt it. Particularly where Axel is concerned. I know he's your little brother and Derek is mine, but even *he* has said that Axel can wear him out. And they're the same age." She glanced at the round clock on the wall. "Gotta run. Hope things go well today."

Leandra hadn't even gotten her "thanks" out, before Sarah had hurried out the door.

She exhaled, her gaze slipping around the confines of the kitchen. Currently, it was painted in muted green tones. There were pretty pale yellow canisters lined neatly on the counter, matched in color by the placemats on the table and the woven towel draped over the oven door latch. The only mishmash of anything was the collection of photographs sticking to the front of the off-white refrigerator door.

She hadn't looked closely at Sarah's collection before. Hadn't dared.

She still didn't really want to look but, for some reason, her feet inexorably closed the distance until she was standing only inches away. Her heart was in her throat. Nausea twisted at her insides. She felt hot and cold all at once as she looked.

Her mind automatically dismissed the tiny snapshots that were distinctly school photographs. Sarah's students, undoubtedly. And she really didn't pay much attention to the assortment of milestones marked by someone's trusty camera.

But the more she looked, the more she'd convinced herself that she did *not* want to see that beautiful, perfect face, the more she realized that the one face that was *not* captured here was the one face Leandra most wanted to see.

Her daughter's. Emi.

Eyes burning deep inside her head, Leandra turned away. She felt shaky and her stomach pitched even more turbulently.

Sarah had removed Emi's photographs.

There was no doubt in Leandra's mind that her cousin's refrigerator door had once been graced with many pictures of Emi.

Emi's birth had marked the beginning of the family's next generation. There had been dozens of pictures. Leandra had sent them herself. Taken them herself.

Her heart ached and she bolted for the bathroom, overwhelmed by nausea. But even after, huddling on the cool tile floor with a washcloth pressed to her face, there was no peace for her.

Coming home to Weaver, no matter how temporarily, was only making the pain inside her worse.

When she heard the distinctive ring of her cell phone from the kitchen, she dragged herself off the floor. There was only one caller programmed into her cell phone with that particular ring tone.

Beethoven's Fifth.

It had been Ted's idea of a joke when he'd been messing around with Leandra's latest cell phone to link the dramatic tune to their boss's phone number. Leandra hadn't had a chance to figure out how to change it. Given her propensity for losing cell phones at the rate of two or three per year, was it any wonder that she didn't sit down with the programming guide every time?

She made it to the kitchen and wearily pulled out one of the chairs as she flipped open her latest phone. "What's up, Marian?"

"Have you talked to that vet of yours yet about our problem?"

A fresh pain crept between Leandra's eyes. Only this pain, at least, was not one that tore her soul to shreds. "I don't consider Evan's love life our problem, Marian. That's not the focus of *WITS*. Remember?" Her tone went a little dry. "We're presenting his life as a veterinarian."

"Hon, if that were all we were doing, we'd call *WITS* a documentary. Not reality TV."

The only reason Marian wanted to call her show *reality TV* was because it sounded more contemporary. More appealing than a documentary series to her all-important demographic—women aged 24-35. The fact that *Walk in the Shoes* had been just that—a small, but relatively well-respected documentary series about people and the careers they chose—before

Marian came on board over a year earlier was obviously unimportant to all but a few.

And arguing the point had been getting Leandra absolutely nowhere. "I'll see what I can find out." She crossed her fingers beneath the table. Childish, perhaps, but the best she could do for her conscience.

"Don't just *see,* Leandra. *Do.* This guy you found may be eye candy, but sweets only go so far. I want spice!" Marian's voice rose. "Either you find it for me, or I'll find someone who will." Marian let out a huge breath. "Now," she said more reasonably and Leandra could picture her sitting there, smiling through her big white teeth. "Are we on the same page here?"

Leandra grimaced. "I understand your page perfectly, Marian. Unless there's something else, I need to get on with it. We'll be taping again in a few hours."

"Fine. But don't forget. Spice, Leandra, *spice.*"

Leandra hung up her phone and shoved it in her purse. "Spice," she muttered. No doubt the reason why Marian had sent Ted unannounced into Evan's house that morning. A quest for *spice.*

"Artificial insemination. Ought to look sexier than it is."

Leandra frowned at Ted. It was late afternoon and they'd been taping since midmorning. It was a toss-up who was more tired. Leandra and her crew set up on the outside of a small arena, or Evan and his, working with a showy black horse on the inside.

"Breeding horses is not just a business. There's an art to it." She kept her voice low, not wanting to add any more disruption to the day's already frustrating attempts. "And the insemination isn't happening right now, anyway."

"No, they have to get that black horse to shoot his—"

"Yes," Leandra cut him off. She'd been listening to jokes about the semen collection process long enough.

"Well, I guess you'd know all about it, growing up here."

Here was Clay Farm, the horse ranch that her father had founded when he and her mother had been newly married. "Mmm-hmm." She kept finding herself more distracted by the action they were trying to film than by her duties behind the scene. More specifically, she was more distracted watching *Evan.*

It was ridiculous, really. The man stood the same height as her own father, Jefferson, who was working alongside Evan. He wore similar clothing—dusty blue jeans and a T-shirt. His short black hair was slightly disheveled and there was definitely a hint of a five-o'clock shadow darkening his jaw—and it was only around two in the afternoon.

What was it about the guy that was so intriguing?

"Earth to Leandra."

She moistened her lips, dragging her gaze from Evan to focus on Ted. "What?"

"I asked if you'd ever done that to a horse?"

"Only a stallion," Leandra reminded wryly, ignoring her cameraman's suggestive tone, "and, yes, I've helped collect semen before. And before you start making comments, it's *business.* Big business. Do you know how high stud fees can run for a really impeccable pedigree?"

It was a moot question, since they'd been talking about such matters most of the day. Northern Light had yet to prove himself at stud, but his sire had commanded stud fees in the six figures. "They're having some problems with Northern Light there because he's never been ground collected before. He's inexperienced."

"Inexperienced?" Ted grinned slightly. "I'll bet it's more like he wants a warm body to snuggle up to instead of that cold tube thing Evan's holding."

"It's called an A.V.—an artificial vagina. Oh, heads-up,"

Leandra warned. "Howard is bringing out the mare again to tease Northern Light."

Ted trained the camera again on the group of men surrounding the stallion and started filming. Leandra stepped slightly away, watching Northern Light's reaction to the mare. His ears perked. The horse's gleaming black coat twitched. His tail swished.

Bingo, Leandra thought, smiling to herself as the horse tried to lunge forward against the teasing rail, wanting to get at the mare.

Her father, at Northern Light's head, kept the stallion from getting light in the front, making the horse resist his natural urge to rear up and mount something. Preferably the mare that had clearly, finally, spurred the young stud's libido.

Even Ted jumped a little at Northern Light's sudden interest, and in Leandra's memory, there were few occasions that managed to startle the cameraman. But, she was pleased to note, the camera didn't waver.

A nervous hand tugged at Leandra's elbow from behind. Janet Stewart, another crew member, was frowning mightily, looking worried about the sight of the half ton of horse flesh seeming to struggle against his handlers. The girl put her mouth close to Leandra's ear. This was only her second shoot, but so far Leandra had been pleased with the quiet girl's work. "The horse can't hurt the men, can he?" she whispered.

Leandra shrugged. The truth was, a stallion could crush a man if he chose. But she'd grown up around horses. She knew her father's capacity to handle the animals. He might be in his 60s now, but he was fitter than many men half his age. And she knew Evan's capacity equaled her dad's.

Evan, who happened to glance their way as Northern Light gave another thwarted lunge. The gleaming black tail spiked and they could all hear the horse's breath streaming from his nostrils.

Janet drew in a hissing breath. "Ee-uu-ww. Is he going to, uh—?"

Leandra frowned, putting her finger to her lips, silently hushing her. The answer to her production assistant's half-formed question was clear in the satisfied actions of the men as Northern Light's interest subsided in the mare still standing safely some distance away.

Howard, her father's oldest ranch hand, took away the collection tube carrying Northern Light's soon-to-be-pricey contribution to the breeding process. Leandra knew this particular specimen would only be used for analyzing. Leandra's father led Northern Light back into the shadowy interior of the barn, where he'd be closed in his stall with fresh feed and water until his next encounter with the A.V.

Evan's presence wasn't ordinarily required at such proceedings, but since he and Axel were co-owners of the stallion, he had a vested interest. As he headed toward them, his gait was loose-hipped and easy and in Leandra's mind, she envisioned the slo-mo and music that could accompany the movement once they put the piece together.

Eye candy, exactly as Marian had said. Oh, yes. Definitely eye candy.

"You realize that Northern Light was distracted by all of you over here." Evan directed his irritation straight at Leandra. "What took most of the day should have been accomplished in a third of the time. It's a wonder that Jefferson allowed you to even tape here today."

"I guess that's one of the perks about being the boss's only daughter." Her voice was as cool as his. She didn't appreciate the lecture, particularly when she was very much aware of the delay they'd caused.

Evan's lips thinned. He glanced at the camera. "I suppose you're still filming."

"That was the agreement, remember?" Despite that very fact, Leandra stepped closer to Evan. "Our crew follows your daily activities for a month and a half. How else can our viewers expect to *walk in your shoes?*"

"With boots," he drawled. "And I remember the agreement. Doesn't mean I have to love it. Definitely doesn't mean I appreciate extending that inconvenience to my *clients*. And daddy of yours or not, Jefferson Clay is one of my best clients. We're planning to breed one of his mares to Northern Light, and I'd still like him to stay one of my best clients even after you've taken your sweet tush off onto your next escapade."

"Cut," Leandra told Ted, barely managing to get the word through her clenched teeth. "Janet, you and Ted go over to the lab where Howard's working and catch what you can. There's quite a bit of science involved in this. You never know what might come in useful." She could feel her phone vibrating silently at her hip, where it was clipped to her pocket, but ignored it. She didn't have to guess hard to figure it was Marian. "Then we'll take a stroll through the horse barn and call it a day."

The idea of ending shooting even an hour early clearly appealed to Janet. Leandra knew she and Paul Haas, the other crew member, were planning to drive down to Cheyenne for the weekend. Both in their midtwenties, they figured their free time would be a little more lively there than it would be if they remained in town. Ted, however, was staying put. He had a wife and a toddler back home in L.A. and, though he hadn't said anything specific, Leandra had the impression that things weren't entirely smooth between the couple. They'd all be back in Weaver on Sunday, though, in time to watch the show on television.

When Ted and the camera were no longer there as silent witnesses, Evan leaned his elbows on the metal rail between them. "You showing off that you're the boss, Leandra?"

"When it comes to this, that's exactly what I am."

"As long as Marian lets you be."

She stiffened, ignoring the jab. "Regardless, I don't need you taking me to task in front of my people just because you occasionally find this situation a little less than comfortable."

"Occasionally?" His eyebrows lifted. "Have *you* ever had a camera following you around all damn day? You don't know what it's like. You only know what it's like from behind the lens."

The fact that he was right didn't help her beleaguered conscience any. Nor did the phone cease vibrating. She snatched it off her belt, flipping it open. "Yes?"

There was a brief pause, then a short, masculine laugh. "Judging by your voice, I can tell you're happy to hear from me."

It wasn't Marian at all. "Jake." Leandra greeted her ex husband. Evan's shadowy jaw cocked and he turned, stepping away from the rail. "I thought you were Marian calling. What's wrong?"

"Who said anything had to be wrong?"

"You don't usually call me when I'm on location." Her ex husband called about once a month, insisting on checking up on her. He'd been doing it for as long as they'd been apart. At first, it had been simply painful. Then, it had been…simply simple. That was Jake.

They might not have made it as a couple—particularly after Emi—but that didn't mean that they didn't care about each other.

"As it happens, I was calling to see how Ev was doing."

Ev was twenty feet away from her now, joined by her father, who'd ambled out of the barn a few moments earlier. "Why? He's a big boy."

"Yeah, but he hates attention. You know that."

"Then he shouldn't have agreed to the shoot. I still don't know why he did. I know he regrets it. It would have been heck of a lot easier if you'd agreed to do this, Jake. I would never have had to come to Weaver. You didn't even tell me your good excuse," she reminded him. "Just that you had a reason."

"I did. Do. So, put the man on the phone, would you? I need to talk to him."

"Oh, so that's why you called my phone," she teased wryly as she crouched down and slipped through the horizontal space between the wide-set metal rails. "Not to talk to me after all, but to your good buddy."

"At least from him I might get the straight scoop on how you're really doing." There was no joking in Jake's voice.

Leandra stopped next to Evan and extended the tiny phone. "Here, spy man. Your accomplice wants to talk to you." She jiggled the phone. "Jake."

Evan took the phone. "Yo."

Leandra grimaced and turned away.

Her father caught her gaze, his dark blue eyes unreadable. "You still talk to Jake?"

She shrugged and he fell into step with her as she walked away from Evan, heading toward the big, state-of-the-art barn. She didn't really want to hear whatever report he might be giving Jake.

The fact that there might be any *reporting* at all annoyed her right down to her bones. She was having lustful thoughts about Evan and *he* was merely keeping tabs on her for Jake.

"Don't worry, Dad. We're not getting back together or anything." There was too much water under that bridge. And Leandra wasn't up to emotional entanglements, anyway.

"Jake was—is a good enough guy." Jefferson's low voice was wry. "Maybe not good enough for my girl, but—"

She tucked her hand under her father's arm. At six-plus feet, he still towered over her. And though his blond hair had a good portion of silver now, it was still thick and often longer than his wife's shoulder-length hair.

"Nobody would be good enough to suit you, Dad."

"Me?" His lips quirked. "It's your mother who's the hard one to please." He nodded his head toward the slender, dark-haired woman who was striding toward them. "Tell her, Em," he said when she reached them.

"Tell her what?"

Leandra suffered a head-to-toe examination from her mother's all-seeing brown eyes. She was ten years younger than Jefferson, and more than once had been mistaken for Leandra's sister, rather than her mother. "He's claiming that instead of him, it's you who thinks no man is good enough for me."

Emily smiled. "Well, we both know what a tale your father can spin. So, how much longer are you going to be following poor Evan around? You know we're all going into town tonight to meet at Colbys, right?"

"Sarah told me."

"I really wish you could stay out here with us." Emily closed her arm around Leandra's shoulder. "I know it's not too practical during the week because of the drive, but what about the weekends?"

A part of Leandra wanted nothing more than to escape to the sanctuary of her childhood home. To sink into the comfort and care of parents whose love was a constant in her life. A bigger part of her resisted those very same things for fear that she'd never make her own way. "I'll still be working on the weekends," she told them truthfully. "We just won't be actively following Evan."

"Working on the weekends." Emily sniffed wryly. "Why does that sound familiar?"

"Because you grew up on Squire's ranch," Jefferson drawled. "And there ain't *no* time off on a ranch."

Emily tilted her head up, looking at her husband. "Oh, and you're so different from your father, are you?"

Jefferson closed his hand around his wife's hand. "Hell, yes. I'm nothing like Squire Clay."

Leandra snorted softly. Her mother laughed and her father smiled before dropping a kiss onto his wife's forehead.

There was no way that Leandra could ignore the contentment radiating from her parents. It blossomed around her as surely as the sun rose and set. "I've got to round up my crew and get them back to town," she told them. "So I'll see you later at Colbys."

"Even if you're not staying with us, I'm glad you're here." Emily kissed Leandra's cheek. "It's been so long since you were home."

Not since Emi.

Leandra kept her smile in place, but it suddenly took an effort. And she knew that her parents were aware of that fact, which made the effort even harder. "I know. So…later." She hurried away from them, retracing her steps back to the small arena.

Evan, though, was nowhere to be seen.

Paul and Janet were busy loading up the rental van with equipment. "Looking for this?" Janet handed over Leandra's clipboard.

She hadn't been, but that didn't mean she didn't need the jumble of schedules and notes and other assorted items that were clipped together on the large brown clipboard. "Where's Evan?"

"He left a few minutes ago."

For some reason, the news startled Leandra. "When?" She hadn't noticed his pickup truck driving away from the ranch, but then she'd been on the opposite side of the barn, facing away from the road.

"A few minutes ago. We're still finished, right?"

"Right." Leandra realized she was looking in the direction of the road, as if she would be able to see Evan's departure. They probably wouldn't see each other until Sunday, when the show aired and the crew threw a promotional event in town to play up Evan's debut. The thought nagged at her, and she deliberately looked down at her clipboard. She was there to work and that was all. Work was good. Work was safe.

And amid her work was a big pink note, taped on top of her collection of pages. *Call Marian.*

She automatically reached for her cell phone.

Which she'd given to Evan.

"Don't suppose he gave you my cell phone before he left?" Janet shook her head. "Nope. Sorry."

Well, if for no other reason than to retrieve her cell phone, Leandra would be seeing Evan before Sunday, after all.

"Guess you'd better lend me yours, then," she told her assistant.

The young woman handed it over and Leandra dialed Marian's phone number.

Even the prospect of talking to her half-sane boss *again* wasn't enough to dull Leandra's sudden burst of cheerfulness.

She wouldn't be waiting until Sunday, after all.

Chapter Three

"Does your daddy know you still play pool?"

Bent over her borrowed pool cue and the side of one of the pool tables situated inside Colbys Bar & Grill, Leandra's stroke hesitated. When had Evan arrived at the bar? She angled her chin, looking beside her. "Does *your* daddy know you've taken up drinking beer?"

The corner of Evan's lips twitched. "I'd have to say he did since he's the one who bought it." His fingers were looped around the slender neck of the bottle and he tilted the bottom of it, gesturing. "He's at the bar over there."

Leandra followed the gesturing beer bottle. Sure enough, Drew Taggart was standing at the bar.

From Leandra's vantage point, it looked as if the only thing that had changed about Evan's father were the strands of silver threading through his black hair. He was talking with one of her uncles. Tristan Clay was as golden blond as he'd ever been, and standing there, the two men—one dark haired and one light—made a striking image.

"I thought you were going to Braden this evening." She distinctly remembered him saying as much that afternoon.

"Plans change." He shifted beside her.

"You said your parents have been to Florida?" She focused again on lining up her shot, instead of on his well-worn jeans.

"Got back yesterday."

The cue ball struck the racked balls with a satisfying *thwack*, scattering them nicely. "Were they gone long?"

"Two weeks." Evan set his bottle on the wide ledge of the pool table and pulled a stick from the selection hanging on the wall rack. Colbys might serve the best steak in town, but it was still a bar, complete with jukebox, wood floors, a very long, gleaming wood bar and a half-dozen pool tables. "They came back early. Because of the show being on television." His voice sounded disgruntled.

"I'll have to catch up with them and say hello," Leandra murmured, stepping around the table and lining up her next shot. She hoped Evan didn't get any grumpier about the shoot. She truly didn't like the idea of making someone miserable just so she could achieve her own goals. "Where's your sister been staying while they were gone?"

"Tris and Hope's. Though she's eighteen now. She could have stayed by herself at the house. Jake doesn't know anything about Ed-wa-ahrd."

Her shot went wide, the ball banking uselessly off the side cushion. She straightened, propping the end of the stick on the toe of her tennis shoe. "What did you do? Ask him about it when he called?"

"Yes."

An invisible band seemed to tighten around her skull. "I

told you it didn't concern Jake. It doesn't concern *you*, for that matter."

"Sounding a little defensive there, Leandra." Evan leaned over and sank two balls in the corner pocket.

So much for her sympathy. She had an intense urge to smack him over the shoulders with her own pool cue. "And you are sounding pretty interfering there, Evan. What does it matter, anyway? Why do you care?"

He was studying the table, his head slowly tilting to one side, then the other. "Jake's one of my best friends."

"So out of loyalty to him you figure he needs to know about Eduard?"

He leaned over again, his movements with the pool cue infuriatingly confident. "Does he?"

Despite her intense concentration on them, the infernal balls didn't have the sense to thwart his rapid shots. They went sailing exactly where he wanted. At the rate he was going, he'd have the table cleared in minutes. "I've already said there's nothing for him to know. Why are you making a deal about this?"

"You're the one being closemouthed." Only the eight ball remained. He lined it up. A second later, it rolled neatly into the pocket. Looking smugly superior, he straightened.

"Bet you can't do that a second time."

His lips quirked, amused. "Bet I can. Don't forget, sport, I've been hanging out here at Colbys since before you moved away."

"Maybe I hit the billiard circuit in California."

"You're a rotten liar. Have been ever since you tried to convince Mr. Pope that you didn't cheat on that junior high math test."

"I *didn't* cheat!"

"Have you convinced yourself of that in the years since?"

"I don't have to convince myself of anything. I know what happened with that test whether Pope—or you—believed me or not." She walked around the table to the other side, facing him. "If you must know, it was Tammy Browning who was cheating off *my* test. I've never cheated on anything. And you're trying to sidestep the bet. What's the matter, Evan?" She leaned over, propping her forearms on the side of the table. "You afraid of losing to a girl?"

"Wouldn't matter if you *weren't* a girl. How much?"

She rolled her eyes in thought. "Twenty."

"Sissy bet."

"Forty."

He waited.

"Fine." She pulled some of the cash from the front pocket of her blue jeans, counted through it. Slapped several bills down on the rail. "Fifty."

Of course, *now* the man smiled. Slow and easy. As if he'd been the one baiting her all along.

It annoyed her to no end.

"Rack 'em up, sport."

She made quite a production out of it. "What's with the 'sport' thing?"

He leisurely chalked the tip of his cue, watching her. "You're the one dressing like a Little Leaguer."

She looked down at herself. Blue jeans and a zip-front sweatshirt. Well, okay, she *was* wearing a ball cap with the show's *WITS* acronym sewn on it, but that was hardly a damning fashion statement. Most of the crew wore the caps. Even people around town were sporting them.

She captured all of the balls within the triangular rack and rolled it back and forth, finally positioning it at the footspot. "Knock yourself out, Doc."

He hit a sound break, solids and stripes bursting outward in a rolling explosion. He waited until they all came to a rest, his blue gaze studying the positions.

"Getting cold feet?" Her voice was dulcet.

He snorted softly and leaned over to begin smoothly picking them off, one by one—and sometimes two—into the pockets. He didn't miss a single shot.

"Who taught you to play, anyway?" She silently bid her money a farewell.

"My dad."

"Figures. And I know he must have played plenty with my uncles during their misspent youth." The Clay brothers, and Tag, had all been notoriously wild teenagers.

"And your dad. He's one of the worst ones when it came to playing hard."

"Worst as in best," she muttered. Not once in her life had she been able to best her father at the pool table, whether it was the one housed in their basement or elsewhere.

"It's all Squire's fault." Sarah had come up to stand beside Leandra. "He's the one who taught his sons how to play in the first place."

Leandra nodded. "True." Their grandfather had raised his sons alone after the death of his first wife, Sarah, after whom Leandra's cousin had been named. According to the stories, he'd been a hard-nosed man with little softness afforded to his boys after his wife's death from giving birth to Tristan, their youngest. And then Leandra's mother, orphaned before she was even ten, had gone to live with Squire and all of those boys. And all of their lives had been forever changed.

Evan sank two more balls. The table was nearly clear again, and Leandra's hopes that Evan would make even one small misstep were dwindling.

"He's going to keep running the table if you don't do something," Sarah murmured as she lifted her soda to her lips. She'd changed out of her schoolteacher clothes into jeans that were nearly identical to Leandra's. But instead of a shapeless gray sweatshirt, Sarah wore a pretty pink crocheted top over a matching camisole, and instead of scuffed tennis shoes on her feet, she had pointy-toed black boots with killer heels that made her look even more leggy than she really was.

And Leandra was beginning to feel decidedly frumpy. She turned on her heel, looking at her cousin. "What am I supposed to do about it? I already feel stupid for putting the money down."

Sarah shook her head slightly and her long hair rippled over her shoulders. "Distract him."

Leandra wanted to snort. Her cousin was a distracting-type woman. Leandra was not. She was not especially tall, nor especially curvy and her last haircut had been at the courtesy of her own hands because she'd been too darned busy to keep a hair appointment. "Just what am I supposed to distract him *with?*"

Sarah rolled her eyes. "Have you forgotten everything we used to know? You're wearing something under that sweatshirt, aren't you?"

"An undershirt."

"Is it completely disgraceful?"

It was thin, white and sleeveless. "It's clean."

Sarah laughed softly. "What would you advise someone on your show? And you'd better hurry up. At the most, he only has three shots left."

Frowning at the lengths she'd go to in order to save her fifty dollars, Leandra unzipped the sweatshirt and tossed it onto the nearby high-top table. Picking up her cue stick again, she sauntered around the table until she was opposite Evan once again.

She leaned the stick against the side of the table and braced her hands on the rails. "Want to go for double or nothing?"

He didn't even glance her way. "We could just save the time and have you hand over the money, instead."

Leandra rolled her eyes. Caught Sarah's gaze. Her cousin nodded encouragingly.

Swallowing an oath, she slowly moved around the table, taking advantage of the time Evan was spending as he studied the table and the not-so-easy position of the remaining balls. She stopped beside him as he began to line up his next shot and murmured close to his ear. "Maybe I think three times is not going to be the charm for you."

He jerked as if he'd been bitten. She almost chuckled at the comedy of the moment. But she managed to contain herself when he straightened again, not taking the shot after all, and she found her nose about five inches away from the soft brown shirt covering his chest.

Or, rather, the chuckle nearly turned into choking because the man was just too *male* for her stunted senses.

"What are you doing?" His voice was mildly curious.

She would not blush. She was a career woman, for heaven's sake. Blushing was not supposed to be part of her repertoire.

She still felt her cheeks warming and thanked the heavens that the bar was crowded and slightly warm as a result. She'd blame it on that. Much more palatable than thinking he could reduce her to a blush so easily.

Searching desperately for an answer, she spotted Sarah, who lifted her eyebrows slightly, meaningfully.

"Just cooling off," she assured. "Don't you think it's getting warm in here?"

His lashes drooped, his gaze moving over her from her face to her toes.

And dammit, she actually shivered. Shivered!

Maybe she was coming down with the flu. Maybe she was simply off her rocker. *That* was far more likely.

"Yeah, it's warm all right." His voice dropped a notch. "A hundred bucks? *You* sink every striped ball and I'll pay you a hundred bucks."

"Interesting idea. But this wasn't about my ability. It was about yours."

He set the bottom of the cue stick on the floor. The tip of it stood higher than Leandra's head. "I don't think either one of us question my ability." He took Leandra's hand and wrapped it around the shaft of the stick, keeping it in place with his own hand around hers. "Do we?"

There was a knot in her throat, making it difficult to breathe. His hand felt hot against hers.

"Well?" He prompted when she failed to answer.

She shook herself, snatching the stick and her hand away from him. Ignoring the faint smile that touched his wicked, wicked mouth, she turned to the pool table only to find that at least a dozen people had joined Sarah in watching them.

She felt her face flush even hotter.

Her parents. Her cousins. Ted. They were all there. Even the players at the other pool tables had gone silent.

Great.

"One hundred dollars," she said brusquely. "You sure you're good for it, Taggart?"

He cocked an eyebrow.

Making a face, she pointed the cue at the table. "Rack them up, then. Striped balls, any pocket."

While Evan gathered all of the balls in the rack, Sarah scooted next to Leandra. "You were supposed to be distracting *him,* remember?"

"Yeah, a fine idea you had," she muttered. "I'm going to make an ass out of myself, right here in front of everyone. Even Ted and his little camcorder, there."

Sarah glanced over at the cameraman. "I didn't even realize that thing he's been playing with all evening was a camera."

After more than a year of working together, Leandra wasn't the least interested in Ted and his penchant for electronics. Instead, she kept her focus on Evan's work at the table. He removed the rack with a goading smile, and waved his hand over the table, as if inviting her to humiliate herself.

"Just take your time," Sarah advised under her breath. "Remember everything we've ever been taught about pool."

The first thing Leandra had been taught was not to place a bet that she wasn't absolutely certain of winning.

She centered the cue ball over the headspot, settled her left hand on the felt, making a bridge for the stick and sliding it slowly back and forth, experimentally, as she focused on the leading ball of the rack.

"Gonna take all night there, sport?"

She drew back and let fly.

The racked balls exploded. Two balls, one solid, one striped, plowed into the corner pockets.

A couple of hoots followed from the peanut gallery.

Leandra closed them out.

It was not so easy to close out Evan, though, as she moved around the table, studying the position of the remaining striped balls. He leisurely moved out of her way when she pointedly stopped next to him.

"Sure you want to try that shot?" His voice was solicitous. "You're gonna have to cut the eleven ball to get the right angle."

Shut up, she thought. She leaned over, lining up the shot. He was right, though. She'd have to hit the cue ball into the striped ball exactly to one side of center in order to gain the forty-five-degree angle she needed for the ball to head toward the corner pocket. Narrowing her eyes, she drew in a breath, and made her stroke.

The balls clacked together and old eleven rolled right into the pocket. More slowly than she'd intended, but at least it dropped.

"That's my girl," she heard her father say.

"Five more to go," Evan murmured as she slipped by him yet again.

As a distracter, he was much more effective than she'd been. "I should have let Ted tape you snoring all night long."

"Who says I snore?"

She leaned over and sank two balls, slam bam. "Jake. You *were* college roommates." She straightened for only a moment before leaning over again. "Hope you don't need that hundred too badly, *sport.*"

He'd moved around the table, opposite her. "Did you know that I can see right down your shirt?"

She barely kept the tip of her stick from hitting the felt. Her skin prickled and she fought the urge to straighten. To press her hand against the scooped neckline of her T-shirt and hold it flat against her meager chest, just in case he was not merely spouting tripe.

Whether or not he could see down her shirt, she still felt her nipples tighten, and prayed that he wouldn't notice.

Three striped balls to go, she reminded herself, and she would get out of the bar, go home and not have to see Evan again until Sunday evening.

She set her jaw, kept her grip on the stick loose and stroked.

Only when the green-striped ball toppled into the pocket did she let out her breath.

"Looking a little stressed there," Evan murmured. "Sure you don't need a break?"

She rounded the table, knocked into his shin with the butt of her stick and smiled sweetly. "So sorry."

He merely lifted his beer bottle and sipped.

She envied him a bit. Her mouth felt parched. And when she leaned over for the next shot, she couldn't help but glance down to see how, exactly, her T-shirt behaved.

It was as snug against her torso as ever and when she

looked up, the glint of laughter in Evan's expression was unmistakable.

He'd caught her looking.

She slammed the sixth ball into a corner pocket. Only one striped ball remained. But it had a nightmare position, nearly blocked by two solids and frozen against the side cushion.

She could hear the murmur from the peanut gallery and didn't dare look their way. Knowing the family as she did, she was afraid they might well be placing side bets.

"Feeling the pressure?" Evan leaned down on his forearms beside her, acting for all the world as if they were bosom buddies. "Not even sure I could make that shot, truth be told."

For as long as Leandra could remember, there had always been a haze of smoke clinging to the interior of Colbys. Now was no different.

Yet despite the smoke, she could still smell the fresh, clean scent that she was beginning to identify with Evan and *only* Evan.

"I can make the shot," she assured, lying right through her teeth.

He shrugged. "Maybe. Or you could just fess up about Edwa-ahrd, and we'll call it even."

She narrowed her eyes, ostensibly studying the table. "A person might think that your curiosity where Eduard is concerned has nothing to do with Jake, and everything to do with you."

"Maybe it does."

She bit down on her tongue, not at all expecting that admission. She'd just been tossing out the accusation to goad him.

"You going to give up, Leandra?" Ted's voice drew her attention. He had moved closer to the pool table from the hightop where she'd last seen him, and was holding up his palm-size video recorder.

Evan was still watching her.

And she had an unbidden vision of him lowering his head toward hers, brushing his lips across hers.

Feeling thoroughly unsettled, she shook her head in answer to Ted, but just as much to shake the image of Evan kissing her from her head, and lined up the shot.

The stripe missed the pocket by a good six inches. Smiling wryly, she turned to face the gallery, shrugging. "Them's the breaks," she said lightly as she extended the cue stick toward Evan.

What was she doing, thinking about Evan kissing her? The only time he'd ever kissed her had been on the cheek at their high school graduation.

She pulled her cash out of her pocket again and counted out another fifty, picked up the cash that was still sitting on the rail, and folded it all together. "There you go, Doc. Add that to your lunch fund."

Evan eyed the woman and the cash she was holding out. He didn't want Leandra's damn money. He *wanted* to know who the hell the French guy was and what he'd meant—or still meant—to Leandra. Loyalty to Jake was only an excuse.

A poor excuse, since Evan's feelings where Leandra Clay were concerned *weren't* exactly loyal.

But Evan knew what Leandra didn't—that Jake was engaged to be married again and he didn't have the *huevos* to tell his ex-wife about it for fear of hurting her even more than she'd been hurt. But if Leandra had been involved with some other guy, then maybe Jake could take off that particular hair shirt of thinking that Leandra was so damn fragile, and get on with his life.

And Evan could maybe get on with his.

When he didn't take the cash, though, Leandra finally stepped toward him. The top of her tousled blond head didn't even reach his shoulder, but he still swore he could smell the enticing scent of her shampoo.

Then she reached out and tucked the money into the front of his leather belt. "Enjoy the dough," she said smoothly, and turned away.

It was all he could do not to grab her by the shoulders and haul her up against him.

The fact that half the patrons of Colbys—including Ted and that toy-size camera of his—were watching, kept his hands firmly at his sides.

Then Leandra lifted her hands and addressed the crowd. "Don't anyone forget. Sunday evening at seven right here at Colbys to watch Evan's television debut!"

Evan endured the hoots and hollers and reminded himself that six weeks wasn't *really* all that long of a time.

He could survive it.

Maybe.

Chapter Four

"**Y**ou know what I like about Saturdays?" Leandra was stretched out on the couch in Sarah's living room. Her cousin was sitting on the floor, surrounded by school materials as she made lesson plans.

"Hmm?"

"The possibility of endless sleeping."

"Having Snow White fantasies again? Like the idea of those seven short guys?"

"As long as they're catering to my every whim?" Leandra smiled lazily. "Sounds okay to me."

"Sort of boring, though, laying there in the glass case, waiting for your prince to come and lay some lip on you."

What would Evan's kiss *be* like?

Leandra threw her arm over her closed eyes, mentally brushing at the thought, but it kept circling like some pesky mosquito buzzing around her head. "Well, note that I said the *possibility* of sleeping. It's nice to just ponder the whole idea of it. Not that I'll be doing it or anything. Too much work to do." Which reminded her that she'd forgotten all about her cell phone again.

Leandra would go to Evan's later and retrieve the phone.

She pressed her lips together, trying to stop the tingling.

Maybe she'd have developed some self-control over her wayward notions by them.

She turned on her side, propping her head on her hand. "Sounds like we'll have quite the crew around next month for Squire's birthday party." Before the ill-fated pool table episode, the family had gone over the developing plans while crowded around several pushed-together tables in the restaurant portion of Colbys.

"We still don't know if J.D. and Angeline will make it back from Atlanta. J.D.'s schedule is probably easier than Angel's, though, given the way she's on call so much."

Angel was an emergency medical technician in Atlanta. J.D. lived in that vicinity, too, working at some blue-blooded horse farm. "And nobody's been able to get hold of Ryan?" Ryan was the oldest of the cousins, serving in the Navy, like his father, Sawyer, had once done.

Sarah continued flipping through a project idea book. "Between you and Ryan, it's a toss-up who has been home to Weaver less."

"Well, I'd guess he'd win, since I'm here now."

"You're here because of the show. But we'll take what we can get. And it's ideal that Squire's birthday falls during your visit." Sarah set aside her book and propped her elbows on the coffee table in front of her. "So…you really like working in show business?"

"Documentary filmmaking. And, yes, I do."

Sarah watched her for a moment, as if she wanted to say

something. But she just lowered her arms again and picked up her oversized book once more.

"What?"

Sarah shook her head. "Nothing."

"*What?*"

"Nothing. Really. I was just going to say that it is amazing the places that life takes us."

Leandra really didn't want to get into that particular discussion. Only pain colored that philosophy.

"Do you think if you hadn't gone to France you and Jake might have gotten back together?"

It wasn't quite the comment she was expecting, but it was easier than discussing Emi. "No."

"You two were crazy about each other."

"Yeah, but we never really managed to know each other very well before we got married. And when…when…things got bad, instead of helping each other through it, we blamed each other."

"I'm sure Jake didn't blame you."

Arguing the point now served no purpose. "I did." *I still do.* Leandra swung her legs down from the couch and pushed to her feet. "So is there anything I can help with around here?" The house was as tidy as a pin. The yard outside was even more so, seeming to lay in wait with its lingering summer colors before autumn truly hit with all of its glory.

"Not unless you want to come up with arts and crafts ideas for two elementary school classes."

Even that humorously meant offer made her hurt inside. "Thanks, but I think I'll pass." She brushed her hands down the front of her jeans. "I'm going to head over to Ruby's Café for something to eat. Do you want to go with me?"

"Not this time. I need to get this done. There's a meeting with the parent association this afternoon."

"They meet on Saturdays?"

"They do when half of them have to drive over from Braden."

Even though Weaver had grown considerably since she was a little girl—mostly because of the computer gaming business her uncle Tristan had started here—it was still at heart a ranching community. "Some things never change."

"If Justine has any cinnamon rolls, bring a few home, okay?"

"Will do." Justine Leoni was the granddaughter of Ruby Leoni, the café's founder. She was also the mother of Tristan's wife, Hope. And fortunately for the town, Justine had inherited not only the café after Ruby died, but she'd inherited her grandmother's ability to make the most delicious cinnamon rolls.

Leandra didn't bother with her purse. She merely tucked some cash into her front pocket—which unfortunately reminded her again of the previous evening—pushed her feet into tennis shoes and headed down the road.

There was no need to drive.

Ruby's was located barely two miles away and the weather was pleasant. Bright blue skies. Morning briskness giving way to the sun's warmth, hanging strong despite the steady breeze in the air. Leandra knew it wouldn't be long before that warmth was only a memory for the residents of Weaver. With the lengthening year would come shorter days, cooling temperatures, and in another month or so, there could easily be snow on the ground.

She looked across at the park as she walked along the street. Homes on one side, green grass on the other. During the wintertime, there would be an ice-skating rink covering part of what was now the baseball diamond, where a handful of kids were even now tossing around a ball.

A young man was mowing the lawn in front of one of the houses she passed. She didn't recognize him.

Not surprising. There were a lot of people she didn't recognize anymore in Weaver. That's what happened when someone moved away and stayed away for years at a time.

The logic was sound. The feeling in the pit of her stomach didn't seem to care.

Sighing, she quickened her step, rounding the corner onto Main Street. She could see Ruby's from here. The door stood open to the fresh air, and when she angled across the road, waiting for a slowly passing car first, and walked into the café, she couldn't help but smile.

Here, everything was familiar. The only missing element was Ruby herself. But she'd died when Leandra was away at college.

The entire town had attended the diminutive woman's funeral. But Leandra hadn't returned for it, even though Ruby had been part of her extended family—great-grandmother to Leandra's aunt, Hope. No, Leandra had been too busy to come home for that event. Too involved in her studies, too involved in her own life.

She stepped through the doorway.

The first thing she smelled were the famous cinnamon rolls.

The first person she noticed was Evan Taggart.

He sat at a booth, facing the doorway, and, as if he'd been waiting for her arrival, he was watching her with not one wisp of surprise in his expression. She gave him a brief nod as she moved through the somewhat-crowded café toward the counter, but the casualness of the motion was belied by the butterflies that were suddenly batting around inside her stomach.

"Hey there, Leandra." The girl behind the counter smiled widely as she poured coffee for the patrons sitting at the counter in front of her. "You need to tell my brother that I should have some face time on your show."

"Tabby, if we put your pretty face on *WITS*, nobody is going to be interested in watching your brother," Leandra teased as she slipped onto the only vacant red stool at the counter.

Tabby dimpled. She really was as striking as her brother. "Yeah, that's what I was afraid of." She sighed dramatically, managing to deliver a plate of corned beef hash and eggs without spilling a drop of coffee as she continued topping off coffee cups. "You here for breakfast? Daily specials are up on the board."

Leandra glanced at the chalkboard that was propped on a shelf. It, too, was a familiar sight. The looping handwriting, though, was undoubtedly Tabby's. "Just give me the special," she said. "And a half-dozen cinnamon rolls to go for Sarah, if there are any left."

Tabby nodded. "I'd already saved in back a dozen for my brother. But you can have half. He won't mind."

Leandra wasn't so sure. She resisted the urge to look over her shoulder back at the booth where he'd been sitting.

"You want to join him, I'll bring your food on out in a sec."

No, Leandra didn't want to join Evan. But even as she told herself she wasn't going to, she was aware of more people entering the café. She was taking up a seat at the counter out of cowardly orneriness.

She took her coffee cup—flipped over and filled up by Tabby without a word—and headed over to Evan's booth. She was halfway there, and everyone in the café knew it, when Leandra's feet dragged to an abrupt stop.

The coffee sloshed over the cup's rim, stinging hot on Leandra's hand.

Evan wasn't alone.

A pint-size little girl sat opposite him in the booth.

She had striking blue eyes, creamy white skin and shining black hair that was as dark as midnight.

She looked like a miniature, female version of Evan, and the sight of her was a blow to her midsection.

She'd heard of Evan's niece, of course, but she hadn't expected to come face-to-face with her.

And she'd never known that she was so like her uncle she could have been *his* daughter.

Evan breathed a soft curse as he saw the color drain from Leandra's face. He was already moving out of the booth and heading for her when she seemed to sway a little, spilling coffee over her hand.

She looked up at him as he took the coffee cup from her. Her eyes seemed to dwarf the rest of her small face. "I'm sorry. I didn't expect—"

"I watch Hannah for Katy sometimes." Katy was his half-sister by blood and his cousin by marriage. Mostly, though, she was Hannah's mom.

She blinked once. Twice. "Right. Of course."

He could see the reluctance in Leandra's expression as it began edging out the shock that had encompassed her. He could also see that she looked decidedly shaky.

Jake had warned him that Leandra still found it difficult being around small children. But seeing it with his own eyes twisted something painful inside him. She looked like a wounded, trapped animal.

He didn't even think about it. He just slid his arm around her and nudged her down onto the bench, across from where Hannah sat, watching them both with her evasive way of viewing the world around her. "Hannah," he said calmly as he sat down beside the little girl, "this is my friend, Leandra. Can you say hello?"

She kept her gaze half-averted from them. "Say hello," she repeated obediently. Her thumb steadily stroked the wheel of the matchbox car she was holding, turning it again and again.

"Tabby." He caught his little sister's attention as she was bustling around behind the counter. "Can we have some more coffee over here?"

"Coffee here," Hannah repeated softly. She shifted, pressing her shoulder against Evan's side. He smoothed his hand through her shoulder-length hair. Despite the convoluted history entwining their families, she was a light in his life.

"I should be going," Leandra said.

"Wait until Tabby has a chance to top off your coffee. And when's the last time you ate? I heard you order the special. So unless you plan on walking out on the order, you might as well relax."

Her lashes shielded those dark, dark brown eyes. Bambi eyes, he used to think. Round, velvety soft and surrounded by lashes that were long and delicate, all at the same time.

Tabby arrived with the coffee carafe, saving him from his teenage, angst-ridden memories. "Your food will be up next, Leandra. Ev, you or Hannah want anything else?"

Hannah had made a typical mess of her toast and scrambled eggs, eating half of each and decorating the table with the other half. "We're good, Tabby. Thanks."

"No prob." She was moving off in a flash.

"For some reason, I'm always surprised at how good she is at this. Tabby's worked here for more than a year now, but it is still a surprise."

"Your thoughts have her perpetually stuck in pigtails, playing with dolls?"

"Playing Little League baseball, more like. But, yeah."

Leandra's lips curved ever so faintly. The tiny smile was heartbreakingly sad, though. "I know the feeling."

He hadn't gone to California for Emi's funeral.

He should have.

He was Jake's best friend, wasn't he?

Something, though, had kept him away. And he'd never forgiven himself for that particular display of cowardice. But before he could form any words, Leandra was looking—somewhat stalwartly, he thought—at Hannah.

"How old are you, Hannah?"

She didn't look up from spinning the wheels on her little car. "Leandra is talking to you, Hannah," he prompted calmly.

"Talking to you," she repeated.

"It takes her a while to warm up to new people," he excused.

"I understand."

Did she? He wasn't all that certain. Leandra Clay may have grown up in Weaver, but he knew her life had been fairly charmed—at least until the devastating loss of her daughter. And now she worked on a show that followed veterinarians around, for God's sake. She observed life now, instead of living it.

"Four," Hannah suddenly said.

If Leandra was surprised by the belated response, she didn't show it. "Four is a fun age to be. I like your car, there. Is it your favorite one?"

"Yes. It's red." Hannah didn't look up as she replied.

"I like red, too."

Hannah's thumb spun the wheels. She didn't reply.

Tabby delivered Leandra's meal, as well as two neatly wrapped packages of cinnamon rolls, and disappeared just as quickly. Leandra picked up her fork, but didn't move it near enough her food to suit him. "How is Katy doing these days? Is she still in the service?"

"She's in Afghanistan."

Her eyebrows drew together, and he caught her sliding a glance at Hannah. "Scary," she murmured.

"Yeah. But she's supposed to be home soon."

"You all must be relieved."

He nodded. "Hannah's been staying with her grandparents in Braden while Katy's been serving overseas. She had been living in North Carolina near her base, but when she got sent to Afghanistan about a year ago, she brought Hannah here to Wyoming."

"What about—" she hesitated for a moment "—Keith?"

He was surprised she remembered the name, since he was pretty sure Leandra had never even met his half-sister's husband. "Yeah. Keith. He split a few years ago. Permanently."

"Will Katy stay in Wyoming when she gets back?"

He shook his head. "She plans to go back to North Carolina."

She slipped a glance at Hannah. "Does she visit you often?"

Not as often as he would like. "She spends a day with me now and then. Gives Sharon a break."

She was silent for a moment, studying him, as if she were trying to put together a puzzle she'd never before noticed. "You'll miss Hannah when she goes," she finally observed.

He didn't bother denying it. Just nodded and wondered darkly why the hell Leandra would sound so surprised by the realization.

"And your… Katy's parents. How are they?"

His lips twisted. "You mean Darian, I suppose."

"I mean both of them," she said.

Given the way her brown eyes had flickered, he doubted it. "Sharon is fine." If you didn't count her increasing propensity for pretending Hannah was just like any other kid around Braden and Weaver.

"And Darian?" Her chin had come up again in that way he remembered from days of old.

"My old man is the same as ever," he drawled.

Her lips tightened. "Drew is your dad."

Thank the good Lord. And he felt his usual tangle of guilt for feeling the way he did when Drew *was* his dad in every way that ought to matter. "Yeah, and we all know why that came about." Drew had married his mom after his half brother Darian had gotten her pregnant and left her flat.

Her eyebrows pulled together, making a crease in her pretty face. "Nobody in this town has *ever* thought that way."

He let that slide, since she was probably right.

His feelings about Darian were his own.

Didn't make it any easier to get rid of them, though.

"Is your grandmother well?"

"Other than that she still hates my mom, dotes on Darian, pretty much ignores Hannah and sort of tolerates the rest of us, she's fine."

"She never was the brightest of women," Leandra muttered. Her cheeks turned pink. "Sorry."

He shrugged. "Not everyone has grandparents like yours."

"Well, Squire is a one-of-a-kind man." Her lips curved faintly. "And Gloria's pretty much a saint."

"How're the plans for the party shaping up?"

"Good." She seemed almost as relieved as him at the change of subject. "The trick of course, is to keep Squire from finding out. Not an easy task when practically the entire town will be turning out for the fete."

"He and Gloria are still out of town?"

She nodded. "I can't believe he's turning eighty-five." She didn't seem to realize that she'd forked up some scrambled eggs, and looked at the results with some surprise.

"But he's a *healthy* eighty-five."

"True." With nothing else to do with the food, she tucked the fork between her lips. Slowly drew it out.

He realized with an inward groan that watching Leandra eat was just one more thing about her that charged his batteries. But he was sitting in a bustling café, with Hannah leaning against his side. It ought to have been as effective as a cold shower.

But then again, this was Leandra Clay he was dealing with.

Or not dealing with.

And that meant that any reasonable thought processes were hard to come by.

She tilted her head slightly. The sunlight streaming through the window beside them caught in the wispy feathers of her funky hairstyle, making each strand gleam like it had been dipped in gold dust.

His fingers itched.

He ignored the desire to feel her hair between his fingers and smiled instead at Hannah. She smiled back.

Leandra took another forkful of food. "My family has been blessed that way," she said. "You know. Good health. Nothing bad happening."

"I wouldn't say nothing bad had ever happened."

"To me," she said. "But not to them."

He brushed a handful of crumbs away from the edge of the table before they could fall on Hannah's lap. "You think that Emi's death didn't hurt them, too?"

He heard the breath she sucked in when he spoke her daughter's name. "I didn't say that." She stared at her forkful of eggs, only this time she didn't partake. She set the utensil ever so carefully down on the plate and shifted in her seat, pulling money out of her pocket. She dropped several bills on the table.

The interlude was definitely over.

"Hannah—" she looked at the little girl with a determined smile as she picked up one of the packages holding the cinnamon rolls "—it was very nice to meet you. Evan, I'll see you later."

He wanted to say something, to stop her from racing out of Ruby's. But whatever words that might have taken, he didn't seem to possess.

So he just sat there and watched her hurry out of the café. She barely slowed as she crossed the sidewalk and headed out into the quiet street, the package of rolls clutched against her chest like some sort of life preserver.

"She's sad," Hannah said suddenly.

"Yes," he murmured, still watching through the window. "She is." And though he wished he could help her change that, he was pretty sure that he was not the man to do it.

After all, they were just friends.

Weren't they?

Chapter Five

"Axel, just do me one favor and pick up my phone from Evan's, would you?" She couldn't believe that she hadn't given the cell phone one single thought when she'd run into Evan earlier that morning.

Leandra's brother gave her a lazy look. He was sprawled on a kitchen chair in Sarah's kitchen, a can of soda balanced on his belly. "God, Leandra, are you that lazy? He's five minutes away."

"Exactly. It won't take you long. And as you can see—" she waved her hand over the pile of materials that had been delivered by courier about the same time that her little brother had meandered up Sarah's neat walk "—I'm sort of busy."

"So am I."

She lifted an eyebrow. "Doing what?"

"Enjoying the company of my errant sister."

"Think *errant* describes you more than me. You've been out of college a year now, right? Still sponging off Mom and Dad?"

His lips twitched. "Damn straight."

She shook her head, amused despite herself. She set down her pen and focused on Ax. They had the same brown eyes, and though he was blond like she was, his hair was a much darker gold than hers. Only, in the irony of the universe, he not only had longer lashes than she did, his hair was thicker, too. He was four years younger than she was; she loved him to death, but she felt like she was a lifetime older than he was.

"You've spent the last year traveling around the world, seems like. So what *do* you plan to do? Seriously?"

"Maybe I'm already doing it," he said.

"Drinking cola?" Not even the diet kind. No, her brother was graced with a metabolism that didn't worry about that sort of thing, either.

"I work for CeeVid," he reminded her, and she was surprised at the hint of defensiveness in his voice. "Just because it's Tristan's company doesn't mean I don't earn my keep."

"I wasn't suggesting that. I just didn't think you got a degree in political science so you could ride a desk right here in Weaver."

"Some people like Weaver, Leandra. Not everyone figures it's a place to escape."

"I wasn't escaping. I was…living." And what would have happened if she *hadn't* left Weaver? Would she have been a better wife? A better mother?

If she hadn't left Weaver, she'd never have married Jake, so the questioning was entirely pointless.

"What's your phone doing over at Evan's, anyway?"

Because, twice now, she hadn't managed to remember the darn thing. "I loaned it to him yesterday out at the farm." It was true in a sense.

"Heard you sat with him this morning over at Ruby's."

She should have known. Her little brother had always had a bodily connection to the Weaver grapevine. "So?"

"Why didn't you get it then?"

"What does it matter to you?"

"You're the one who wants me to play errand boy."

She picked up her pen, determined to remain nonchalant. "Forget about it. I'll get it later."

"What'd you think of Hannah?"

She squelched a sigh. "Axel, I have *work* to do, here. Aren't there any available females around anymore?"

"I save that for later in the day, when the sun goes down and stars come out." His eyes gleamed. "So? What'd you think?"

She shoved her pen behind her ear and fixed her gaze on her brother. "I think she's a very pretty little girl who looks a lot like Evan."

"And Katy."

"Undoubtedly. They are related."

"She's autistic, you know. Hannah, I mean."

"I figured it was something like that."

"Did Evan say so?"

"He didn't need to. Some things I can actually discern for myself. Now, either go get the phone, or go drink soda elsewhere."

He jackknifed his legs and rose. "You haven't changed since you were ten, you know. Still bossy as hell." He rumpled her hair as he passed her on his way to the living room. "Dad would be proud that you're displaying the Clay genetic trait so well."

She shook her head, but she was smiling as she turned her attention back to the production notes that Marian had sent.

There was a ton of work yet to be done on Evan's shoot, particularly with the first episode airing the next day. There was also a mammoth amount of work going on for the next series, set to feature a young cheerleading coach who was trying to break in to singing. The only problem was the girl—beautiful and wonderfully fit though she was—couldn't carry a tune in a bucket. There would be plenty of ear-splitting, wince-inducing footage of her efforts, no doubt.

Marian, currently filming it, predicted that the viewers would love it, and Leandra supposed there was some truth in that.

Thank goodness Evan's story wouldn't include anything so embarrassing. It wasn't as if she was exploiting any of his dearest dreams the way Marian was with Whitney Sanchez. But the business was weird. For all Leandra knew, Whitney could end up as famous as she'd ever dreamed as a result of *WITS*.

Leandra heard her brother's footsteps behind her. "Twenty bucks," she offered. "Easy money, Ax."

"I'm all for easy money," a voice—not her brother's—answered. "As proven by last night at Colbys. What's the gig this time?"

She looked around to see Evan standing there. Of Axel the rat, there was no sight. "Nothing," she assured him. "I hope you have my phone." Better to get it out quickly, lest she forget yet again. When it came to her thought processes around Evan, she was beginning to wonder about herself.

Fortunately, he pulled the small phone from his pocket. An action that *unfortunately* drew her attention to the shape of the man beneath the soft blue denim.

His fingers grazed her palm as he dropped the phone into her outstretched hand. She set it aside on the table, quickly looking away from him. "Thank you. Where's your niece?"

"Having a nap at my mom's. And I ought to thank *you*. That phone rings every hour on the hour, practically. Made me want to curse Beethoven's composing skills. It's no wonder you weren't in any hurry to get it back."

"I—" she bit off the denial that she *had* been anxious for the phone. How would she explain her reason for continuing to forget it was tied entirely to the way he had of scrambling her brains? "Sorry," she said instead. "It does ring a lot. Comes with the territory." Even as she said the words, the little phone vibrated against the table, and sent out its first tinny note.

He made a humorous grimace and turned out of the kitchen as she picked up the phone. "Hello, Marian," she greeted. "I got the courier pack. I'm nearly finished."

She held the phone a few inches away from her ear as her boss went into her latest litany. Through the doorway from the kitchen, she could see Evan standing in the small living room. He seemed completely out of place among the fine lines of Sarah's furnishings. He was much more suited to rustic woods and knobby fabrics than to Chippendale and English chintz.

"Dig up his old girlfriends," Marian was saying when Leandra belatedly tuned back in. "I'm sending a second crew to New York to get some background."

"Wait a minute. Why? For what?"

"Not for what. Who. Why did I have to learn from Ted that your hunky hometown vet had a thwarted love affair with a citified ballerina? You're holding out on me, Leandra, and I don't like it."

"Lucy Buchanan comes from Weaver, too," Leandra said quietly, not wanting Evan to hear. "And that story goes back way too far to be of interest. They dated in school, for heaven's sake."

"Well it's the only love life that apparently exists for studly Evan Taggart. Or maybe he's more of a dud than a stud. Is that it, Leandra? Is Evan more interested in the gents than in the ladies?"

Leandra pressed her fingers against her temples. "Marian, I can assure you that Evan Taggart is *not* gay. And even if he *were,* it would have no relevance to our shoot! *WITS* isn't about his sex life. It's about his career."

"Honey, if you haven't learned yet that *everything* is about sex, then you're in the wrong business."

"Maybe I am." Leandra's temper sizzled. Which was

exactly the reason why she wanted to get out from beneath Marian's thumb. There were interesting stories and people all around the world. Informative, empowering stories. Stories that could change people's lives, even. And they didn't have to be steeped in titillation to be told. "But right now, this is where I am at."

"And don't you forget who put you there."

"Eduard put me here," Leandra reminded just as coolly. She'd been on the *WITS* crew longer than Marian had been.

The reminder was enough to silence Marian, for once. After all, Eduard Montrechet was the money behind *WITS*. Marian worked for him just as much as Leandra did.

"I'll send my production notes before Monday morning," Leandra said more calmly. "Is there anything else we needed to discuss?"

"Get them to me by tomorrow night," Marian snapped, clearly still feeling a need to establish her authority. "Before the show airs. I'll probably have to work all night just to get things in order for Monday's taping."

"Fine." Leandra let the insult pass. "You'll have them by tomorrow night."

Her answer was a click. Marian had hung up.

Leandra sighed, closing the phone. Escape, she thought faintly. Just let me escape.

"Why are you doing this, Leandra?"

She couldn't look at Evan. Not yet. She lifted her shoulder and set aside the phone, keeping her attention on the schedules and lists and budgets that were spread across the kitchen table. "You have your living, I have mine. Thanks, again, for the phone."

"Why were you talking about Lucy?" He pulled out the chair beside her and sat on it. Sprawled, really, much the same way Axel had done. He picked up the cell phone and toyed with it, balancing it on end between his palm and the table top. "Can I only hope that you're thinking she'd be a subject for *WITS?*"

Following a New York City ballerina around would definitely be interesting—and it had definitely been done before, something that *WITS* tried to avoid. "Marian heard that you and she were high school sweethearts."

"And?"

There was no reading the expression on his face. His voice was calm, also revealing exactly nothing.

There was no point in prevaricating, even if she'd wanted to do so. Evan would know soon enough what was in the wind. "And Marian wants to pursue whether or not there remains any interest or involvement between the two of you." Her voice was flat.

His lips twisted a little at that. "The local yokel and the girl who made good?"

"Lovers thwarted by whatever reason."

"What do you think? That Lucy and I are thwarted lovers?"

She shifted, gathering pages together in a careful pile. "It doesn't matter what I think."

He didn't respond to that. After a moment, he stretched out a long arm and plucked one of Sarah's photos off the refrigerator. "Remember when this was taken?"

She glanced at it. Five girls. Five boys. The girls dressed to the nines and the guys looking like they wanted to rip off their bow ties. "Prom night."

"Weaver and Braden had to combine their high school proms. Only way they could get enough kids together to qualify as a prom."

"I remember."

"They still do it the same way, even now. Trade locations each year. One year in Weaver. The next in Braden."

"The trip down memory lane isn't necessary. I remember how it was."

"Do you?" He set down the photograph. It was facing away from Leandra, but she had no trouble seeing the image. Evan's arm had been looped around Lucy's shoulder. Except for those brief few weeks in high school when Evan had claimed to be crazy for Leandra, his arm had nearly *always* been around Lucy's shoulders. Even at that age, Leandra had known not to take the word of a guy who was in love with someone else.

"Of course I do." She signed her name to the bottom of Janet's latest expense sheet and added it to the pile, then reached for Paul's report.

Evan caught her hand, pen and all, before she could reach it. "You think Lucy and I were lovers? That I've spent all these years—an entire decade—pining for her?"

Her hand tingled. "I've already said that it doesn't matter what I think. Could I have my hand back, please?"

He ignored the request. "That I didn't have the where-withal to go after a woman I wanted, even if it meant going all the way to the big…bad…city?" He finished with an exaggerated drawl.

"I don't know, Evan. Do you?" All the irritation she felt probably showed in the look she gave him. "You're the one who—with the exception of veterinary school—has pretty much stuck close to home. Unlike nearly every other single man of your age in this town, you're still unattached. Who *wouldn't* think you were pining for Lucy? For a while there in school, you guys talked about getting married, remember?"

"We were kids. That's all. And believe me. I usually do go after what I want." His fingers tightened on hers. "Sometimes the smarter thing is *not* going."

She frowned at him. Heat was seeping—no, it was tingling

its way right up her arm. "If that's some sort of comment on *my* leaving Weaver, then—"

"Then what?" He leaned closer to her. "If you don't like what I say, Leandra, just what are you going to do about it?"

She was trembling. She was actually trembling. And there was no way the man could be unaware of it. "I'll give Ted his rein and he and his camera will dog every footstep of yours twenty-four-seven from now until we wrap."

A dimple slashed his hard cheek. His voice dropped a notch. He leaned even closer, until she could feel the whisper of his words on her face. "Why am I not the one shaking in my boots?"

She couldn't respond. Her head was blank.

No, it wasn't blank. It was filled with color. Sapphire-blue color.

Like his eyes.

And her head was filled with scent. Piney and lemony and outdoorsy.

Like him.

And she was filled with want.

For him.

His thick lashes lowered. He was looking at her mouth. She pressed her lips together, wanting to deny everything.

The moment.

The possibilities of what it would feel like to once, just once, have his mouth on hers.

"Whoops. Guess you really didn't hear me come in."

Leandra jumped back from Evan, staring stupidly at Ted, who was standing in the hallway, looking into the kitchen. "What?"

"Your brother was outside. He told me to come on in." Ted was grinning. "Didn't know I was interrupting something."

Her face couldn't possibly get any hotter. "You're not," she assured him blithely. "Have you finished your expense report, yet? I didn't see it in my stuff."

"That's what I came over for." He pulled a slightly crumpled, very folded-up piece of paper from a pocket on the side of his khaki cargo pants and handed it over. "Sorry it's late. To make up for it, I'll take your stuff to the courier when you're finished up to send back to Marian."

That was a particular task that would require a drive over to Braden, since the local carrier's office was already closed. "Guess you decided hanging around town all weekend wasn't so interesting, after all?"

He looked slightly uncomfortable, but just shrugged. "So, we cool?"

"Yes. We're cool." Leandra unfolded the paper, glanced over it before signing and handed it back to him, along with a thick bundle of papers and several videotapes. "She wants it before tomorrow night."

"No prob." Ted grinned at Evan. "I'll let you two get back to it."

Leandra wanted the earth to open up and swallow her right then and there. Her mind, sadly, had no problem whatsoever conjuring a dozen scenarios involving a very specific "it" and she felt as if that particular fact might as well be tattooed on her forehead in flaming scarlet letters.

She turned blindly to the cupboards, opening and closing them. Dragging down a bowl. Scattering wooden spoons onto the countertop.

"Now what are you doing?" Evan asked.

What *was* she doing? Besides losing her mind and feeling like her body was on the verge of some sinful conflagration? "Baking." In more ways than one. At least in her current frenzy she'd pulled out a boxed cake mix, so the explanation held a modicum of credibility.

"Any particular reason?"

"I need something to do." She resolutely tore open the box, and it ripped right in two. The sealed bag of mix inside tumbled out. She tossed aside the box.

Did he really have to stand there watching her like he was?

Eggs. She needed eggs. And oil. Or something. She tried fitting the two pieces of the box back together. Yes. There was a picture of three eggs. Thank goodness the instructions were excruciatingly elementary. Her mind was working on only two cylinders.

"Why are you acting weird? Jake also said you never baked."

She yanked open the refrigerator door and pulled out the egg carton. "Maybe I just never baked for Jake. Why are you so preoccupied with him, anyway?" Eduard. Jake. What *was* Evan's problem? She fumbled one of the eggs as she pulled it from the carton and it wobbled across the counter, heading for the edge.

He caught it easily, closing one hand over it. "You're nervous."

"I am not." She pushed her finger at his hand, wanting the egg.

"Yes you are."

"No I'm not! What are we? Five years old and playing in the sandbox?"

His lips quirked and even though she was irritated with him for some truly unfathomable reason, she couldn't help but respond. She gave a half laugh, shaking her head. "Could I please have the egg?"

"I'm not pining for Lucy." He took her wrist in his fingers and turned her hand, placing the egg in her palm. "Talk to her, do whatever." He folded her fingers around the egg, but didn't release her. "There's nothing interesting there."

What was interesting was the way she was suddenly short of breath again. "Why not?"

His thumb slowly stroked over the veins pulsing in her wrist. "Why not…what?"

She swallowed. "Pining?"

"For Lucy," he murmured. His thumb stopped moving, seeming to press directly over her pulse. "I said I wasn't pining for *her.*"

She needed to pursue that. Marian would want her to pursue that. Only doing her job was not anything she wanted to be doing just then.

"Evan—"

He seemed to be watching the progress of his hand as it moved up her wrist to her forearm. A sliver of blue between thick black lashes. "Hmm?"

"What are we doing?" Her voice was barely a whisper.

His hand paused at her elbow, palm curling around it.

Her nerves tightened.

He looked at her. "Something I've wanted to do for a long time," he murmured.

And he lowered his head, covering her mouth with his.

Chapter Six

Evan had kissed her once. A long time ago.

This was nothing like it.

This was not like anything.

His lips grazed hers, barely a whisper. One that sounded through her like a full-bodied orchestra. A soft sound came out of her from nowhere. She felt the egg rolling out of her lax fingers, and wanted to sink into him when his arm closed around her, pulling her close.

He caught her face in his hand, tilting her chin higher, and she dragged in a breath when he lifted his mouth for a moment. She thought she heard him swear, then his mouth was on hers again and the whisper had become a shout.

This was Evan. What was she—what were *they*—doing?

It didn't matter. Reason didn't matter. Her mouth opened under his, her hands dragged through his hair. She couldn't get enough, couldn't get close enough and he must have felt the same for his hands dragged down her spine, caught her waist and she felt her feet leave the ground as he lifted her higher.

She gasped, and still he kissed her. Deeper. Hotter. Her mind spun as his belt buckle dragged against her belly. Her breasts flattened against his chest until she could feel his heart beating against hers.

"Yo, Evan."

Yes, this *was* Evan. How had she managed to miss this all the years they'd known one another? She wanted to wrap herself around him and absorb him into her very being.

"Yo, oh, *dude*." The voice turned pained. "Get a room, would you, please?"

Protest rose in her as the source of all things wonderful pulled his mouth away from hers. Just as rapidly, she realized that they were no longer alone.

Her forehead hit Evan's shoulder for a nanosecond and then she was scrambling away from him. Eyeing with some shock the way his shirt was half buttoned. The way his hair was disheveled.

Leandrà didn't know if she needed to thank Axel for his interruption or strangle him. "What do you want?"

Her little brother was eyeing her with a thoroughly irksome amusement. "Don't shoot the messenger, Leandra. Evan's phone's been ringing for ten minutes, easy. We heard it all the way from his truck. Whoever is calling is pretty persistent."

Phones. What was the significance of all this *phone* business in her life?

Then it hit her. Belatedly, of course. That's the problem when a woman's mind—and body—was fogged with lust. The brain cells starting operating on half time.

"We heard it," Axel had said. *We.*

She managed to focus beyond her brother to the man standing

behind him. Ted. Well, it just figured, didn't it? If she were going to be found making a fool of herself, why not be found by a co-worker of hers as well as by her annoying little brother?

Evan wasn't saying much of anything, but he was watching Leandra. She wished she could tell what he was thinking. Feeling. Chagrined? Embarrassed? Thwarted?

She felt all that and more. And she didn't much like having witnesses to it. "Ted, the courier service closes in a few hours. You planning to make it or not?"

"Yeah, it's cool. Just got caught up talking with Axel for a few minutes." He was still holding the paperwork she'd given him. "I'll get going now."

The sooner the better, as far as Leandra was concerned. She looked at her brother. "I thought you'd left, too."

His lips twitched. "Obviously."

The man was enjoying her discomfort far too much. Clearly, their parents hadn't disciplined him enough as a child. "So…why are you still loitering around here?"

"Wanted to talk to Ev about Northern Light."

Leandra lifted her eyebrows. "What about him?"

"Has your name changed to Evan Taggart?"

She made a face. "Fine. Talk away. I have work to do, anyway."

"Leandra."

That was all it took. One utterance of her name in *his* low voice and she was melting all over again.

Yes, she definitely preferred having her libido in cold storage. Being at the mercy of it like this was more than her nerves could take. And having her brother as a witness was more than her pride could take. "I have to run to the grocery. For…um…oil. Sarah doesn't have any oil." She had no way of knowing that, since she hadn't looked, but as an excuse it would do since she was fresh out of imagination.

"Leandra." Evan held out his arm, stopping her dash from the room.

She looked at his hand, suffered an appallingly vivid image of those long, calloused fingers running over her bare flesh, and knew some creative cells were still in treacherous operation.

"I'll see you tomorrow. At Colbys for the party."

His lips twisted. "Don't know why there has to be a damn party just 'cause your show is going to be on television."

"There is a party because everyone in town wants to see *you* on TV for the first time," she countered. "We always do it. Good community spirit and all that. Ted will be filming, too." She skirted his hand, ignoring Axel and trying hard to ignore the narrow-eyed gaze of Evan's that followed her cowardly escape.

She drove her small rental, and instead of hitting the old grocery that had been located in the center of town on Main Street, she drove to the far end of town where all the newer establishments were centered around the sprawling structure that housed CeeVid.

There, the grocery store was nicely impersonal. There were no former schoolmates tending the shelves or parked at the soda fountain counter sharing the latest gossip. There were wide aisles and piped music and she could have been in any supermarket from California to Kansas.

She located the oil and paid for it, and back in her car once again found she was a chicken of such magnitude that she didn't want to go back to Sarah's just yet. It would be just like Axel to hang around waiting. And who knew what would be just like Evan. *He* didn't seem to be the man she remembered, at all.

Who knew he could kiss like that? Or that he could set her skin on fire just from a touch of his hand?

When she drove back through town, she passed Evan's two-story house. The clinic—larger than the house—was behind it, and she could see his dusty pickup truck parked in front of it.

Well, at least *he'd* gone home.

Ninny that *she* was, though, her foot hit the gas a little harder as she sped past. As if he were standing behind the big picture window just waiting to catch her driving by.

The man was probably just amusing himself with her. For no reason that made any sense to her, though.

He and Jake were really good friends, after all.

But Leandra and Jake were finished and had been for a long time.

She turned onto Sarah's street, trying to shut off the ping-pong debate going on inside her head, and coasted to a stop in front of the little house.

Just get through the shoot and move on, she reminded herself. This little detour in Weaver is just that. A detour. Another step on the path where her life couldn't be destroyed again by her own failures.

She nearly jumped out of her skin when someone knocked on the window right beside her head. Sarah looked in at her, concern drawing her eyebrows together as she juggled her book bag. "You okay?"

Her heart slowing again, Leandra nodded. She grabbed up the cooking oil and her purse and left the car. "I was woolgathering, I guess."

Sarah eyed the oil. "I hope that's for mundane purposes and not because *WITS* is heading off into previously unexplored adultlike directions."

"I was baking a cake."

Her cousin stopped in her tracks halfway up the walk. "No kidding. And you didn't see the oil in the cupboard?"

Leandra shrugged, her face warming.

Sarah grinned. "I ran into Axel on my way here. He told me you were here with Evan."

Her fingers flexed around the plastic bottle. "That's all he said?"

Sarah nodded and took the last few steps to the door. "That, and the fact that you had your tongues down each other's throats." She smiled brightly and opened the door.

"I'm going to kill my brother."

Sarah chuckled. Leandra followed her to the kitchen, where she dumped the unnecessary purchase on the counter. The eggs were still resting on the counter, uncracked.

Her cousin looked at the display. "Wow. You really *were* planning to bake a cake."

"Why is everyone so shocked by that fact? I cooked breakfast for Evan just yesterday."

Sarah dumped her satchel on the table. "And a surprise that was, too. Probably because you once vowed that anything to do with a kitchen—other than eating what came out of it—held no interest to you. So, what was it like kissing Evan?"

"Fabulous." The truthful answer came out unexpectedly and she felt her cheeks heat even more.

Sarah laughed softly. "Let's just be glad that *someone* is kissing someone, okay? God knows I haven't had a reason to touch up my lip gloss in a good long while."

"But he's *Evan!*"

"I know." Sarah's eyes twinkled. She picked up the eggs and deftly cracked them in the bowl. "Six foot something, black-haired, blue-eyed Evan Taggart."

"Six foot two," Leandra murmured. She knew exactly, because they'd asked him for the information for the promotion they were doing for his episodes. "You're not interested in him, are you?" she asked suddenly. Surely her cousin would have said something if she were.

Sarah looked shocked, as if the idea had never once occurred to her.

Leandra kind of knew how that felt. Until recently, the idea had never particularly consumed her, either.

"No," her cousin assured her. "So, it wasn't just a kissing session, then. You're *interested* in the man."

Immediate denial sprung to her lips, only to go unvoiced. "I don't know what to think," she finally admitted. She sank down on one of the kitchen chairs and watched her cousin mix together the rest of the ingredients. "He's a *friend*."

"Yeah." Sarah measured oil and water into the bowl and handed it to Leandra, along with a wooden spoon. "So try not to break each other's hearts while you're at it."

She snatched the bowl and began stirring. "I've never broken anyone's heart."

"What about Jake?"

The spoon paused for a moment. "No. To be fair, he didn't break mine, either. What broke us both was—" Her voice strangled to a stop. She stirred harder. "Don't we need a cake pan or something?" She pushed the words out, wanting desperately to change the subject.

Sarah pulled out a pan and silently set it in front of her. "What broke you both was losing Emi," she said quietly. "It's more than any person should have to bear. But—"

"I don't want to talk about it." She pushed out of her chair and turned on the oven with an abrupt twist. Talking about kissing Evan was easier than talking about Emi. And she didn't really want to discuss either.

Sarah's gaze was unflinching. "One of these days you're going to need to talk about it, don't you think?"

"You tell me," her voice suddenly shook. "You're the one

who took all of her pictures off your refrigerator." She shoved the pan in the oven despite the fact that it was not even close to being preheated, and strode out of the kitchen.

"Leandra!" Sarah called after her, but Leandra just shook her head and kept moving, right out the front door.

She made it across the street and through the park before her anger gave way and she sank down on the grass, watching two girls playing on the swings in the playground.

She pressed her head to her knees, feeling the soft breeze flow over her head. The girls' chatter was indistinct, merely a soothing sound on a quiet afternoon.

What was wrong with her, snapping at Sarah like that? She knew her cousin had only been trying to make things easier for her by removing the pictures.

Coming to Weaver was just making her crazier than ever. Sniping at Sarah. Kissing Evan. What would be next?

She groaned, pressed her head harder to her knees and told herself to just get…a…grip.

"You look like you've lost your best friend."

It wasn't the comment that sent ripples down her back, but the voice. She couldn't even pretend to be surprised, though. Evan seemed to be everywhere these days. Why not at the park on a Saturday afternoon?

"Are you following me?" She looked up at him, shaking a strand of hair out of her eyes and was startled at the sight of Hannah leaning against his leg. Her head was on a level with Leandra's, and the little girl gave her a long stare before blinking her silky lashes.

"Hannah likes the swings. And since she had a good nap, she gets the swings." He crouched down and turned the child until she was facing the playground. Two of the three swings were still occupied by the older girls. "Go ahead," he encouraged.

Leandra was not entirely surprised when Hannah took

about five steps onto the sandy play area, then stopped. She sat down on her rear and began running her toy car up and down her jeans-clad leg. Her tiny tennis shoes tapped against the sand beneath her. Evan didn't coax her any further, though. He just smiled when Hannah cast him a sidelong look, and then sat down next to Leandra.

"Tabby's terrier got loose earlier and licked Hannah's hand. She was upset for an hour. Couldn't tell it looking at her now, though."

"Is she staying all weekend with you?"

"Nah. I'll take her back to Sharon's before supper time. So, what's wrong?"

"Nothing."

"Sure?" He stretched out his legs. They seemed ridiculously long, and she was vaguely surprised to see that he wore white tennis shoes rather than the cowboy boots he typically favored.

"Quite sure."

He plucked a long blade of grass and held it up to study. "Then why are you hunched down here in the park all alone?"

"Sometimes I *like* being alone," she said pointedly.

He slanted a look her way, then turned it back to the grass. He apparently found it wanting, for he tossed it aside and plucked another. He ran his fingers along it, then carefully positioned his fingers, held it to his lips and blew.

A sharp whistle sounded.

Hannah looked back at him and laughed. The breeze tugged at her hair, making it dance around her narrow shoulders.

A smile creased his face and he whistled through the grass again.

Not even two hours ago, she'd been climbing up the man like he was some tree and she a loved-starved monkey. Now, he was whistling through grass to make a little girl laugh. She sighed faintly, smiling a little even though there was a part of her that wanted to cry. "You should have children of your own," she finally said.

He let the grass go and it flitted about in the breeze before settling on the ground. "Then I'd need a wife."

"Well, not technically, though it's the nice way to go about it."

"Only way I'd go about it."

"I don't know, Evan. Accidents happen. Haven't there been women you've—"

"No."

She lifted her eyebrows. "No? Just what does that no mean?"

He leaned back on one arm, his gaze as vivid as the cloud-bejeweled sky above them. "You asking because of the show, Leandra, or because you want to know who or how many women have been warming my bed?"

"I couldn't be the least bit interested, personally," she assured him.

His smile was slow. And it made her twitchy all over, just seeing it. "Right," he drawled.

That's what she got for telling bald-faced lies. She'd never been good at it, not even when she was five years old and in cahoots with her grandfather to sneak away with her mother's brownies. "Well?" She managed the challenge, anyway.

"I'm no saint, but I can assure you, there aren't any unclaimed Taggarts running around. Not from me."

She felt like groaning all over again. Naturally he'd feel that way. It was because his mother had become pregnant with him and abandoned by Darian that she'd ended up married to Darian's half brother, Drew. "I didn't mean—"

His eyebrow lifted, obviously waiting.

She sighed again. Seemed she was in rare form that day for saying the wrong things to people. "I'm sorry."

"Tell me who Eduard is and we'll call it even."

"He owns the production company that produces *WITS*," she informed, her voice abrupt.

"And?"

She tugged her ear. "And nothing. He's seventy years old, if he's a day, all right? I work for him. He's promised me a new show if I can prove myself with *WITS*."

"Yet he taught you how to make fancy eggs."

"So? It wasn't for breakfast after we'd spent a tawdry night together, I assure you. I crewed on a cooking show he produces in Paris. He was always trying out recipes on us that he'd learned from the show."

He looked oddly frustrated. "Why didn't you just say so in the first place?"

"Because you were making such a fuss about it!"

His jaw shifted to one side then slowly centered. "You are one ornery woman, you know that?"

"I'm not a Clay for nothing," she muttered.

"That's for damn sure."

"If you find it so terrible, then why do I keep tripping over you every time I turn around?"

"You're the one who came back to *my* town, Leandra. You left a long time ago."

She stared past Hannah. The two older girls had lost interest in the swings and were skipping away from the playground toward the opposite side of the park. She and Sarah, J.D. and Angeline had played in much the same way when they'd been young.

Leandra had never had a chance to teach Emi to skip. She'd been too young.

She brushed her hand over her eyes and looked back at Evan. "And since I left, I'm not allowed to claim Weaver as my home anymore? Seems pretty harsh."

"Where *do* you call home? California? Jake said you have

an apartment a few miles from his but that you never spend any time there because you're always off on location somewhere. You've cut off friends. Hell, you practically cut off your family."

"I never realized that I was such a topic of interest between you and Jake. What does he do? Call you to rehash all of my oddities? Do you check in on me with my folks here, too?"

He shook his head, looking annoyed.

She wasn't sure she believed him.

"Jake wants you to be happy again," Evan said after a moment.

Leandra pressed her lips together for a moment. It was a struggle not to cut and run right then and there. "I want him to be happy, too."

"Have you told *him* that?"

"Of course."

"Are you sure?"

She frowned. "What are you getting at?"

He shrugged, suddenly looking as casual as if they were watching June bugs beside the swimming hole on a summer evening, and she didn't believe the ruse for a second.

"Just seems to me that you might still be more involved than you think," he commented.

"Trust me. We're not."

"You called him to do the show."

"Because he's perfect for the camera, just like you are!" She stretched her legs out, only to draw them back in and cross them. "Criminy, Evan, what does it matter?"

His jaw tightened for a moment. "Because he's trying to move on and so should you."

"I'm not keeping him from moving on."

"Are you so sure?"

She eyed him harder. "What is *with* you?"

"I don't think you want to move on."

"What would you call that bit of *moving* around earlier today in Sarah's kitchen?" She realized her voice had risen and closed her mouth tightly.

"Lust," he said smoothly and even though she'd called it that herself, she still felt stung by the word.

Well, what had she wanted? For him to profess some unspoken adoration of her or something?

This was Evan Taggart here. She knew him too well from days of old. He'd pulled her hair when he'd sat behind her in third grade. He'd put a frog in her lunch box one time. Not that she'd minded all that much—she'd sort of been into frogs when she was ten.

But adoring, he was not.

"I don't *do* lust," she assured him repressively.

He laughed.

Annoyed, she balled her fist and slammed it into his arm, knocking it out from beneath him. He hit the ground flat, and still he laughed.

Harder.

She wanted to pummel him.

Hannah was watching them, a half smile on her pretty face, as if she were equal parts curious and equal parts amused over his behavior.

"Go ahead. Laugh it up, Chuckles." She pushed to her feet, but Evan reached out and grabbed her ankle.

"Don't go getting in a snit. It's too nice an afternoon for it." He was still grinning that wicked, wicked grin. "Besides, who are you kidding?" He made a face and mimicked her. "I don't do lust."

She shook her foot, but dog that he was, he had a hold. "Someone is going to see us," she warned, trying not to smile, herself. How utterly ridiculous they must look. "Look, there are cars driving by right now." She shook her foot yet again and his grip slipped below the hem of her jeans, touching her bare ankle.

It was like he'd touched her with a live wire.

She jumped. He jumped. They stared at each other.

And Hannah suddenly started screaming.

His gaze shuttered and he swore under his breath, pushing to his feet and hurrying over to the girl.

Leandra pressed a hand to her heart that had seemed to have completely stopped for a moment there and took several instinctive steps toward Hannah as well, before she stopped herself and stayed where she was.

Hannah looked perfectly fine. She was still sitting in the sand, her thumb spinning the wheels of her ever-present car. No tears. Just that high, keening scream.

Evan scooped her up. Leandra couldn't hear what he said to the girl, but after a moment, she stopped screaming just as abruptly as she'd started. She pushed at him and he set her back down, but this time, she didn't sit in the sand. She kept her head against Evan's leg and wrapped her arm proprietarily around his knee. Her blue gaze—so like the man who towered above her—studied Leandra.

Leandra didn't really need the reminder, though.

Hannah was the female who counted in Evan's life. Appealing as Evan could be when he wanted to be, Leandra couldn't afford to forget that she was only there because of *WITS*.

When the job was done, she was gone.

Leandra brushed her hands down the sides of her jeans. "I'd better get back."

"Hannah acts out sometimes. Don't let it bother you."

"You don't have to explain, Evan. I understand."

His eyebrows drew together. "Some people around here don't. Sharon told me they were in the grocery store the other day and something set off Hannah and a woman told Sharon to keep her c-r-a-z-y-blanking kid away from the public." His hand smoothed over Hannah's silky hair.

"Consider the source and let it go. The woman was an idiot. Don't take stock of idiots."

"I don't." He took a step forward only to stop since doing so would have dragged Hannah along a foot, also.

"She has a grip like you do," Leandra observed dryly. "I'll see you tomorrow for your big debut."

Once again, he looked several shades less than thrilled at the prospect. But it wasn't the show he mentioned, when he spoke again. "Leandra, about Jake."

"What about him?" He had her full attention, yet he was silent and it birthed a kernel of worry inside her. "What about him, Evan? He's all right, isn't he?"

"You two need to talk."

Even more disconcerted, she nodded warily. "Okay."

He nodded. "Good."

"Well." She swallowed. There was only so much yo-yoing her emotions could take, and the day had held plenty already. "See you later."

He silently lifted a hand.

It was Hannah, though, who spoke. "Goodbye, Leandra."

She started. Evan, too, looked just as surprised. "Goodbye, Hannah," she returned.

Then, feeling more off-balance than ever, she retraced her steps back to Sarah's place.

Chapter Seven

The moment Leandra opened the door, she smelled chocolate.

"Hey." Sarah barely looked up from her paperback book, which she was reading while sprawled out on the couch. "You're just in time to take the cake out of the oven."

Sure enough, the oven timer went off with a buzz the moment she'd finished speaking.

Leandra went into the kitchen and pulled out the cake, setting it on the cooling rack that Sarah had left out on the counter, and turned off the oven. The chocolate smelled as wonderful as chocolate ever did, but Leandra had no particular appetite for the thing. She tossed the hot pad on the counter and turned away.

But the refrigerator door caught her attention first.

Still a jumble of pictures. Still a mass of images.

Only, Emi's face was back among them. Just a trio of pictures. Emi at her third birthday party. She'd been wearing a sunny yellow dress.

Leandra closed her eyes for a moment, letting out a long, slow breath.

Sarah came up behind her and pressed her head against Leandra's. "I have dozens more."

"I know." She turned and hugged her cousin. "I'm sorry. I know you were trying to help." She swallowed, and stepped back. "I'm just a crazy person, I think."

"You're not crazy," Sarah dismissed. "We're all trying to take our lead from you, sweetie. You haven't wanted to even mention Emi's name. I thought putting away the pictures was what you'd want."

"Maybe it was." She pushed at her forehead and the pain that seemed to have lodged itself there, and went into the living room. "Evan told me to talk to Jake."

"Was that before you were necking in my kitchen, or after?" Sarah flopped on the couch beside her.

"We weren't necking." Her forehead throbbed harder. Maybe the pain was her version of Pinocchio's wooden nose. For every lie, the pain got worse. "All right, so maybe we were almost necking. Sort of. Maybe."

"Now you're sounding like a politician." Sarah looked amused.

"And it was in the park just now."

"There was more necking there? Wow. Usually the kids wait until after dark for that sort of thing, but you two—"

"Ha-ha. We weren't doing anything there. We just ran into each other. He took Hannah over there to play at the playground. He told me I needed to talk to Jake."

"About what?"

Leandra lifted her shoulders. "It worries me, though. What if something's wrong?"

"Then you'll deal with it," Sarah said simply.

Leandra frowned. "Because I've proven how well I *deal?*"

She pulled out her cell phone and dialed her ex-husband. When she got a busy signal, she was relieved, which just proved her point.

She tucked the phone back in her pocket and raked her fingers through her hair. "When was the last time you went riding?"

Sarah started to smile. "Your dad's place or mine?"

"Let's go to the Double C. I haven't seen the big house since I got here."

"You're on. You bring boots?"

"I figure you probably have a spare pair lying around."

Sarah did, and hours later, Leandra knew that some things hadn't changed over the years, and the pleasure of spending the afternoon on the back of a horse was, thankfully, one of them.

They took their time, plodding over ground that Leandra had once known as well as the back of her hand. There had been few changes at the Double C since she'd last been there and that was a pleasure, too. A part of her felt guilty for enjoying it so, when she didn't seem to be able to find that easy pleasure at her parents' spread.

By the time they took the horses in, it was evening and Jaimie, Sarah's mother, had the table already set for dinner. Leaving was, of course, out of the question.

The meal was yet another step back in time. Fried chicken, mashed potatoes and gravy. Leandra half expected her aunt to offer her cherry Kool-Aid, which had been pretty much her favorite drink until she was a teenager.

Matthew sat at the head of the big oak table that sat center in the spacious kitchen. His hair was clipped short and his lean, suntanned face made his icy blue eyes look even lighter. Jaimie, an older version of Sarah right down to the long, reddish hair, sat opposite him. And even though Leandra knew they'd been married nearly as long as her own parents had been, she swore they were still giving each other the eye across the table in the same way they had nearly every time Leandra had spent the night with Sarah at the big house.

Not that her parents were any different. Growing up, it had been embarrassing. She wasn't entirely sure that it wasn't embarrassing *now*.

Sarah looked at Leandra over the rim of her iced tea glass, seemed to read her mind and rolled her eyes, smiling and shrugging a little.

"They think we're old coots, Matthew," Jaimie observed, noticing their exchange. Her green eyes danced.

"Maybe I am, Red, but we all know you'll never be old enough to qualify."

Jaimie reached out and patted Sarah's hand humorously. "Your children are your children all their life, darling. You ought to be used to it by now. Some day you'll see." Her smile included Leandra, knowing perfectly well what she'd said. She'd never been afraid of broaching sensitive subjects, and yet she managed to do so without causing pain.

That was her Auntie Jaimie. Bold and loving.

"Now, Leandra. Tell me the truth." Jaimie leaned her elbow on the table. "Were you really making out with Evan in the playground this afternoon?"

Leandra straightened like a shot, nearly spilling her tea down her front. "What?"

"Mom, where did you hear such a thing?"

"Oh, you know Weaver, Sarah. Somebody saw Leandra in the park and they called someone who then called someone and so on and so forth." She smiled a little crookedly, looking much younger than her years. "It was Emily who called me, actually."

Leandra gaped. "My own mother was spreading gossip like that?"

"Well," Jaimie allowed, "she was sort of fact checking,

figuring my daughter—" she sent Sarah a pointed look "—would have filled me in on the truth."

"I don't spread gossip," Sarah said loftily.

Matthew snorted softly and picked up his coffee mug, looking highly amused.

"I just said she was looking for *facts,* didn't I?" Jaimie tsked.

"There are no facts to check," Leandra said firmly, sharing a look with Sarah. They'd shared plenty of secrets over the years. She hadn't expected to be doing it again at their age…like this…about Evan.

Had they entered some weird time warp where they were still thirteen and being grilled over why they'd been late coming home from the winter dance? Or were they really sitting there, in their late twenties, fully capable, mostly functioning adults?

Jaimie chuckled suddenly and patted Leandra's hand. "I'm just teasing you, honey. Surely you know that." She pushed away from the table and grabbed a plate of cookies, passing it to Leandra first. "Matthew heard from Squire and Gloria this afternoon."

"Squire's wanting to come back early from their vacation. So far Gloria has kept them on their schedule, touring Europe for two months, but she's not sure how long she can do so," Matthew added. "You know Squire. He's never liked being away from the ranch for too long at a time."

"I think Squire doesn't like being away from the *family* for too long at a time," Jaimie said dryly. "Still afraid we'll mess things up without his sage advice."

"Interference, you mean." Matthew smiled faintly.

They all chuckled. Squire's interfering ways were known far and wide and though they may have mellowed some in the past few decades, they were by no means extinct.

When Jaimie started to clear the table, Sarah and Leandra

tried to take over but to no avail. Then it was good-nights all around and assurances that everyone would be in town for the "do" at Colbys.

And turn out, they did. By the hundreds.

By Happy Hour, there was not a seat to be had inside Colbys Bar & Grill. People spilled outside onto the sidewalk and into the street that her uncle had conveniently closed off to traffic.

WITS had arranged the half-dozen large-screen televisions that were situated both inside and out. A local country and western band was cranking out tunes. Those who weren't dancing in the street were sucking down lemonade or beer and filling their bellies with free food.

"If the show about Evan is as popular as this party, you're not going to be associate producer anymore." Ted came up and stopped beside Leandra, where she was doling out *WITS* ball caps and refrigerator magnets to the new arrivals who kept straggling in.

"From your lips," Leandra murmured, her smile never leaving her face as she looked at a young school girl who already had three hats in her hand. "Would you like a bag to hold them all?"

The girl nodded and Leandra handed over a plastic sack with the *WITS* logo prominently featured, but not before she dropped in a few pens and some other doodads that brought a huge smile to the girl's face before she ran off.

"Five minutes to showtime," Ted told her.

She appreciated the reminder despite the fact that she was already excruciatingly aware of the time. "Tell Janet—"

"I'm here, I'm here." Janet skidded to a stop behind the table next to Leandra. She had a tall glass of something in her hand and a grin on her face. "Leandra, if your brother could be bottled, we'd never have to work another day in our lives. We'd be rich selling his charm."

"Yeah, he's charming all right, and just as wily." She vacated her chair, making room for Janet. "Evan still inside?"

"Playing pool."

Avoiding the television sets, too, Leandra figured. She left Ted to adjust the sound system he'd tied all of the monitors to, and wound her way through the throng. She saw her parents sitting at a high-top with her uncle Daniel and aunt Maggie, and her father gave her an encouraging thumb's-up. The rest of the family were scattered around, too, all offering their easy support as the evening progressed.

It didn't matter, though. She was still nervous as a cat.

She found Evan at one of the pool tables. "Show time."

He smiled, particularly when her announcement was met with a boisterous round of hoots from those crowded into the bar. But she saw beyond the smile to his discomfort at being the center of all this attention. For some reason, she tucked her arm through his, as if she were going to be capable of alleviating his version of stage fright. "Don't worry," she murmured in his ear when he lowered his head to hear her through the noisy bar. "The network that carries us isn't the *most* popular cable network." It was second, but she didn't figure he needed to hear that just then.

Then the show's theme song blasted out over the sound system, and whatever second or third or tenth thoughts they all might be having were moot.

Somebody grabbed Evan and pulled him closer to one of the large screens, and Leandra found herself falling back, working through the tightly packed bodies until she found a pocket of air and a somewhat removed view of the audience.

Their attention was rapt. As silent as they'd been noisy, as every single person—to a one—craned to see more, to hear every word.

Halfway through the half-hour show, she even allowed herself to believe—just a little—that the interest wasn't entirely owed to Evan. That she might just have had something to do with the engaging pace and content.

Then she stopped watching the audience and watched one of the screens herself.

And her heart nearly stopped in her chest.

In the flesh, Evan was a compelling, impossibly striking man. On the big screen, he was…brilliant.

Beautiful to look at. Wry. Confident.

Single. A state that was played up a little more than Leandra had planned—Marian's doing.

And then, just as quickly as it had begun, the chipper theme song played over the image of Evan and his damnably attractive jeans-clad backside walking away, a beautiful black horse following him along as obediently as a devoted puppy.

Leandra let out a long breath, letting the cheering that had exploded at the notes of the theme song flow over her. She worked her way outside once again, catching a glimpse of Evan, surrounded as people slapped him on the back and called for fresh rounds of drinks.

She went over to the unmanned table where all of the giveaways had been distributed and sank down onto the chair, feeling shaky. But she wasn't allowed much time to collect herself of the nerves that had drained her, because family started descending almost immediately, hugging and laughing and exclaiming that the show was, by far, the most interesting thing they'd ever seen in their entire lives.

Leandra laughed off the exaggeration, but the truth was, she was pleased. And in another blur, the evening wound down until there was just her and Ted still packing away the mess outside while the staff of Colbys finished up inside.

"Wouldn't want to pay that bill out of my pocket," Ted

murmured when Leandra signed off on the final bill for the event and bid good-night to the manager.

"Me, either." She waited until the manager left, then stared around at the sidewalk and street. They'd cleaned up all of the trash and broken down all of the boxes that had contained the giveaways. Aside from the stack of cardboard, there was no sign left of the festivities. "Eduard has never been one to stint on promotion."

"Fortunately," Ted added. "Good job tonight, Lee. You want me to give you a lift to your cousin's?"

"Think I'll walk. Work off some of my energy."

He grinned. "Can't see how you'd have any left, but whatever. See you in the morning, then."

"Bright and early at Evan's clinic."

He waved on his way to the van. Her cameraman knew the schedule as intimately as she did. And in minutes, he was driving away.

She let out a long breath and tugged down the long sleeves of her *WITS* T-shirt as she set off in the direction of Sarah's house. When she heard a car engine come up behind her, she looked back, half expecting Ted to have returned for some reason.

But it was Evan's dusty pickup truck that pulled alongside of her. The windows were down and he had his long arm stretched across the seat as he cocked his head, looking out at her.

"Dontcha know you shouldn't be out alone at this hour?" The tires of his truck slowly turned, keeping time with her pace.

She made an exaggerated perusal of the quiet street, both ways. "In Weaver? Besides, the only one out is you."

"And you."

She heard another car and looked back to see the last of the Colbys crew depart. "And them."

"Want a ride?"

She kept walking. "What for? Nearly to the corner. Another mile after that and I'll be at Sarah's."

Evan eyed her. "Afraid to get in the truck with me?" It was a pretty cheap shot, but accusing her of being afraid of something used to be the surest way of getting under her skin.

And he knew some things hadn't changed when she stopped dead still and gave him an incredulous look. "Excuse me?"

He braked, stopping, as well. "Get in the truck, Leandra." His voice was resigned. "Or I'll just have to follow you the rest of the way."

"You have an overdeveloped sense of responsibility, you know that?" But she reached for the handle and pulled open the truck door.

A rough sound rose in his throat. Right. Responsible.

She joined him in the cab, bringing with her some light fresh scent that teased his nerves in a way he was beginning to get used to.

"I, um, I didn't see when you left earlier." She carefully fastened her seat belt, then pressed her palms together in her lap. "One minute I saw you still in the bar with Axel and Derek and a few other guys, and the next, you were gone."

He didn't kid himself that she would be looking for him for any reason other than *WITS* as he headed down Main Street. "I'd had enough of the freak show."

Her sigh was soft, but still audible. "I really wish you didn't feel that way." Her fingers twined together and she looked out the side window as he turned the corner, heading down Sarah's street.

"Why? Because we used to be friends?"

She looked back at him, her soft lips pressing together for a moment. "That. And the fact that I do have a responsibility to my production. You know, most people have enjoyed their experience once we finish shooting. I, um… Is there something I—we—as a crew can do to make things easier for you? Some way we can get you from feeling like you're a…a sideshow attraction?"

"Keep Ted out of my bedroom."

"Again, I'm sorry for that. It was…unfortunate."

He grimaced. "That's one word for it." He pulled into Sarah's driveway and parked, but when Leandra reached to undo her safety belt, he dropped his hand over hers.

Stupid, but he just couldn't let her go like that. Thinking that his foul mood was because of the show. "Wait."

She blinked and he wondered if she were able to feel the rumba his pulse had danced into when he touched her. But all she did was look at him, waiting.

He let out a breath. "I didn't leave because of the show," he said abruptly. "Not that I particularly like all that fuss and attention," he added darkly, lest she get her hopes up too much otherwise. "I—"

Her gaze searched his face. "What? If you were just tired, Evan, it's okay. I mean, we were *all* tired, and I know you have to keep some pretty awful hours, sometimes."

He finally let go of her hand, and looked out the windshield. "Yeah, that would be the easy excuse," he muttered.

She frowned. "Look, you don't have to tell me why, Evan. Your reasons are your own. It's fine. You were there for the main event—people got to feel involved in the process of the show. And I wasn't complaining that you'd left—just commenting on the fact that I didn't see you leave. I felt bad about that. As if I'd let you down or something."

He ran his hand around the back of his neck. "Don't. Just…don't." He looked at her. "I left because Darian showed up. He missed the show. Not that he cared."

She looked as surprised as if he'd announced he'd gone into

labor. "Then why—" Her expression tightened. "Is Hannah all right?"

"What?" He shook his head a little. "Yeah. Hannah's fine." He supposed he shouldn't feel his own surprise that his niece was her first thought. "Hell, believe me, darlin'. Darian doesn't bother himself over his only grandchild."

She unsnapped her seat belt and shifted in her seat to face him better. "Can I ask you a question?" She didn't exactly wait for his consent as she went right on. "It seems clear to me that you're not completely thrilled with Sharon and Darian taking care of Hannah. Does Katy feel the same way?"

"Sharon and Darian are Katy's parents. Of course she doesn't feel the way I do."

"I didn't mean to stick my nose in."

He sighed again, noisily. "Look, it's not you, okay? For once it's not you," he added in a low voice.

Her too-large eyes looked away, as if he'd insulted her and he felt even worse.

"Sorry," she said. "Look, it's really late. I appreciate the ride—"

"Leandra, I wasn't looking for an apology."

"Fine. Okay. but you need your sleep, too." She shoved open the truck door and smiled brightly at him. "The episode was a hit. *You* were a hit. Better than I could have ever hoped for."

Even better than following Jake around with his celebrity pets? He didn't voice the question. "Leandra!"

But there was no stopping her. "Thanks again." Her voice was deliberately cheerful. "I'll see you in the morning." She shut the door, wincing a little. "Oops. Too loud at this hour. Sorry."

Evan watched Leandra practically jog to the front door, and swore under his breath.

He'd made himself a fine mess of that.

Chapter Eight

Evan still felt like an ass the following morning. So much so, that when Leandra and her crew showed up with their van of cameras and lights and microphones, he invited them into the house where he had breakfast waiting.

Ted took one look at the cinnamon rolls from Ruby's and clapped Evan on the back. "Good man." He grinned and plucked one off the plate, shoving half in his mouth.

"Jeez," Janet muttered, and grabbed a napkin out of the package Evan had thought to toss onto the table alongside the rest of the grub—also scored from Ruby's, thanks to Tabby's connections. "Here." She shoved the napkin into Ted's hands, then picked up a plate, which she handed to Paul, who was nodding and eyeing the food with interest.

Leandra was the last to enter and she closed the door behind her. Her eyebrows raised. "What if we'd already eaten a big breakfast?"

"Did you?" He'd seen what they often ate in the mornings—tortilla chips being a primary favorite as far as he could tell.

She made a face. "No, but we might have."

He lifted his coffee mug and shrugged. "Then I'd have leftovers for the next week. Less cooking. Not a bad deal, either way."

Her eyes narrowed to a slit of chocolate brown, as if she didn't trust a word of it.

Why would she? He hadn't exactly made any of them feel particularly welcome.

He wasn't entirely sure why he was trying to make up for that failure now. Except that his mother would expect him to show some good manners. She and Drew hadn't raised him, after all, to be a complete jerk.

That was just in his genes, courtesy of Darian, who rarely managed to behave with any ethical or moral behavior.

If Evan had needed any more evidence about that, he only had to look at his own behavior the night before when he'd driven Leandra to Sarah's.

"Dig in, Leandra," Janet encouraged. She gestured with her fork before sticking it back into the mound of fluffy eggs she'd added to her plate. "Stop looking a gift horse in the mouth. This is a whole lot better than those granola bars you usually have."

Leandra's cheeks turned a little pink and she avoided looking at Evan. "This really wasn't necessary. But thank you."

He shrugged again. "Consider it returning the favor."

She looked blank.

"The breakfast you fixed me," he prompted.

Her expression cleared. "Oh. Well, for heaven's sake, Evan. That was just eggs and bacon. This—" she waved her hand over the containers he'd put out on the table with something he realized was less than artistry "—is a feast. Eggs, rolls, home fries, sausage, bacon. Sliced fruit. Really—it's too much."

"Shut up, Leandra," Ted told her good-naturedly, "before the guy starts putting the stuff away for someone who appreciates it."

"I *do* appreciate it," she said quickly. Her gaze flickered over Evan again, and the pink was even brighter in her cheeks. "I just…didn't expect it."

"Unexpected doesn't have to mean unpleasant," he said deliberately.

She nodded, a faint smile around the corners of her lips. "Right. You're right. Again."

He picked a paper plate off the stack and handed it to her. "My best china," he drawled.

"Same pattern as mine," Ted said.

"And mine," Paul piped in.

Her fingers brushed against his as she took the plate. "Were you waiting for us, or did you already eat?"

"Yes." He grabbed a plate of his own and added two cinnamon rolls to it. "We'll just consider this seconds."

There weren't enough chairs for all of them to sit, so Evan leaned back against the cupboard and worked his way through the enormous sweet rolls while the others filled their bellies and talked shop.

It was pretty damn surreal.

If anyone would have ever told him there would be a television show filmed in Weaver, much less one about *him,* he'd have laughed his fool head off.

Yet here they all were.

"So she was telling me that on the station she listens to for her morning ride, the deejays were talking about it." Evan focused in to see Janet looking excited.

"Seriously?" Leandra set down her plastic fork. "In Phoenix? That station's number one in their market."

"I know." Janet grinned around a bite of honeydew melon.

"They had listeners calling in, all talking about Evan. My friend told me that she wished she had a dog she could bring up here just for an excuse to see him." Her gaze landed on Evan. "Mostly women were calling, of course. Who can blame them?"

The cinnamon roll lost its appeal. "You've got to be kidding."

"Good buzz is important," Paul said.

He'd spoken more than Evan had ever heard before. "Buzz about the show," Evan said warily. He looked at Leandra. "Right? That's what this is all about. So you can get promoted to producer or something."

She nodded. "It works both ways, though. Good word of mouth about you means that more people might tune in next week. It's a win-win situation." She pushed her plate away, even though she'd consumed barely half of what she'd put on it. "So don't you have patients coming in soon?"

"Yeah."

"Then we'd better get set up." She pushed back her chair.

It was evidently the signal her crew needed to do the same, and within minutes, they were trooping out of his kitchen. Ted, Evan noticed, didn't relinquish his plate. He just carried it out with him.

Leandra hung back. "This *was* really nice of you, Evan. I should help you clean up."

"It's just takeout, sport. No big deal. And clean up just means closing the containers and shoving them in the fridge. Think I'm pretty familiar with that particular process."

"Right." Her lashes veiled her eyes. "Is the clinic open already? Or still locked up?"

"I'll be there in a few minutes." He tossed her the key chain.

She caught it and headed toward the door. "Thanks."

Once again, he was letting her walk away without clearing the air.

He really was a slug.

"Leandra, about last night."

She hesitated, her hand on the door latch. "What about it?"

"Darian had his latest squeeze with him. I don't know why Sharon puts up with his infidelities but she does. I got pissed off about it and that's why I left Colbys."

Her lips rounded in a silent O. "You don't have to explain, Evan. I told you that."

Yeah, he didn't have to. For some idiotic reason he still felt compelled to do so, though. "Anyway, about Hannah's guardianship. You were right. I'd take her in a second, but Katy has refused."

She let go of the door knob. "What on earth for?"

"She's got it in her head that I'd use Hannah as an excuse *never* to find a woman to settle down with."

She made a short sound. "Are you serious?"

"As a heart attack."

She blinked, shaking her head a little as if the idea were unfathomable to her. "I can't believe Katy could be so…" She shook her head again.

"Ridiculous?" Evan supplied.

"Well, yes. Actually. My goodness, *she* is a single parent. Does she think she'll never get remarried because of that?"

"Keith left her because of Hannah. Katy's got a bug in her bonnet about it. And the truth of it is I haven't gone out of my way to convince Katy that I *do* want to settle down. Some day." Admitting it was harder than he would have expected.

She cocked her head slightly. "You wanted to marry once, though. You proposed to Lucy even before we graduated from high school."

"I never proposed."

Her eyebrows shot up into her spiky bangs. "Oh?"

Jesus. He should have just kept his mouth shut about the

whole thing. "I didn't. She just brought up the idea of being married somewhere along the way, and everyone assumed that would come to pass sooner or later."

"Everyone? But not you?" She looked skeptical. "Don't pull that on me, Evan. I know you too well. You and Lucy were practically joined at the hip. Are you saying that if she *hadn't* gone to New York, that the two of you wouldn't already be working on your own litter of kids?"

"We were a comfortable habit. I told you before that I wasn't pining for Lucy, and I know she's not longing for the good ol' days with me, either. She's your cousin. Call her yourself if you don't believe me."

"Then why *haven't* you gotten serious about someone since then?"

Because he was Darian's blood, he thought.

"Everyone around here thinks it's because you never got over Lucy."

"Maybe it was convenient," he said flatly. "Believe me, darlin', it hasn't kept me from having female companionship when I've wanted it." Plenty of it, and none from the girl he'd never been able to get out of his head.

She looked as if she'd suddenly sucked on a sour lemon. "Well, woo-hoo for you." She pulled open the door. "We've got work to do. I'll see you over there."

He watched her stride away and exhaled. There was a reason he worked with animals.

They were a helluva lot easier to get along with.

Despite the promising beginning to the day, Leandra felt grumpy for the rest of the morning.

She didn't have to wonder why.

Female companionship.

Though why she should care about the women Evan had

in his life, she couldn't begin to fathom. It wasn't as if she wished she were one of the hordes, after all.

She wouldn't *be* one of a horde, in the first place.

She wouldn't share her man with other women; wouldn't want a man who wanted others, anyway.

And just because she was saddled with this inexplicable attraction didn't mean that she intended to do anything about it. She didn't want a relationship.

She'd had that, and had failed on all accounts.

So she was grumpy. She knew she was grumpy and there didn't seem to be a darn thing she could do about it. Except try not to inflict her grumpiness on her crew.

So she let them do their jobs without much interference.

Fortunately, they were good at that.

And then, when Evan's morning of appointments was cut short by a call from a local rancher with a horse who was down, they packed up and followed right along with him. After that was an emergency with a cat stuck in a tree.

Evan's assurances that if the cat were able to get *up* the tree he'd be able to get back down when he was good and ready didn't hold much comfort for the teary six-year-old girl.

So Evan climbed the tree. Retrieved the cat and earned himself a half-dozen scratches as a result.

"Why don't they make guys like that back home?" Janet whispered to Leandra as Ted moved in for a closer shot of Evan returning the now-purring feline to its young owner.

Leandra was saved from answering, though, as her phone vibrated and she moved away from the scene to take Marian's call. As icy as her boss had been a few days earlier, she was now positively gleeful over the results of Evan's first episode, taking full credit for the entire effort, which had been Leandra's idea.

Nothing that Leandra wasn't used to, though. She nevertheless felt a throbbing in her temple by the time Marian's enthused litany wound down.

After hanging up, she followed the crew and Evan to Ruby's and then to the weed-and-feed, where he ordered an assortment of supplies and picked up a package of razors and microwave popcorn.

"Think he's planning on having company for the popcorn?" Ted asked Leandra while they followed Evan. "Considering the razors and soap?"

"If he is, you're not going to catch it on tape," Leandra assured him. "I don't care *what* Marian's been telling you to do."

Ted looked distinctly guilty. "You know Marian."

"Yes, I do. But if Evan does have a date, that's his business. Not ours."

Liar, liar, pants on fire.

She mentally drop-kicked the taunting demon into the next county and trailed after Evan and her crew as they continued their parade through Weaver, drawing plenty of attention as they did so.

Not that Evan seemed to notice. Oh, he was still full of plenty of complaints, but Leandra knew enough now to take them in stride.

The man was a natural.

They continued filming as he drove out to his parents' place. It was starting to get dark, which simply meant that Janet and Paul were kept busier ensuring there was enough light for Ted.

Jolie and Drew Taggart came out on the front porch when they heard the commotion of the crew's arrival. If they'd expected their son to drop by, they certainly hadn't expected him to come with the television crew trailing closely behind. Jolie looked distinctly uncomfortable and, as a result, Drew looked distinctly protective.

Unlike their son, natural they were not, but they made the effort for Evan's sake, as they came down off the porch and headed toward the stables behind the main house where Drew kept his string of horses. He was a highly sought-after horse trainer but was also working with Evan on horse breeding. In particular, like Leandra's father, Drew had a pretty mare in mind for Northern Light's foray into daddyland.

By the time the sun went down completely, Leandra called it quits for the day and couldn't help but smile at the relief on Jolie's face when she saw Ted lower his camera and the others begin packing things away in the van.

Leandra went over and thanked them for their patience, having every intention of leaving with them. But Jolie caught Leandra by the hand. "You'll stay and have some coffee and dessert, won't you? Your friends are welcome, too."

Leandra knew her "friends" wanted nothing more than a good night's sleep, since they'd already put in about a fifteen-hour day and had been more than a little vocal about it. And as much as she liked Evan's parents, she wasn't sure she was up to spending more time with their son, particularly in a social setting.

There was definitely something to be said about the security she found behind the camera. Watching lives go on around her, rather than participating in them.

"I'll go ask them," Leandra told Jolie, and the other woman beamed.

As she'd expected, they declined, claiming tiredness. Even Ted, who *rarely* turned down free eats, seemed extremely anxious to get back to the privacy of his motel room. "You stay, though," he encouraged. "These are your people. Chow down."

Leandra's appetite for food wasn't the problem. Her appetite for a certain tall man was. "It's just easier if I drive back in to town with you guys."

Ted snorted a little, shaking his head. "Yeah, right."

"What's *that* supposed to mean?"

Ted lowered his voice. "Look, I've been watching you. You obviously like the guy. Stick around."

She felt her entire body flush. "Evan is a *friend* and that is all."

"Yeah, and my wife loves having me gone all the time," he countered wryly. "But, hey, it's cool. If you're afraid, then—"

"I am not afraid." Admitting the truth to herself was one thing. Admitting it to the cameraman she'd worked with for umpteen episodes was another.

He clearly didn't believe her. "Whatever floats your boat, you know?"

"I'm just as tired as the rest of you," she muttered. "Maybe I want an early night of it."

"Leandra?" Jolie called from the porch. "How would you like your coffee?"

She knew when she was beat. "Fine. Go ahead." She waved at Ted. "I'll see you in the morning." Then she turned back toward the Taggarts' home and raised her voice. "Just black, please, Mrs. Taggart."

"Oh, call me Jolie." The older woman waited until Leandra made it to the porch before turning to go inside. "It's not as if you're still ten years old."

Leandra's gaze fell on Evan the moment they entered the spacious great room. He was standing by the enormous stone fireplace.

Now this was a room that suited him. The thought snuck in without permission.

"Have a seat, honey." Jolie waved toward the leather furniture clustered around the fireplace. "Drew, why don't you start a fire? It's definitely getting chilly in here."

Leandra seated herself on one end of the butter-soft couch. Evan crouched in front of the fireplace himself. "I'll do it, Dad."

Tabby breezed in moments later, not seeming to think a thing of it that Leandra was ensconced in the family's couch. "Hey, there. My mom put on the videotape of Evan's big debut yet? She's watched it like a hundred times."

"Shut up," Evan said, without heat. "Go bug someone else." He set a long match to the kindling he'd packed around the larger logs.

"That show didn't fool me," Tabby told him, grinning. "I know the truth. How bo-oh-ring you really are." But she was grinning as she said it, and before Evan could grab her as he made a move to do, she hustled into the kitchen. "I ate at the café," they heard her tell her mother. "And I gotta finish a report for history tomorrow."

"She puts in a lot of hours at Ruby's, doesn't she? Must make all her homework kind of hard." Leandra looked at Drew.

"Too many hours as far as I'm concerned," he said. "But there's no convincing her of that."

"She keeps her grades up." Evan fitted the fireplace screen in place. "She's stockpiling her earnings so she can see the world when she finishes high school."

"Like your mother is going to allow that," Drew said wryly. "She wants Tabby to stay right here in Weaver."

"And the rest of us don't?" Even though there were plenty of other places to sit, Evan sat next to Leandra on the couch. He propped his boots on the heavy wooden coffee table. "The only one enamored with Tabby's idea is Tabby." He quickly dragged his boots off the table when his mother entered the room.

Leandra bit back a smile. Jolie didn't look fooled for a minute. She probably knew exactly where the scars in that wood—which ironically only increased the rustic-looking charm of the piece—came from.

"Maybe she'll change her mind about leaving for good," Leandra offered.

Evan raised his eyebrows and looked at her. "Did you?" He didn't really wait for the reply she wasn't even sure of herself. "Of course not. You're just as driven as Tabby, only you're further along in the course of it."

"You make ambition sound like a bad thing."

"I didn't say that." He leaned forward and grabbed a cup of coffee, handing it to her. "And I didn't say I was talking about ambition."

"You think I'm driven." His unfathomable gaze met hers as she took the cup from him.

"Aren't you?"

"What's the difference? You're ambitious, too, Evan. You don't want your veterinary practice to fail, so you work hard at what you do to make sure that doesn't happen."

"But I'm not *driven*." He sat forward again, taking a cup for himself, and a couple of small, perfectly round, golden sugar cookies. He dipped one in his coffee and popped it in his mouth. "And you know there's a difference," he said around the cookie.

"You just leave Leandra alone," Jolie said firmly. "Honestly, it's like you were both still playing in the sandbox together. If you didn't like the way she was building her castle, you just ran over it with your truck."

Leandra couldn't help but smile. Particularly when she noticed the hint of pink creeping above the collar of Evan's blue shirt. "You *were* horrible to me."

"No, I wasn't." He dunked another cookie and polished it off. "Even back then you liked playing director, telling everyone what they should be doing and how they should be acting."

She reached over and pulled his hair—the hair that had grown long enough to curl slightly behind his ears. "I never told you to pull my hair, and that's what you did all through grade school."

"You were the one who always sat in front of me."

"So? If Joey Rasmussen sat in front of you would you have pulled *his* hair?"

Evan smiled faintly. "Joey would be happy to have someone pull his hair these days. Guy's already lost most of it and he's not even thirty yet."

"You're missing the point."

"You had long blond braids back then," he defended himself. "You always wore red ribbons tied around the ends. What can I say? You might as well have been waving a red flag."

"Well there's no red flag waving now," Jolie told her son. "So you just behave yourself."

"She's the one who just pulled my hair." He sounded so aggrieved that they all laughed, and before Leandra knew it, more than a few quite enjoyable hours had passed before they were finally taking their leave.

"Don't work too hard at making my son famous, now," Jolie ordered as she hugged Leandra.

"Fortunately, folks around here aren't going to let him get much of a swelled head, despite that 'do' over at Colbys," Drew added dryly. "They've seen him sweeping up horse droppings after the Memorial Day parade too many times." He clapped his son on the back, ordering him to drive carefully back to town, and went back inside the house with his wife.

Leandra followed Evan to his pickup truck, wondering what else there was that she no longer knew about the man. "You really *still* work the shovel brigade after the parade?"

He shrugged and opened her door for her. "Somebody's got to."

She climbed up on the high seat, waiting until he came around and was behind the wheel. "Somebody, yes. Like a high school kid. That's about when you started, right?"

"It's a volunteer job," Evan reminded her, pulling away

from the house. "High school kids, these days, don't shovel sh—stuff like that unless they get paid to do so."

"So what was your excuse? Why'd you do it?"

"No particular reason."

"Just an affinity for little green apples," Leandra drawled, disbelieving. "Who are you trying to kid?"

"You were in a bunch of those parades yourself."

She'd been the junior rodeo princess for more years than she cared to recall. "Remember when Joey Rasmussen's grandfather's covered wagon caught on fire in the middle of the parade route?"

The light from the dashboard illuminated the grin he flashed. "Yeah. Do you remember why?"

She shook her head. "I never knew. But Joey was always getting into some sort of mischief."

"He was trying to smoke a joint. Only it wasn't pot, it was dried cow chips and when he realized it, he dropped his light on the hay bales stacked in the wagon, and the rest is history."

Leandra chuckled. "Well, the covered wagon was certainly history."

"Joey never tried smoking pot again, either."

"Wonder how he ended up mistaking cow chips for marijuana, anyway? And how did he figure out it wasn't?"

"Somebody switched his little plastic bag of the stuff."

"Obviously." She looked at him suddenly. "No. You?"

"Nah. I just told him the truth after he'd taken a few puffs. Ryan was the one to make the switch. He knew his dad was going to bust Joey for possession. It was just a matter of time before he was caught, considering the way he was bragging about it." He chuckled a little. "Man, the way he worked so hard to roll it, and then he dropped it—and the match—on the hay bale. I thought we'd split a gut laughing, and we were also busy scrambling out of the damn thing before it went up around our ears. Think Joey's parents grounded him for about six months for that one."

"Where is Joey now?"

"Moved to Idaho. Growing potatoes, if you can believe it. He and his wife have about two dozen kids, seems like. Maybe it's really only two or three, though."

Leandra smiled, trying to picture the rowdy kid she'd known settled down as a farmer with a family. "Speaking of Ryan… Have you heard from him lately?"

"Usually he keeps up with e-mail, but he hasn't answered the last few I sent."

"Did you ever consider going into the service?"

"Yeah."

"Seriously? I never really thought of you doing anything other than what you're doing. You're great with animals. Horses, dogs, whatever. You've always been that way. I wasn't at all surprised when you became a vet."

"I was surprised when you ended up doing the television thing."

"Why? I studied production in school."

"You also studied psychology, child development, ceramics and fifth-century literature."

"I didn't study literature."

The corner of his mouth had lifted again. "You did the others."

It occurred to her that he knew a lot of details about her college education. Details she'd never specifically shared with him. They'd been friends, but not particularly close when they'd both been away at different schools. "All right, it's true. I couldn't exactly make up my mind about a degree. It was hard, you know?"

"Finding your niche? You think you've found it now?"

"I'm getting there," she assured, more confidently than she felt.

He didn't reply, and she looked out the window at the passing scenery. There wasn't much to see. No city lights illuminated the country for miles the way they did back in California. There were a few lights, of course. Sparsely situated, marking someone's barn, someone's front porch. The area hardly looked any different now than it had when she was a child. "It was hard because I wanted to make a difference," she mused. "In the world, you know? I just couldn't see doing that by staying here in Weaver."

"People here in Weaver make a difference every day. Maybe not in the global scheme of things, but look at Sarah and the kids she teaches. Or your aunt Rebecca. She was the first doctor in a long while to come to Weaver and stay. The hospital that's been here for most of our lifetime would have probably never existed if not for her, or your uncle Tristan bringing CeeVid to town. Hell, most little towns were dying out back then. Weaver grew. It still grows, for that matter."

He was right. "I just…well, I just grew up knowing the stuff my father used to do. He traveled around the world. Built bridges. Helped impoverished people."

"So you think Jefferson canned it all by coming back to Weaver and starting up Clay Farm?"

"No, of course not." Her parents had married after her father had hung up his traveling boots and had come home to Weaver. "And I'm not saying everyone who is here isn't doing extremely worthwhile things. I just never knew how *I* could contribute. I don't want to follow in my dad's footsteps and breed horses. I don't want to follow in my mom's as an accountant. I don't want to work at CeeVid. Tried that when I was in high school. Remember? I lasted all of three weeks as a clerical assistant. I hated it, and I think everyone was relieved when I quit so that they didn't have to go to the trouble of firing me."

"And now you want to produce your own television shows. You think that'll feed your hunger to make a difference?"

"All of television isn't dreck, you know."

"I never said it was."

"Okay, then." She crossed her arms, not entirely certain why she felt as defensive as she did.

"Okay." His voice was peaceable.

He pulled up on the street outside of Sarah's house. This time he left the engine running.

Suited her just fine. She hopped out of the vehicle. "Thanks for the ride."

"Leandra."

She hesitated. "Yes?"

"I hope you find what you need with this TV stuff."

Her breath eked out. "Thank you."

He nodded once and she watched him pull his truck into a U-turn, heading back home.

But it was a long while before she finally went inside.

Chapter Nine

They started arriving the next week, right after the second episode of *WITS* aired.

Women, that is.

Some old enough to be his mother, Evan thought, some young enough to be illegal.

And all of them with the same thought in mind—that he was their soul mate. If only he'd give them a chance to see it.

He'd tried to be polite, sending the first one who showed up on his doorstep to the hotel before driving back to Missouri, where she'd come from. He'd advised the same of the second, third, fourth and fifth.

By the sixth, he was feeling less polite. Particularly when she didn't seem to realize that camping out on his front porch *wasn't* a trait that would endear her to him.

The deputy who'd come out from the sheriff's office had

been mighty amused about the whole thing as he'd finally gotten the woman to move along.

Then there were the phone calls. Messages—friendly and innocent sounding to down-right lurid—left on his answering machine.

When he told Leandra about it, she looked surprised, then sympathetic and suggested he change his phone number. Anyone who really knew him and wanted to reach him used his cell phone, anyway, rather than his home phone, she reasoned.

It was good reasoning, one he'd thought of himself when he wasn't grousing about it. So he called the phone company.

Got a new number.

Too bad moving wasn't a solution as easily accomplished.

By the middle of the week, Sawyer Clay assigned one of his deputies to regular crowd control at Evan's place. "Hotels are getting full up around here," the gray-haired sheriff drawled, standing in the reception area of the clinic and looking out the window at the caution tape his deputy was putting out to corral the crowd—about three dozen women now—from getting closer to the clinic entrance. "Your thing with my niece is turning out to be damn good for tourism this time of year."

"Great." Evan shoved a stack of files to one side of the desk. He needed to hire another receptionist, badly. "Glad to be of assistance."

Sawyer laughed softly, his blue eyes amused. "Don't look so down about it, son. You've got, what? Four more episodes of the show to air? The novelty ought t' wear off soon enough after that."

"You want to put that in writing?" Evan grimaced. "There was a strange woman staring through my living room window when I got up this morning, for God's sake." He wasn't exactly a shy sort, but being caught in his skivvies by a complete stranger had been this side of hard to swallow.

"That's a problem being too eligible," Sawyer said, still grinning. "Might try locking your doors more."

Leandra sailed through the entrance, her clipboard in her hand. "Time to call in reinforcements, I see." She kissed her uncle on the cheek and barely glanced at Evan.

Ever since they'd had dessert that night at his folks' place, she'd been nothing but professional, nothing but work, work, work.

It was almost enough to drive a man insane.

"You never warned me that this might happen," Evan pointed out darkly.

"I never considered that it would." She flipped a page on her clipboard, her pen busy. "Guess there's a first for everything."

Sawyer was still looking out the front window. "You going to put all those women on the next show?"

Evan stifled an oath and eyed Leandra. "Ted's out there filming all of this, isn't he?"

"That's the way it works, Evan."

"Well, my work here is done," Sawyer said. "What you need is a wife, Ev. Scare off all those prospective brides." He let himself out the door, chuckling.

Evan didn't see all that much humor in the situation.

"They're scaring off my regulars," he said to Leandra. "Those *women* out there."

She sighed slightly and her pen finally stopped moving. "I'm sorry. I don't know what more we can do about it, though, aside from cordoning them some distance away like my uncle has done. At least you've got Tommy Potter out there, keeping them all orderly."

Evan crossed the room, dumping magazines on a side table next to the chairs in the waiting room, and a high-pitched sound rose from outside.

That was orderly? He moved back behind the desk and

away from the window. "They're out there screaming," he muttered. "What the hell kind of sense does that make? I'm a vet for God's sake, not some rock star."

"Try to ignore them."

"That's a helpful suggestion, Leandra. Thanks."

She pressed her lips together, finally looking up at him. "The attention will die down."

"You didn't know the attention would rise up in the first place." He plucked the clipboard out of her hands and tossed it on the desk alongside his mess of organized disorganization. "Come on. I'm taking Hannah for the afternoon for Sharon. You can come to Braden with me."

"I thought you were doing surgeries this afternoon."

He waved his arm at the empty waiting room. "Can't if there are no customers, can I?"

Her eyebrows knit together. "You're really serious."

"I said so, didn't I?"

"I can't believe this is affecting your business. For pity's sake, the people here in Weaver ought to know better."

"The people here in Weaver don't like walking through a throng of screaming women to get to my clinic door. Who the hell can blame them? They probably figure waiting another month or so for things to get back to normal is better than heading through the gauntlet there."

She stared out the window. "This has never happened before. I don't know what to say. I'm so sorry."

"Sorry enough to call off the rest of the show?"

Her lashes fell. "I can't. You know I can't. I'm bound by contracts just as surely as you are. It's the way this works."

"Fine." He closed his hand around her arm, and felt the subtle flinch she couldn't quite hide.

"What are you doing?"

"Making sure we're in front of the window so they *all* can see."

She gave him a wary look. "See what?"

He closed his mouth over hers.

Her hands fisted between them. He felt them against his chest.

"Let me go," she said against his lips.

"No damn way," he returned and slid his arms around her back, pulling her up tight against him.

"Evan—"

He was a self-serving bastard, he thought, as the ploy to show the audience outside his clinic that he wasn't quite so available wasn't necessarily his only reason for wanting his hands on her.

That came from night after night of dreaming about her.

His friend's wife.

Ex-wife, a voice inside his head reminded.

Her lips softened under his. "Evan—"

He angled his head, going deeper. She tasted of coffee and chocolate and went straight to his head faster than both.

When her hands touched his waist, slowly sliding behind his back, he wanted to pull her away from the window. Wanted to hide her from the intrusive stares, hide her from everything but him.

The office would work. There was a couch here.

Her head fell back and she moaned softly when he trailed his mouth down her jaw, pulling the collar of her T-shirt aside so he could taste the curve of her neck.

"Ah-hem. Ah-*hem*." The voice was loud and intrusive. "Giving Ted a lot of fodder out there."

Leandra gulped and yanked out of his arms to stare at Paul. "What?" Her wide gaze followed Paul's nod toward the big, wide window where Ted's camera was pointed squarely in their direction. "Oh, *Lord*," she muttered, and hustled out the door, giving Evan a look that scorched along the way.

"Sure you know what you're doing?" Paul's voice was mildly curious. "I know that you know Leandra from way back, but she doesn't get too chummy with people these days."

Evan wasn't sure if Paul was warning him away from Leandra for her sake or for Evan's. "I know exactly what I'm doing."

The other man shrugged and seemed to accept it, and followed Evan out the door when he headed after Leandra.

She was busy talking to the crowd; doling out plastic *WITS* bags with one hand and rolled-up T-shirts with the other. The second that Evan came into their view, though, all attention veered his way.

It was damned uncomfortable, is what it was; made him feel like he was some prized monkey at the zoo. And it was definitely time to put a stop to it.

He walked up behind Leandra and wrapped his arms around her from behind. The bags and armload of shirts dropped to the ground when she jumped and let out a soft squeak. Her head reared back and she looked up at him. "What are you *doing?*"

He smiled into her face, but addressed the crowd of women. "Isn't she the prettiest thing you ever saw?"

Despite the myriad desires that had driven all of those women to travel from far and farther, they still gave out a collective "ah-h." Whether it was that sentimental sound or his arms around her that caused the bloom of color in Leandra's face, he'd never know. But he was dead certain that the dark glint in her eyes was owed straight to him.

"What are you doing?"

"Now, now, now. I know you wanted to keep it between us for now, but these folks here have traveled a long way to get to know us."

"They've come to see you." Her voice was so bright, it could have blinded a sunbeam. "Not us."

"Come on, honey," one of the women called out. "If I had *his* arms around me, I wouldn't be complaining much."

Laughter and nods followed the statement. Evan grinned, too. "She's just a little shy. Prefers being behind the camera, instead of in front of it. But I figure you all have earned the right to hear the news straight from me."

The lithe body in his arms was about as malleable as a rod of rebar. She looked up at him again. The glint in her eyes had turned to shards. "News?"

He ignored the shards and dropped a kiss on her lips, also ignoring the hissing sound that was low enough for only his ears.

"You all can be the first to congratulate us since this lovely lady is going to be my wife." He didn't have to turn her around in his arms; she spun like a top to face him and her "are you insane?" comment was drowned out by the even louder "aw-wh-h" that filled the air at his announcement.

He kissed her lips, drowning out any other comments she cared to add, while applause broke out all around them. "You owe me," he muttered in her ear when she pulled her mouth away from his.

Between their bodies, her fingernails dug into his chest. "Tell them the truth," she said through a clenched smile.

"Dude," Ted said from behind his camera. "Guess there's more going on than even I thought." He finally turned his camera away from them and panned over the crowd, who was acting as if Elvis had just reappeared in the flesh.

Janet and Paul began pulling women forward, getting live comments and Leandra pinched the inside of his arm. "Inside," she said, looking all loverlike.

He was going to be feeling the bruise on his arm for a while, he figured.

He twined his fingers through hers, keeping a good grip just in case she decided to bolt and ruin his charade. "Wither thou goest," he muttered, smiling right back at her. "You all don't mind excusing us for a while, do you?" he asked the crowd at large, and earned them another round of comments and laughter.

The moment they were inside the clinic, Leandra yanked her hand away from Evan's. "Are you *mad?*" She wanted to scream, but managed by some grace of God to keep her tone low. "You can't go around telling people we're getting married!"

"Why not?" Evan leaned back against the reception desk and crossed his arms over his chest. He looked so satisfied with himself that she wanted to kick him.

Or kiss him.

Both choices were completely unacceptable, even though she'd already done the latter. More than once.

And wanted to, again.

Despite his apparent loss of senses.

"Why not?" She propped her hands on her hips. "Why *not?*" Her voice rose and she swallowed hard, taking another deep breath. "Ted was filming all that, you know. Those women are going to expect to see themselves—and us—on the next episode."

"That's the plan."

"The plan. There *is* no plan! And that…that…mockery out there will be edited out. You can count on it."

"You're not going to edit it out," Evan said.

Shock was beginning to gurgle through her nerve endings, overriding the stunned paralysis that had seemed to plague her from the moment he'd put his arms around her. "Of course we are!"

"No, you're not." He grabbed her shoulders and dropped his head close to hers. "Your uncle had a point. If I had a wife, those women out there wouldn't be so damn anxious to throw themselves on my doorstep."

She felt light-headed. "I'm not your wife." She wasn't going to be anyone's wife again.

He looked impatient. "So, they all look pretty happy to me thinking that you are going to be," he said evenly. "I did you a favor doing this show in the first place. Now you do me a favor."

"It wouldn't be honest," she whispered fiercely. "*WITS*— at least when I'm producing it—is not going to be *dis*honest."

"Viewers can draw their own conclusions," he returned, completely unhelpfully, as far as Leandra was concerned. "That's the beauty of it."

The only beauty had been the warmth in her veins caused by Evan's mouth on hers, and even that had obviously been feigned on his part. All for the benefit of his unexpected flock of groupies.

"Find someone else," she said brusquely. "If it is so all-fire important to you. Maybe one of those women who are so ready to be at your beck and call."

She knew her error the moment the words came out, and his blue eyes lit with some unholy amusement. "Now isn't that interesting," he murmured softly. "You almost sound jealous there."

"Not in this lifetime." The words felt like they were ground out between her teeth.

He shrugged. "Doesn't matter. The deed's already done. They think you're going to marry me, and they can go right on thinking it until you pack up your cameras and take your sweet butt right out of town."

"This isn't just about complete strangers, Evan! People you know, *we* know, are watching this show. How are they going to feel if they see that…that…farce you just acted out?"

The corner of his lip lifted. "You think they won't have heard the scoop before then? Honey, this is Weaver, remember? Grapevine here is more effective than the almighty

Internet. By the time we get out to Braden to get Hannah, your mama will be getting ready to order napkins engraved with our names."

"Exactly." Her arms went up. "That's *exactly* what I mean! They're going to think that there's something between us!"

His lips twisted. "Pretty unbelievable, is that it?"

Her mouth opened, but no words jumped to the fore. "Well, yes," she finally managed. "Why would they believe it?" Her voice gained strength again. "Why would we want them to believe it?"

"Then tell them it's a front. Tell them whatever the hell you want, Leandra." He looked decidedly grim. "But make sure they keep it to themselves, so that they," he nodded toward the window where Ted was thoroughly surrounded by women anxious to get themselves on television, "can move on and find some other oddity to occupy their time."

"I'm not going to ask my family to participate in any sort of deception."

"Sounding a little uptight and prim there," he murmured.

"So what if I do? Are you telling me that you're perfectly content asking your family—even Tabby—to act as if you and I are heading into wedded bliss when they know nothing of the sort is ever going to happen?"

His lips twisted again. "Ever?"

Her stomach danced anxiously, as if she'd shot up an elevator shaft, then plunged right back down again. He was trying to annoy her; the same way he'd tried to annoy her through most of their childhood. All because his life had gone more topsy-turvy than any of them could have expected. She didn't blame him for his reaction, but she wasn't anxious to lay out over the train tracks so he'd feel better. "I'm not even going to discuss this." She'd edit out his outrageous nonsense and that was that.

"Suits me. Arguing's not high on my list of things I want to do today."

The easy capitulation made her even more wary. But she wasn't enamored with arguing, either. "Fine. Good. So I'll tell the crew that we're hitting the road today, instead of taping here."

"No."

She lifted her eyebrows. "Then where?"

"Nowhere. You can tell your crew to pack it in and go on home, because we are done."

Her stomach headed right back into the elevator shaft. "Evan—" She broke off, not entirely sure what to say. He was leaning easily against the reception desk, but there was nothing easy about his set expression. "You mean done for today, right?"

He slowly shook his head.

The elevator shot down to the sub-sub-basement. "You can't just quit. You signed a contract."

"Sue me."

He didn't realize that the production company could, and would, do just that. "Evan, you can't afford a lawsuit like that." She spread her arms. "You could lose your practice, even!"

"And you'll lose that promotion that's so all-fire important to you."

Her arms lowered. She stared at him. "I swear, there are times I don't know you at all."

He stared back at her, blue eyes as deep and inflexible as a black glacier. "Don't edit it out."

"That's blackmail."

"Consider it a favor for an old friend," he drawled.

She winced. That had been *her* argument when she'd approached him about the show. "Pretending to be engaged to you is not exactly the same thing."

"Ought to be a helluva lot easier." He straightened. "That's the deal, sport. One favor in return for another. If it makes you feel better, tell your folks the truth. I imagine they can keep a secret pretty well." He looked amused for a moment.

"And when the show wraps? What then?"

"Tell the rest of the world that you changed your mind."

As if that would make up for lying to everyone? As if that would salve her conscience? As if that would make working with him as closely as they'd been one whit easier?

"Fine, then," she said, matching his careless tone with an effort. She hated the fact that she felt stung by his attitude. "I guess we'll both be getting what we want."

His gaze didn't waver. "Yes, ma'am. Would seem that way, wouldn't it."

It wasn't a question.

Instead, she had the sinking fear that it was more of a sentence.

Chapter Ten

The news spread like wildfire.

Before the day was over, nearly every member of her family had descended upon Leandra, mostly goggle-eyed and mostly thrilled.

One of the hardest things she'd had to do was tell her parents the truth, and watch her mother's face fall when she realized that Leandra wasn't *really* going to be making her home in Weaver, after all.

They were at Sarah's place, and Leandra's cousin—already cued in to the real scoop—quietly excused herself, leaving Leandra to face her parents alone.

She watched her father slip his palm over Emily's shoulder when she broke the news and felt her throat tighten. "I'm sorry," she said.

Emily waved her hand, but her dark brown eyes were still sad. "Don't be sorry, darling. I just couldn't help…

hoping that you'd—" She shook her head and smiled. "Well, it doesn't matter. Has Evan told Jolie and Tag?"

"I suppose he has." She felt inexplicably foolish that she wasn't certain. After all, they *weren't* engaged—why would they confide everything to one another? "He went to Braden earlier. I haven't seen him since."

"What about the rest of the family?" Jefferson asked quietly. "You going to keep up the charade for them?"

"Not if I can help it." She pinched the bridge of her nose. "The problem is, if word gets out that the engagement is a fake, then it could cast a poor light on the integrity of *WITS*." And her future with the production company would be zilch. "There was just no reasoning with Evan, though."

Jefferson made a soft sound. "Peanut, if I had to put up with what that boy's had to put up with, I'd have been damn desperate, too."

Leandra's throat felt tight. "Me, too," she admitted, feeling miserable. The only one to blame was herself, for bringing all the attention onto Evan in the first place. All because she was desperate to prove she could do *something* right. Something worthwhile. Something that did not hurt anyone else.

Emily stepped away from Jefferson and brushed her hands together. "All seems like spilt milk to me," she said briskly. "This is not life and death, here. It's a television show." Leandra was enveloped in a cloud of soft fragrance as her mother gave her a swift hug. "As for anyone who thinks engagements are never broken, they obviously don't understand the reason why people do get engaged, and they can just get over it." Her mother stepped back and Leandra couldn't help but smile.

"I love you, Mom."

Emily's expression softened and she cupped Leandra's cheek for a moment. "Backatcha, sweetheart." Then she angled a look at Jefferson. "Now, I'm trying to get your father to take me to the movies. He only wants to see some action thing."

"She wants to see some kissy thing," he returned, looking amused. "Told her we could have plenty of that at home without paying money for it."

Leandra covered her face. "Too much information, Dad."

Her mother laughed. She kissed Leandra's cheek again, then her dad gave her a tight hug and in minutes, they were out the door.

Leandra watched them from the window. Hand in hand, to the truck parked at the curb. Her dad opened the door for Emily, then lifted her right up inside. She saw her mother's grin flash, and the way she swatted at Jefferson's hands before he closed the door and rounded the vehicle.

"Ever watch your parents and wonder if you'll some day have what they have?" Sarah stopped next to Leandra, watching through the window, too.

"I used to," she murmured.

"Did you think you had it with Jake?"

"When we first married? Sure. But even before—" she swallowed hard "—before we lost Emi, I knew that we didn't."

Sarah sighed faintly. "I thought I came close once, too."

Leandra hugged her cousin. It was rare for Sarah to refer to that. "Couple of sad sacks, aren't we?"

Sarah's lips curved. "And here you are, all engaged and everything."

Leandra rolled her eyes, but inside, she felt shaky. Mostly because she couldn't get out of her head the wondering about what belonging to Evan might really be like. "Let's go to Colbys."

"You want a drink?"

She wanted distraction and that was one place that might provide it. "Pool," she said.

Her cousin didn't look particularly fooled, but she grabbed her purse and they headed out.

At Colbys, however, Leandra was just treated to more well-wishers, and when Sarah got distracted by a few teachers she worked with, Leander excused herself. "I'm going to walk home," she assured Sarah over her protests. "I'll see you later."

Her cousin walked her to the door. "I'd go with you, but I want to get these two on one of my committees and this is the first time they've shown an interest."

"Then you've gotta stay and work your magic."

Sarah rolled her eyes, but headed back to the table and Leandra went outside.

The moon was high, and the air felt cool after the warmth and busyness inside the bar. She walked quickly, for some reason half expecting yet another congratulatory soul to come trotting after her.

A car went careening past, and she made a face after it, glad she'd kept to the sidewalk. Even Weaver wasn't immune to speeding dolts.

At the end of Main, she turned the corner and headed along the row of houses opposite the park. The ever-present breeze drifted over her, chilling her skin into bumps, and she quickened her step. The boots she wore rang out on the sidewalk. A dog barked. She saw the shadow of it racing through the park.

Then she heard the race of a car engine again and turned to see the same car screaming down the street.

She almost expected it to happen before it did. The car. The dog. She was running before the dog went still and the car continued on as if nothing had ever happened.

"Oh, God." The dog lay on its side. She crouched down beside it, gingerly reaching out to touch him. She didn't want to hurt him more, but she also didn't want to earn herself a dog bite, either. "It's okay, puppy." She held the back of her hand near his nose, letting him sniff her before she felt along his neck for a collar.

There was none.

He looked at her, flopping the end of his feathery gold tail a few times, and let out a whine as her fingers touched something wet.

Blood.

Murmuring softly to the animal, she carefully slid her arms under him, wanting to get him out of the street before another car came past or worse, the idiot who'd hit him came back around. She could see the taillights of the vehicle even now driving around the far side of the park. A few more turns and he'd be right back where they were.

The dog whined harder, but didn't struggle. Unfortunately, he also weighed a small ton, and there was no way she could carry him farther than the edge of the sidewalk. She yanked out her cell phone, peering at the dim display as she dialed Evan.

"Taggart." His voice was terse as he answered, but she still felt calmer just hearing it and she managed to relay the situation in a voice that didn't shake quite as much as her body did.

"I'm about five miles out," he said. "Got anything to cover the dog?"

"I could get something."

"Do it. I'll be there in a few minutes."

She shoved the phone back in her pocket and ran her hand down the dog's head again. "Stay." Stupid command since the dog wasn't going to be going anywhere under his own steam.

She ran back to Colbys, going through the rear door. Nobody even noticed her as she snatched up a stack of cloths that were folded on a shelf in the kitchen. She was tucking them around the dog when Evan's pickup truck pulled up next to her.

He stopped with a lurch, and she ran around the hood of his

vehicle going to his side. He was already getting out, his expression dark. His hands grabbed her shoulders. "Is that blood? Are *you* hurt?" Before she could blink, he'd lifted her onto the seat and was leaning in over her. "What exactly happened?"

She tried fielding the hands he was running over her arms and legs, but had little success. She finally caught his fingers in hers and squeezed. "*I'm* not hurt. Just the dog."

He let out a breath, his eyes closing for a moment. Then he straightened. "Give me a freaking heart attack," he muttered and turned to tend to the still dog.

She hovered next to him, feeling useless. "Some fool was speeding. The dog's conscious, but he's bleeding."

"There's a tarp folded up under the seat. Grab it, will you?"

Leandra felt around for the item, scraping her knuckles on the oddball collection of tools and other items before she found the tarp. She pulled it out and joined him on the sidewalk where he was examining the dog.

He was no longer beating the end of his tail. Not even the tiniest bit.

Leandra felt cold inside. She folded her arms around her waist, hovering next to the truck.

"His leg is definitely fractured, and he's going to need stitches for that cut."

"Maybe I shouldn't have moved him from the street."

"Lower the tailgate would you? We're gonna have to lift him up there." He began working the tarp beneath the unconscious dog. "And we've gotta go fast. He's going into shock."

The tail gate fell open with a noisy clang when her fingers slipped. Emi had been in shock when they'd pulled her from the swimming pool.

"Leandra." Evan's voice dragged at her. "I need your help to lift him."

She crouched down beside him, pulling the tarp taut the

way he instructed. If she didn't think beyond the moment, she was okay.

Shock.

"On three," Evan said. "One. Two. Three." He lifted the dead weight of the animal far more easily than she did. When he'd carefully slid the injured dog into the truck bed, Evan touched Leandra's shoulder. "You can drive or you can hold the dog. Your choice."

"D-drive."

"Sure?"

She nodded.

He tucked the cloths from Colbys gently around the animal and pulled himself up into the truck bed with an easy motion. "Drive around to the back of the clinic. Park by the rolling door."

Just get to the clinic, she told herself.

Shock.

She fumbled with the gear shift, and the truck lurched forward. Her heart was in her throat, making her feel nauseated. Trying to drive more smoothly, she pulled a U-turn, barely managing not to bounce over the curb on the park side of the street, and headed back around the corner and toward the clinic.

She slowed at the red light in the center of town, hurriedly looking over her shoulder at Evan and the dog. He was leaning over the animal and she realized he was administering CPR.

She pressed harder on the gas and sailed through the empty intersection despite the red. Another few blocks and she turned into Evan's drive, going around the house, gravel spitting beneath the tires as she headed for the clinic that was farther back. It was a single story and considerably longer than his house, surrounded by a grassy area and pens on one side, and smooth cement parking on the other. The office and two examining rooms were at the near end—for the folks who brought in their companion animals. Cats. Dogs. Even a ferret or two, Evan had told her when they'd first started filming. Midway down the building, though, was the rolling door. She pulled up so the tail of the truck was closest to it and jumped out of the cab.

He was still giving CPR, only now he was doing chest compressions on the dog. "The code on the door is oh-five-oh-three."

She fumbled open the metal covering for the control panel and rapidly punched in the numbers. With a comforting rumble, the metal door began rolling upward. "Don't you know you're not supposed to use things like your birthday for security codes and passwords and such?" She lowered the tailgate of the truck again.

"If I didn't, I wouldn't remember them. Get a gurney. Should be one by the wall. Lights will come on automatically when you go inside."

And thank goodness for that, she thought as she stepped into the black cavernous opening. A moment later, overhead lights began flicking on in an orderly grid. She grabbed the wheeled cart and ran it out to him, managing to hit the wall and the side of the truck as she did so. "Sorry," she mumbled, scooting it a little more carefully around where he gestured.

He didn't stop his CPR until the last possible second, and then he jumped down from the truck bed and single-handedly lifted the animal onto the gurney. "You're going to have to help me inside," he told her, wheeling the cart around with far more expertise. "He's breathing again, but I don't know if it'll last."

He turned toward the front of the building, rolling the gurney up next to a high, steel table that sat in the center of the surgical area. "Grab that instrument stand. Roll it over here." He moved the dog onto the table, strapped him down and grabbed his stethoscope. "I only saw the one cut on his hind leg. Press the gauze pads—yeah. The large ones."

Leandra blindly ripped open the package that was on the tray along with an array of instruments. Two pads tumbled to the ground.

"Don't worry about them." Evan didn't even seem to be watching her as he filled a needle and shot it into the dog. "Press several pads against the cut. Gently, though. You're not applying a tourniquet or anything."

He dragged a rolling contraption around, and she realized it was some sort of monitor when he began attaching leads to various points of the animal. "Can you tell if the bleeding has stopped?"

She lifted the compress, and smoothed the matted hair away from the cut as best she could, mostly afraid that she would be causing the dog pain. "There's only a small amount of fresh blood."

"Good. There are elastic bandages in that drawer behind you. You can strap one around the pads on his leg and then help me splint his fracture."

She swallowed and blindly followed his instructions, which seemed to come in an unending flow. She didn't stop to concentrate. Just did what he said. And after what seemed hours, he finally straightened and pulled the stethoscope from around his neck, laying it aside on the tray where the implements no longer lay in such pristine order.

"That's it," he said. "Now, we wait."

Leandra brushed her hand through the dog's luxurious ruff. "What are his chances?"

"Pretty good." Evan crossed to a sink and began washing his hands and forearms. "Haven't done anything in this clinic for days without your pal Ted following me around with that camera of his. Feels a little strange."

Leandra hadn't even given *WITS* a single thought. And now that she did, she knew that Evan's actions would have made great footage.

So why did she feel so glad that Ted *hadn't* been there?

She realized that Evan had asked her a question. "What?"

"Did you see who hit him?"

"The car, yes. But not the driver. He was definitely speeding."

"Judging by the size of our patient there, I imagine the car will be sporting a good-size dent now."

"I hope so." Now that Evan had stopped barking orders at her, she was feeling distinctly woozy. She reached behind her for the counter and locked her knees.

Evan was adjusting a blanket around the dog. "You did good. Sure you don't want to consider a career change?"

She shook her head, which did nothing to clear her vision. It just seemed to grow hazier and dimmer.

And the last thing she was aware of as her knees turned to liquid was the widening of Evan's blue, blue eyes.

Her pretend fiancé's eyes were bluer than the sky, she thought faintly.

And then she didn't think anything at all.

Chapter Eleven

Evan looked up in time to see the remaining color in Leandra's pale face drain away. Her eyes rolled and she pitched forward.

He barely caught her before she knocked herself on the end of the surgery table where the dog still lay. Cursing, he lifted her in his arms and carried her through to a back room that doubled as a break and storage room. There was no expensive lighting system in there. Only a bulb hanging from a forty-year-old fixture in the ceiling.

He settled her on the couch that he'd bought for its comfort rather than its aesthetics, and felt for her pulse, then reached up and yanked the chain for the light.

Already her eyes were fluttering open.

He hunkered down beside her, resting his palm along her neck. Not because he really needed to.

She blinked a few times and he waited, watching the grogginess clear and clarity take its place. The moment it did, she was trying to jackknife herself off the sofa.

"Take it easy," he murmured. "You fainted once already. Don't want a second round, do we?"

She subsided. "Don't suppose *we* do," she murmured. Her eyes were as dark as molasses and he could feel himself getting sucked into their sticky allure. "Jake never liked me watching him work. Guess this is probably why."

Evan didn't particularly want to hear about Jake just then. Particularly after fending off questions about his sudden engagement to Jake's wife.

Ex-wife.

He straightened and grabbed a paper cup, shoving it beneath the spout of the water dispenser, and took it to her. "Here. Drink."

"Sit. Stay." But she did sit up a little and accepted the cup, drinking it right down. Then she let her head fall back on the arm of the sofa. "I'm sorry."

Except for the sofa, there were no other places to sit other than the scarred coffee table that held a healthy collection of sports magazines and professional journals. So he sat there. "Sorry for what? Passing out?"

She looked pained. "Yes."

"You're not the first one who has." He propped his forearms on his thighs and looped his fingers loosely together between them. Maybe that way he could keep himself from touching her again. "Don't sweat it. I'm glad I caught you before you hurt yourself falling."

"Oh. Right. Thank you for that, then, too."

"Too?"

"Well, you helped the dog."

He smiled faintly. "That's what I do. Just part of the job, ma'am."

"We did a show last year with a single mom in Florida who

was trying to break into fashion design. They had a dog needing some treatment and because they couldn't afford the bill, the vet refused to treat the dog. I don't think it's part of the job for *every* veterinarian."

Evan couldn't pretend he was shocked. He'd met plenty of animal care providers who felt the same. He could pretend that he hadn't seen the episodes when they aired, though. Just as he pretended to have rarely seen the show, ever. "It probably wasn't because the vet didn't care, but that he didn't have the resources to keep taking on patients who can't pay."

"Have you ever done that?"

He shook his head. He'd been paid with an assortment of goods and services in the few years since he'd established his practice—from having his house painted to having that fancy lighting system installed out in the main rooms. "I'm the only vet in the area," he dismissed. "Your Florida mom probably had other alternatives."

She made a face and tried sitting up again. This time, she moved more slowly and he kept his infernal hands to himself. "Figures you'd take the high road even on behalf of someone like that."

"I'm not taking any roads. I'm just saying you may not have had the entire story."

"Are you feeling that same understanding for the jerk who hit that dog? I told you the driver was speeding." She swung her legs off the couch. "Or maybe you think the driver had no choice but to hit him."

"I don't think anything of the sort. Would you relax? You've given me heart failure more than once tonight. Can you just stay still for a little bit and give me a break?"

Her chin jutted pugnaciously. "I wasn't trying to give *anyone* heart failure."

"Believe me, darlin'. You appear before anyone with your

shirt covered in blood, and you're going to upset a soul or two." He didn't know what he'd thought when he'd seen her that way. He knew what he'd felt, though.

Murderous.

"What did you expect me to do, Evan?" Her voice went so high it nearly squeaked. "Leave him lying there in the street? Act like he's just some piece of roadkill for someone else to deal with?"

He scrubbed his hands down his face. "I'm not suggesting you do anything other than exactly what you did! If the dog makes it through the next few hours, he's going to be fine, so stop getting yourself all worked up."

"That's right! *If.* The dog might not make it. The dog might, might go into shock again, or…get an infection…or have internal injuries that you don't know about yet." Her words were coming so fast, they were practically running on top of each other. "Maybe if I'd been faster, or had stopped the dog from running out in the street, or—"

"Stop." He reached out and caught her face between his hands, making her look at him. Sometimes he was such a bloody idiot it was a wonder he had opposable thumbs. "What happened to this dog was not your fault. If you hadn't gotten help, he would have probably died out there on the street. You cannot blame yourself for this. It wasn't your fault." She tried to look away and he leaned closer. "Losing Emi was *not* your fault, either."

The shudders racking through her slender body stopped as if he'd plunged her into frozen storage. Her brown eyes seemed to grow even darker until they were almost black. They roved over the room, never stopping, never focusing and certainly never looking back at him.

And the pain inside her seemed to blast from her pores in a mushroom cloud.

He moved his hands to her shoulders. "It wasn't your fault," he whispered.

Her restless gaze finally stilled, settling midway down his chest. "You don't know." Her voice was low. Raw.

But he did know. Because Jake had told him. Jake, who'd needed to unburden himself one night after his marriage had fallen apart and Leandra had escaped to Europe to lick her wounds, alone. And it was Jake who'd told Evan—just mere weeks earlier—that he was certain Leandra still had not talked to anyone about what had happened the day Emi died.

"She climbed over the gate in your backyard and fell in the pool."

"And she died because of it," she finished flatly.

"It was not your fault."

"You think if you say that often enough, it's going to magically make it be true? It doesn't work that way, Evan. You don't know. You'll *never* know."

"That doesn't mean I don't know about loss," he said evenly. "Grief."

"Bully for you." She pushed herself off the couch, trying to brush past him, but he caught her around the waist, stopping her cold.

It galled the hell out of him that he was trying to help her and he could still be so easily sidetracked by desire. What did that say about him? That he was more Darian Taggart's son than Drew's?

He let go of her waist. "You need to clean up," he said, moving away from her before his baser instincts gave him the answer he didn't want to acknowledge. "You can take my truck home if you feel like you're steady enough to drive. I can't leave the dog yet."

She plucked at her T-shirt, looking down as if surprised that the bloodstains were still there. "I...I want to wait and see how the dog is."

He could have argued. Could have told her he'd call her, just the way he called any of the other pet owners who'd left their animals in his care for one reason or another. He could have gotten her out of his range by a half-dozen means, yet he just moved to the cupboard in the corner and opened it up. He pulled out a set of scrubs and held them out to her. "They're clean."

She reached out to take them.

Their fingers brushed.

Her lashes lowered, hiding those too-dark eyes of hers. "Thank you."

He shoved his hands in his pockets. He'd manipulated her to suit his own purpose, and as a result had made touching her even more impossible. "You can use the shower if you want. There's one in the bathroom there." He nodded toward the narrow doorway on the other side of the couch. "It's not fancy, but—"

"Thank you."

He nodded again and forced his feet to move out of the office. Thank God for the dog. It gave him something to occupy his mind and his hands as he checked him over again and transferred him to one of his larger kennels. The clinic was deadly silent except for the faint sound of hissing water.

He flipped on the radio and cranked the volume high enough to drown out the sound.

He was mopping up the floor in surgery when she reappeared. The pale green scrubs were meant to fit him, so on Leandra they were a couple million sizes too big. The arms barely stayed up on her shoulders, and she'd rolled up the bottom of the pants so she wouldn't trip on them.

She held a bundle at her waist. Her own clothes. Blue jeans. Blood-stained T-shirt.

He should have looked away when he spotted a hank of white lace bundled together with the rest, but he didn't. He just plagued himself wondering if there was anything between his cotton scrubs and her bare skin.

He flipped the mop back over the floor. "Watch out. Floor's slick."

"You really do handle everything around here, don't you?"

"Pretty much." But he knew the question was rhetorical. After all, she'd been the one asking questions from behind the camera during the second day of filming when she'd had him sitting on a wooden fence rail—as if that were where he spent a good portion of his workday—and wasted hours describing every way from Sunday how his practice worked. She knew that, until recently, he'd employed a part-time bookkeeper. Only Gretchen had left Weaver to be closer to her daughter and grandchildren, who lived in Cheyenne. And she knew he had two rotating assistants who helped with the companion animals.

"Jake only handles surgeries and what he calls the prima donna celebs at the animal hospital." She skirted the center portion of the floor that still gleamed wet. Her ex-husband's real interest was research, though, and the practice he had made enough money to fund it. "I guess you know that, though." She set her bundle on the end of a stainless-steel table. Then she snatched it up again. "That's not sterilized or something is it?"

He shook his head. "It's fine."

She set the clothing back down again. Crossed her arms. Uncrossed them, then crossed them once more.

He shoved the mop in the kick bucket filled with disinfectant. "You can go see the dog. Just around the corner there. He was awake a few minutes ago."

She didn't look at him as she slipped out of the surgery.

He pressed his forehead to the end of the mop handle. What on God's green earth was he doing?

He dumped the mop into the bucket. The floor was as clean

as ever. Mopping it again wasn't going to change that any more than reminding himself why Leandra was off-limits changed his wanting her anyway.

He stepped around the wall to see Leandra sitting on the floor in front of the kennel. The dog was slowly licking the small fist she'd pushed between the bars. As he watched, she reached through with her other hand and gently worked her fingertips over his head, crooning softly.

He leaned his shoulder against the empty cage beside him. "I don't suppose you have any pets at home."

She shook her head. Her hair was slightly damp and it stuck out in feathery spikes, reminding him of a bird. The back of her neck looked pale and soft. The shirt had slipped toward her shoulder, baring a trio of freckles.

If he touched those tiny, enticing spots—the only marks on that smooth sweep of velvety skin—would she startle and fly away?

"I'm not home enough for a pet. But when Jake and I were together, he sometimes brought home strays."

"Jake said you were the one to bring home strays."

She was silent for a moment. Then she lifted her shoulder. "Maybe." The V-necked shirt took another run at slipping off the point of her shoulder, but she pulled her hand out of the cage and stopped it. "Why don't you have a pet? Too busy taking care of everyone else's?"

"Yeah."

"When did you and Axel go in together on Northern Light?" She seemed determined to discuss prosaic matters.

"A few months ago. We wanted Ryan to buy in, too, but he's been out of touch. Once we hear from him, if he still wants a share, we'll arrange it."

"I didn't know you were so interested in horse breeding."

"Neither did I." He watched her shirt slip again. There was

definitely no bra strap impeding its wayward progress. "I'm in it for the money. Axel's just experimenting around with it. He knows your dad would be pretty happy for him to take a bigger interest in the horse farm."

"I don't think Axel knows *what* he wants to do."

Evan pinched the bridge of his nose. Axel knew exactly what he wanted to do, and the effect it would have on his family if and when he did it. Since the Clays already worried enough about Ryan's naval service, Axel wasn't inclined yet to add to it by revealing he'd pitched his hat into a similar ring. "Maybe," he hedged.

"Besides, what do you need with the money? Isn't this place paying its way? I mean when you don't have your groupies around scaring off the customers."

He grimaced. "There are some other things I'd like to do."

"Expand?"

He shrugged. But even as he was prepared to let her think that, he told her the truth. "I want to help pay for a special school for Hannah."

Her lashes lifted and she looked at him. "Wow."

"It's no big deal," he dismissed. "Just that Katy's a single mom on a serviceman's salary, you know? So if I can help—"

"You will," she finished. "Well," she turned her attention back to the cage. "I know what I want."

He seriously needed to get his mind off those freckles that kept peeking out at him. "What's that?"

"To sleep with you."

He hadn't heard right. "'Scuse me?"

She didn't look at him. Her fingers continued fondling the groggy dog. "I want you to take me to bed," she enunciated clearly as if he were not overly familiar with the English language.

There had been a day when he would have jumped at an

offer like that—like a starving man jumped on a morsel of food. But that had been when he was twenty-one and doing anything and everything to forget the fact that the girl he'd never had, had fallen head over heels for his friend. "Why?"

She turned her head at that. But she still didn't manage to meet his gaze and there was a splotch of color riding her cheeks. "Do I have to draw you a picture?"

Unfortunately, no extra effort on her part was required. "Why *now?*" he pushed.

"We are engaged," she reminded him tartly as she faced the kennel once more. "But if you're not interested just say so."

He let out a harsh breath. "You'd try the patience of a saint, you know that? My *interest* is pretty damn evident, as you well know."

"Then what's the problem?"

"The problem is you're going around offering sex like it's a cup of coffee."

"If your percolator is out of commission—"

"Dammit, Leandra!"

Her shoulders moved, and the annoying shirt slipped another inch. "Look, just forget it. I changed my mind, anyway."

"Yeah, that solves it all, doesn't it," he muttered. "Let's just pretend we never had this conversation."

"Exactly."

He grabbed her arms from behind, hauling her to her feet. She let out a gasp, her eyes widening.

"No, not *exactly.*" His teeth were clenched. "You don't put something out there like that and then pretend it never happened."

"You're the one who blackmailed me into pretending we're engaged. And you'll want to pretend *that* never happened when this is all over."

"Bugs you, does it? Hasn't even been a full day, yet. You think it's just one big joke, is that it?"

She glared and brushed at his hands, but he had a hold and wasn't remotely close to letting go.

"I know how you used to behave," she said tightly. "Jake told me all about it. Once Lucy was gone, you had a different girl every week."

"Which is it that you prefer, Leandra?" He barely managed not to shake her. "Thinking that I was moping around brokenhearted because Lucy chose New York over me? Or thinking that I was some get-laid-quick guy in college? Which one would make a better story for *WITS?*"

"This isn't about *WITS!*"

There were tears in her eyes. Dammit all to hell.

He let go of her so fast she stumbled, and he felt even more like the front-runner for crumb of the year. "Don't ask me to sleep with you just because you're bored," he snapped.

She managed a reasonable glare that was only slightly mitigated by the shimmer in her eyes. "I thought it was only women who were supposed to act all offended when presented with such a…situation."

"Proposition."

"Don't think that applies, given our affianced state. It doesn't matter, anyway, because like I said, I've changed my mind. In fact, I wouldn't sleep with you now if you begged."

He'd sit, stay and roll over and play dead if he believed she were serious. Though he seriously doubted that a single instance of lovemaking would get her out from beneath his skin. Not when she'd been lodged there as long as she had been. "That's a fact, huh?"

"Yes." She snatched at the shoulder of the shirt, twitching it back up again. "So what do we do about the dog? He has no collar, and you obviously don't recognize him. Do you think he's a stray?"

He barely managed to get his mind off Leandra and him

and a bed—or any convenient surface. If he'd needed any confirmation that she really *hadn't* wanted what she'd said, he definitely had it now. "I doubt it. Aside from the injuries from the car, he's in good condition. As for what we do about it, I'll file a complaint over at the sheriff's office, but that probably won't lead to anything, either. All you have is a car description."

"So we just forget about it as if it never happened?"

"What *do* you want to do? Run a door-to-door search for the car? I'd like to see the driver punished, too, but believe me, there's not much more that we can do about it."

She looked even more distressed.

There was one thing he could say about Leandra. Every emotion she felt was usually broadcast on that expressive face of hers.

She knelt next to the cage again and reached through to pet the dog. "What happens to him, then?"

"We'll post a notice or two, see if someone comes out to claim him. He looks well cared for. Chances are his owners will be looking for him."

"And if they don't?"

"Then I try to find someone to take him."

"And if you can't?"

"You have more questions than Hannah, you know that?" He hunkered down beside her.

"What happens?"

He reached through the bars and gave the dog a gentle scratch. "Animal control will take him."

"No!"

"What do you want me to do? Keep him? If I kept every stray that crosses my path, I'd have my own zoo."

"But you're a vet."

And he'd done plenty of volunteer stints for a host of

animal services. "I'm a vet who can't afford his own zoo," he said. His father had attained a certain level of success, but Evan hadn't been born into a family with the kind of resources that she had. "Don't borrow trouble. The owner will probably turn up."

"If he doesn't, I'll take the dog."

"You just said you're not home enough for a pet. And even if you were, this guy won't fit in an apartment. He'll need space to run."

"There are parks." She shot him a look. "Don't you think I can take care of a dog?"

And just that quickly, they were back in quicksand, where everything he said was measured against the death of her daughter. "I think you can do anything you try to do. As long as it's for the right reasons."

Her shoulders sagged, as if she hadn't expected such an admission from him. The shirt slipped yet again. "Thank you," she whispered.

Even though there'd been no begging—other than in his feeble mind—and even though he'd made himself a year's worth of promises otherwise, he touched his finger to that smooth, beckoning trio of freckles.

She froze. He swore he could hear her swallow, and then the slow exhalation that followed.

She reached up and covered his exploring finger with her hand, pressing it against her flesh.

His hand flattened, fingers splayed. He could feel her pulse fluttering beneath his index finger.

"I'm not bored," she said after a moment.

"I know." He moved his thumb over the nape of her neck. Her hair was nearly dry, and it was as silky as anything he'd ever felt. "But we can't sleep together just so you can stop thinking about your daughter."

Her eyes closed. He felt her instinctive wish for flight. But she didn't move. Didn't take her hand from atop his. Didn't do anything but sit there, her pulse beating frantically against his fingers. "And…if I'm not thinking about that?"

"Then I'd still say no out of self-preservation. Can't take being ruined for all other women for the rest of my life."

She made a disbelieving sound. Then she patted his hand briskly and pushed to her feet. "No matter what anyone says, you're a good friend, Evan Taggart."

He grimaced. She thought he was giving her a palatable way out. And maybe he was.

But that didn't mean he hadn't meant every word he'd said.

Chapter Twelve

Facing Evan when they resumed shooting the next Monday morning took about all the courage that Leandra could muster.

It wasn't just the airing of "the" episode, either. Though she'd gotten calls from friends and coworkers and even Eduard, who'd considered the entire matter *très romantique*.

It was the fact that she'd thrown herself at Evan, and he'd turned her down.

She'd put off going to his clinic until the last possible moment, not until Ted was calling her on her cell phone, wanting to know if she'd had an accident or something because she was *never* late.

She should have known not to worry, though. The minute she joined her already-set-up crew, Evan—who was talking to a girl about her kitten and the shots he needed to give it— barely gave her more than a passing glance.

Having spent every minute since she'd thrown herself at

him fretting over this very moment, his lack of reaction was...deflating.

Ted had everything well under control. It was a day of pretty straightforward stuff. Evan had appointments all morning long in the clinic. Clients coming and going, bringing dogs and cats, even a goat. They would shoot continuously and during editing would pull and combine moments for the most effective results.

As Janet termed such days, it was a bit of a snooze.

Leandra sat quietly well behind the cameras, lights and sound equipment, making notes and fielding calls from Marian. When she wasn't doing that, she found herself becoming entirely distracted just watching Evan be Evan.

Even Ted caught Leandra seeming stuck in a daze as she watched the man and teased her about looking lovestruck. Evan caught the comment and Leandra felt herself flushing. Of course, they were *all* watching Evan, but she was in the disquieting position of knowing she wasn't watching him in a professional capacity. Everyone else thought they were engaged—even the crew—but Leandra knew better.

She rose from her chair and gestured silently to her cameraman that she was stepping out.

He nodded and mouthed "cool."

Because the film equipment blocked the area leading toward the rear of the building where the kennel cages were kept, Leandra went out the front door and walked outside the building, re-entering through the door through which they'd brought the injured dog.

He was still in the cage, but he lifted his tawny head and slapped his tail against the blanket beneath him when he spotted her. She crouched next to the bars, tucking her fingers through them. The dog immediately began licking them. "Yeah, you're feeling a whole lot better aren't you," she murmured. "Evan's pretty good at what he does." She rubbed the dog's silky ears and he made a sighing sound. "Wonder what your name is. Where you belong."

"Too bad I'm not Dr. Dolittle so he could tell us."

She bumped her shoulder against the kennel, turning so quickly. Evan stood there, looking very official in his white lab coat. "I didn't hear you come in."

"Sorry." He didn't particularly look it. He crouched beside her and pulled a treat from his pocket, feeding it to the dog, who lapped it up with greedy glee. "I put in a report with the sheriff's office. Just in case something turns up. Maybe the driver'll get stopped for speeding or something. And if anyone reports their dog missing, the county animal control has the info, too."

Leandra focused on Evan's hand, stuck through the cage bars beside hers and tried not to notice how good he smelled. Some combination of fresh air and Taggart that went to her head.

If he moved his thumb even a fraction of an inch, it would brush her hand where it lay, buried in the thick coat of butter-scotch-colored dog hair.

She made the mistake of glancing at him, only to notice that his hair was starting to curl a little behind his ear. She made her fingers be satisfied with stroking dog fur, though, since running them through those gleaming black strands was really quite out of the question. Particularly after he'd turned her down. Flat.

She turned and stared again at the dog.

"We okay?" he asked after a moment. "You and me? You know. After the other night."

Her skin started to burn. "Why wouldn't we be?" She hoped she didn't sound like she was bluffing. "We're engaged, aren't we?" Her voice was flippant.

But he sighed and dastardly moved his hand just enough

to close over her fingers. She was glad she was sitting on her butt, because she probably would have fallen over had she merely been in a balancing crouch the way he was.

"Then why are you acting so jumpy?"

"Too much caffeine. Don't take any notice of it."

"Easier said than done," he murmured.

She swallowed. *Why* wouldn't he move his hand? For that matter, why hadn't she moved hers? "Don't you have a patient waiting or something?"

"Overweight beagle. Owner's always late."

She moistened her lips, nodding.

He fell silent, too.

To say the air was thick would have been a huge understatement. Yet Leandra couldn't think of a single sensible thing to say. And she couldn't exactly afford to let her tongue run away with her again. It was bad enough that she'd propositioned him once and been turned down.

If she offered herself again she'd have to do something drastic to herself. Like cut out her tongue.

His thumb moved over the back of her hand. "Leandra—"

Couldn't he see that he was destroying her? What on earth was wrong with her that she didn't move away from him? Put some distance between them. Remember that he was just a friend from her home town.

Just Evan Taggart.

Nobody special. Nobody out of the ordinary. Nobody who made her lose track of anything and everything but him.

She swallowed past the vise constricting her throat. "Yes?"

His thumb caressed her hand again. No, he wasn't caressing her. He was petting the dog. Her hand was simply in the way.

Willpower finally found her and she pulled her hand away from the dog. Ensuring that willpower didn't desert her again just as quickly, she slipped her arm out of the cage, even scooting back a few inches on the floor as she curled her fingers into a fist in her lap.

Evan still hadn't said whatever was on his mind. Her fingernails dug into her palm. "What, Evan?"

He looked at her.

And the expression in those blue, blue eyes reached down inside her and twisted. "What's wrong?"

He made a sound, partly impatient, partly wry and mostly effective in tightening her nerves even more. He pulled his hand from the cage, too, sliding his palm under her fist. "Conscience versus wishful thinking."

For some ridiculous reason, she suddenly felt like crying. But the scrape of a shoe on the floor behind them had Evan's head whipping around just as rapidly as hers. Their hands parted as if they'd been caught doing something naughty.

Ted stood there, his attention on his heavy camera. He'd obviously caught the moment on tape. "Beagle's here."

"What did I tell you? Fifteen minutes, every single time." Evan straightened, brushing his hands down his lab coat. "Coming?" He stuck his hand back out.

She took it, trying to act as if everything were perfectly normal as he pulled her to her feet and quickly released her. She was perfectly aware that Ted was still filming. Not that there was anything unusual in that. It was the way they put together a show, after all. Reality.

And since Evan's big "announcement," she was even more a part of the odd reality.

She moved around behind Ted, and they processed back to the waiting beagle.

For the rest of the afternoon, Leandra kept her nose firmly where it belonged—in the show. They were just packing up the equipment while Evan was cursing over the mess of files and paperwork on the desk when the door to the clinic opened and Darian Taggart stepped in.

Leandra shot a quick look at Evan.

He continued sorting file folders, barely looking at the older man. "What's wrong?"

Darian spread his hands, smiling. "Who says anything is wrong?"

Evan turned to a filing cabinet and dumped a pile inside the drawer. "You're here." His voice was flat.

Leandra saw Ted flip off the cover of his very small, very portable recorder and deliberately stepped in his path, cutting off the view. "Let's head to Colbys. My treat."

Janet and Paul were plenty enthusiastic about that. Ted, however, just eyed her.

She didn't move out of his path.

"This isn't the way we do this." His voice was low. Curious.

"It is today." She lifted the camera out of his hand and fit the cover back over it.

He hesitated, but after a long moment where she dreaded having to pull rank on him, he shrugged and hefted the last bag of equipment on his shoulder and followed the others outside. "We'll be in the van."

She nodded and looked back at Evan. "You're still doing rounds in the morning, right?"

"Yeah." He strode over to her and ignored the stiff surprise in her face as he dropped a kiss on her mouth. "I'll see you later."

She pressed her soft lips together, obviously believing he'd kissed her strictly for the benefit of Darian. She mumbled "later" and headed out the door, her cheeks pink.

For the first time that day, Evan was glad to see the back of Leandra. Whatever had brought Darian around, he figured it wouldn't be pleasant. "And I'm leaving by five in the morning whether your musketeers are here or not," he warned, calling after her.

"We'll be here." Her dark eyes flicked past him to Darian and she smiled as she excused herself.

Evan passed Darian, who was watching her walk toward the van, and reached for more files.

"She's a hot thing, but I can't believe you're going to bother marrying her. Easier to just sleep with 'em, I think," Darian announced.

"Which explains so much about your marriage to Sharon." He stuffed the files into the drawer; there would be hell to pay when he needed to look something up, but the desk needed clearing. The haphazard filing was better than setting a torch to all the paperwork, he figured. Much as getting rid of all the papers appealed. "You still haven't said why you're here."

"Have to be a reason to see my son?"

Evan looked over at the man. "Not your son in any way that matters to me and, yeah, there has to be a reason."

Darian made a face. He stood barely an inch shorter than Evan, and looking at the man, he had a pretty good idea what he, himself, would be like in another twenty years.

Practically carbon copies.

He shoved the last batch of files in the bottom drawer and jammed it shut. "Spit it out, Darian. I've got things to do."

"Picking out china patterns?"

"Maybe." If it got rid of Darian, what was one more lie? Evan had told his folks the truth; it was enough to keep his conscience relatively clear. "China, invitations, the whole bit."

Darian looked suspicious. "Don't fool me, boy. You're not the kind to settle down."

"Like you, you mean?" Darian didn't know what being settled even meant. Marriage sure in hell hadn't stopped him from entertaining himself elsewhere.

"Sharon's all right," Darian said carelessly. "She accept me the way I am."

Because she's either a saint or a damn fool, Evan thought not for the first time. And Darian still hadn't said why he'd come; it wasn't as if the man made regular trips to the clinic

Grabbing the keys, Evan went back to the front door an pushed it open, holding it there.

Outside, the van was just pulling away. He could se Leandra's tousled blond head through the window.

"Katy's coming home next week. We just got an e-mai from her yesterday. Sharon wants to have a party."

He was glad to hear about his cousin's return. "Something wrong with the phone? You didn't have to come here in person.

"I was in Weaver, anyway."

Evan eyed the man. "So you used telling me about it as a excuse to be in Weaver. Pretty thin, don't you think? Mayb Sharon isn't as accepting of your behavior as she used to be Who is it you're really here to see? The same woman you wer with the other week?"

Darian's eyes narrowed and Evan knew he'd hit the nail o the head. Not that it was a particularly tiny nail—give Darian's perpetual behavior, it was about the size of a cow pie

"A week from Saturday."

Evan had no respect for Darian, but that didn't extend t Katy. "I'll be there."

"Bring your girlfriend."

"Fiancé," Evan drawled.

"We'll see about that. Last fiancée you had didn't want t stick around Weaver, either."

Evan let the jab slide. He and Lucy hadn't been any mor engaged than he and Leandra were. "Unless you want to sta locked in with seven dogs, two cats and a ferret for th night...?" He pushed the door wider and Darian finally left

Evan pulled the door closed and locked it. Two minutes later, his cell rang and with little surprise, he answered Sharon's call. "Yeah, he was here," he told her when she asked if he'd seen Darian.

"Oh, good." Sharon sounded relieved. "We're so thrilled for you, you know. About you and Leandra. So romantic. You know, Darian followed me to Braden way back when. Reminds me a little of you two, now."

The similarity escaped him, but he listened to her prattle on a while about how nice it would be for Katy to be back for the wedding, and speaking of which, when would it be?

"We haven't set a date," he told her.

"Oh, well. Plenty of time for that," she assured him cheerfully and soon rang off.

Evan pocketed the phone and closed the rest of the clinic down, thinking he was as big a fraud as Darian.

The house was quiet when he went across, and even though he'd spent a lot of years telling himself he preferred it that way, it quickly got on his nerves. He showered and found some clean clothes and drove out to Clay Farms.

He didn't go up to the house; just headed around to the stable to check on Northern Light. Not a necessary endeavor; he couldn't trust anyone more than Jefferson Clay when it came to horses.

He turned the stallion out in the corral, then climbed on the fence rail to watch the horse work out his friskies.

"Used to come out here and watch the horses when you were just a boy. Em always said it was when you were chewing on something. Otherwise you went to your folks' place."

Evan was used to Jefferson's silent approaches. He settled his hat lower over his eyes to shade against the setting sun. "Married yourself a bright woman."

"I always thought so." He winced as he swung himself up

beside Evan and swore under his breath. "Getting old ain't for sissies." He adjusted his own hat and eyed the horse. "Best-looking stud we've got on the property. Sure you don't want to sell him to me?"

"As sure as I was the last time you asked."

"Stubborn. But smart." Jefferson grinned faintly. "I wouldn't part with him, either."

The sun sank a few inches lower on the horizon, sending long red fingers across the landscape.

"I s'pose I should ask if you wanna talk about it or something."

Evan chuckled humorlessly. "Rather you didn't."

"Suits me. But Emily. She'll ask, you know."

"Nothing to tell. Just finding myself stuck between a rock and a hard place."

Jefferson straightened out one leg, then bent it again, propping his boot heel back on the rail. "Hard wanting someone you think you shouldn't want." He grimaced slightly when Evan shot him a look. "Hell, boy, you think I like talking about this? She's my daughter."

"The engagement isn't real. I know she told you that."

"You wishing it were?"

Evan stared back at the sunset. "It's not. I'm not the marrying kind and she's got her sights set elsewhere."

Jefferson snorted. "You're a vet. Oughta know better than to think that dog's gonna run."

He wasn't going to sit there on the man's fence and debate whether or not he wanted the man's daughter. "Squire coming back soon?"

Jefferson's teeth flashed. "Next weekend."

"Going to be plenty of parties going around. Sharon's throwing one for Katy's return the next weekend."

They sat there and watched the sun take its last dip. "Well, my butt can only take so much these days and Em's got dinner going inside. Welcome to come join us if you'd like." Jefferson climbed off the fence.

"Thanks." He'd shared many meals with them. "I'll take a rain check, if you don't mind."

Jefferson shrugged. "You'll want to be checking with Howard soon. He's got a list of people already interested in Northern's services. You and Ax are going to be neck deep in the business before you know it." He headed off toward the long stone house with a wave.

Evan hoped Jefferson was right about the business. If he were going to pay for Hannah's tuition, he'd be needing funds and the sooner the better, given Katy's impending return.

He climbed off the fence and rounded up the horse and led him back to the state-of-the-art horse barn. He coaxed the animal into his stall with fresh feed, then washed up and headed back to town.

The familiar van was parked outside of Colbys.

He thought about stopping.

Even slowed his truck down to a crawl.

Their engagement was not real. It never would be.

He put his boot harder on the gas and drove past.

Chapter Thirteen

Leandra sat up with a start, staring around the darkened bedroom at Sarah's, letting her heart settle, trying to get her bearings.

She let out a deep breath and lay back on the bed, bunching the pillow under her cheek.

A noise at her window had her bolting upright again, and she realized it was that same noise that had wakened her.

Then she heard her name. A crackle of something against the glass window. Followed by her name again and a somewhat less-quiet oath.

She threw back the blanket and went to the window, yanking up the shade.

Evan stood on the other side and she gasped, jumping back a foot, nearly tripping over the shoes she'd left lying on the floor.

He lifted his hand in a sketchy wave, as if they were just passing on the street.

She stepped to the window, shoving it upward. "What are you doing?"

He leaned in, smiling harder, and she got a whiff of alcohol through the window screen. "Visiting my fee-on-say."

"Good grief." She looked past him. The bedroom faced the street. Anyone and their mother's brother could drive by and see him tottering outside her window.

Not that there was a lot of traffic at—she glanced at the clock on the nightstand—two in the morning. "You've been drinking."

"Yes, ma'am."

She hadn't seen him drink more than the occasional beer since she'd returned to Weaver. "Why?"

He propped his elbows on the windowsill. "Because I am a parched man," he enunciated, more clearly than she would have expected, given his state. "Living in a desert with no hope of water."

"You're tanked," she muttered. "Just…stay there. I'll get dressed and drive you home."

He smiled again. "Knew you would. Seems like something a fee-on-say would do."

She wished he'd stop calling her that.

She grabbed a sweatshirt from the drawer and dragged it over her head, stuffed her feet in the shoes she'd tripped over and quickly let herself out of the house before he woke up Sarah and the neighbors, too.

He was waiting right where she'd left him. "Well? Come on." She gestured, her keys jangling in her hand. "It's cold out here. You don't even have on a jacket."

"More fee-on-say-uh-lee words." He stepped carefully around a bush, managing to put his boot right in the center of it. "Sorry."

"You can plant Sarah a new one when you're sober." She grabbed his arm and pulled him toward the car, trying hard not to be alarmed. "What's wrong? You don't drink anymore." She knew he'd once done plenty of it in college, right alongside Jake. But those days were long past. "Were you at Colbys or somewhere else?"

"Chaps. Out by CeeVid. Couldn't go to Colbys. You were there."

"Hours ago. Please don't tell me you drove here."

"Do I look that stupid?"

"You look that drunk," she said tartly. But there was no sign of his vehicle on the street.

"I walked."

"Been closer to walk to your house." She opened the passenger door and waited for him to fold himself into the close confines.

He caught her hand when she stepped back to close the door. "I did." He sounded weary. "There's a strange woman sleeping in my bed."

Her lips parted. Since the episode with his announcement had aired, the flocking women had abated considerably. "You picked up a stranger?"

He made a face at her. "Not these days."

His thumb was moving back and forth over her wrist in a very distracting way and she pulled away, only to have him loop his arm around her waist instead. Off balance, she leaned against the car, trying not to fall in his lap. "Evan—"

"Only ones in my bed should be us."

Her mouth ran dry. "Easy for you to say now," she said striving for lightness, "given the way you've already turned me down."

He shook his head and it brushed against her belly. He tightened his arm around her waist, and she hovered, precariously caught with one hand on the opened door and the other on the cold roof of the car. "Had to." His voice sighed against her.

She didn't want to examine that too closely. "Did you call the sheriff? About the woman in your house?"

"Mmm." He turned his head against her abdomen. "Smell good. Always do. Anyone ever tell you that?"

She couldn't say that anyone had. "Evan, what did you do about the woman in your house?"

"Left her there. She was sleeping."

"Thought you'd started locking your doors."

He shrugged. His hand slipped down her waist, cupping her hip, fingers splayed. It was an effort to keep her thoughts controlled. The woman could be robbing Evan blind for all they knew. "You have to call the sheriff's office. Who does the night shift these days?"

"Dunno." His fingers flexed against her hip, and she bit her lip against the rush of sensation he was causing. Then he did it again, and she began wondering if he was doing it deliberately. "Dave Ruiz," he said suddenly.

She grabbed his hand and peeled it away from her hip. "Do you have your cell phone on you?"

He leaned back and spread his arms wide. "Wanna check?"

She did, drat it all, and despite his inebriated state, he seemed well aware of that fact. "I'm going inside to call him." Her voice was prim in the face of the heat ripping through her veins. "Maybe he can meet us at your house. Just wait here." She didn't wait to see if he did so; she just spun on her heel and hurried back inside.

She was dialing the phone in the kitchen trying to be quiet so as not to wake Sarah when she heard a shuffle, and turned to see Evan coming through the small living room. He knocked his shin on the corner of the coffee table and swore softly, hurriedly catching the pretty glass vase of Sarah's that sat on top of it.

The dispatcher answered and she quickly relayed the information before Evan could make even more noise.

"It'll be a while before the deputy can get there," she was told. "He's out on a car accident. We've got a few others on call, though. You say the intruder is sleeping?"

"That's what Evan said."

"Bunch of crazies coming to town lately," the dispatcher said, her voice tart. "Give me a few minutes to raise somebody. Tell the doc not to re-enter his dwelling until we've given the clear. Can he be reached at this number?"

"Yes."

"Right. I'll get on it immediately. Oh, and congratulations on the engagement."

Leandra stared at the phone, feeling a little like she'd fallen down the rabbit hole. She slowly hung up the phone and turned to Evan.

He was leaning against the kitchen doorway. His eyes were narrowed against the kitchen light and his hair was rumpled. His dark T-shirt was coming untucked from the waist of his jeans. Dark stubble shadowed his hard jaw.

He was drunk yet looking at him still jangled every feminine instinct she possessed into shivering attention.

"You're not supposed to go back to the house until they call." She folded her hands together at her waist, feeling uncommonly nervous. "Do you want some coffee or water or something?"

"Something." He lifted his hand. "Come 'ere."

She stood stock still, not taking a single step toward him. "Coffee, I think." But she didn't head toward the coffeepot, either.

"I'm not Jake."

The comment came out of nowhere. She frowned at him. "Shh. Nobody's confusing the two of you. Least of all me."

His lips twisted. "You still love him." His voice was soft, but she still heard him.

Her stomach dipped and swayed. "I divorced him, remember?"

"You haven't replaced him."

"People don't get *replaced*. You haven't ever gotten serious about anyone since Lucy went away, and you insist that isn't because you're still in love with *her*."

"Always'll love her. Just not...love her."

"There you go, then." She crossed her arms. "And keep your voice down or we'll wake up Sarah."

He straightened from his slouching lean and stepped closer. "Say it."

"What?"

"That you're not in love with Jake."

Annoyed, she stretched her arms out, holding him at bay. "I just did." Heavens, there had been two calls just that week from him that she hadn't even returned.

"Not the words." His lips twisted again. "Maybe you can't."

"Oh, for Pete's sake. I am *not* in love with Jake! I'm—" she clamped her lips together, scrambling for the composure that had clearly deserted her. "You're drunk," she said flatly. "If you weren't, you'd be keeping a ten-foot pole between us."

His lips suddenly twitched. "Even I'm not gonna exaggerate about myself that much."

She blinked. What?

Then he closed his hands on her shoulders and yanked her against him, and she realized belatedly just exactly what he'd meant. So much for the theory that inebriation made a man incapable—

Her brain cells scrambled when his hand slid up her ribs, and grazed over her breast. "Evan—"

"Getting right fond of this kitchen." His lips nibbled along her neck.

She tried not to moan and instead, sank her fingers into his hair and pulled.

"Hey!"

"We are *not* doing this. Whoa!" He'd lifted her onto the counter. "Hold it."

He ignored her, stepping between her thighs and tugging her snug against him. "I'm trying to hold you."

Her head fell back against the cupboard behind her. Giving in would be oh, so easy. "This is a pretend engagement," she reminded him a little desperately.

"This—" his hand delved beneath her sweatshirt and camisole and slid wickedly along her spine "—isn't pretend."

She realized her fingertips were kneading his shoulders, and she yanked her hands back. "The other night you wanted nothing to do with *this*. Remember?"

"Shows you I'm not as nice a guy as you thought." He kissed her, almost roughly.

And though she'd expected to taste alcohol, she tasted him; laced with only a hint of coffee and whiskey. Heady.

He sighed against her, his lips softening, coaxing, then sinking deeper into her. She knew there was some reason she should be resisting him; she just couldn't quite put her finger on the reason. Particularly when her fingers were busy smoothing through the thick black locks that they'd so recently pulled.

His arm slid behind her rear and pulled her even tighter against him. Her legs slid around his hips, ankles looping.

"Too many clothes," he muttered, and worked her sweatshirt up.

She let go of him long enough for him to draw it over her head. "You've got more on than me." Her voice was husky. Raw. A match to the way she felt inside.

The sweatshirt hit the floor and his hands came between

them, molding her breasts through the stretchy thin fabric of her camisole.

Desire had been flooding her already. Now it was pushing headily at the dam. She bit back a cry when his fingers teased her nipples into even tighter peaks, and nearly came off the counter when his head dipped and he caught one, fabric and all, between his lips.

He made a low sound, male and satisfied and wanting all in one, and whatever dwindling sense of reason she still possessed fled for good. She just thanked the stars that Sarah was as sound a sleeper as she was. Her hands dragged at his T-shirt, working her hands beneath it, wanting to feel him, more of him, all of him. "Evan—"

"Leave a message." He discovered her other nipple, leaving the first bathed in damp fabric. "I'm busy here."

She traced the waist of his jeans around to the front. Felt the metal button at the top of his fly, and the flesh pushing hard from beneath.

He made that low sound again, the one that sent tingles streaking down her spine, and grabbed her hand, only to slide his between them. Her thin, cotton pajama pants were no protection against his teasing, intimate touch, and she sucked in a hard breath. "Evan—wait."

"Can't." His marauding hand found the thin excuse of a waistband and pulled at it, swirling and delving beneath until he touched only her. "You can't wait. I can't wait." He inhaled on a hiss as he dragged his fingers through the wet desire she couldn't hide, then sank into her. "Just this," he murmured, his mouth hot against her ear. "Just give me this one thing. Come for me."

There was no reason for his demand, his plea, for she was already convulsing against him, her body spinning out of control. She was still trembling when he let go of her and moved away. She reached for him, protesting. She wanted more, so much more than just his hand on her, in her. "No. Where—"

His expression was fierce, his breathing hard. He lifted one hand, calming, and reached for the phone she hadn't even realized had been ringing with the other.

Adjusting her disheveled clothes, her face feeling on fire, she slid off the counter, only to have to grab it again for her knees were barely strong enough to hold her up.

The sheriff's office calling, of course.

Talk about timing.

She pushed her shaking hands through her hair. Where had she left her car keys? In the car? Or had she brought them back inside with her? She'd need to drive Evan back to his place—

"When?" His voice was harsh and she flinched, watching his face turn pale.

Alarm slithered through her and she pushed a kitchen chair toward him when he seemed to reach out, needing something.

He sat down, the phone glued to his ear. "Is Darian there?"

Not the sheriff, then, she thought with even more alarm. Evan's gaze lifted to hers and she mouthed, "Who?"

He just shook his head, but grabbed her hand in his, practically a death grip. She swallowed. Her head was suddenly pounding and nausea swirled inside her belly.

"I'll find him," he said, his voice flat. Hollow. "I'll get there as soon as I can." Then he dropped the phone on the table. It was an old-fashioned corded kind, affixed to the wall. The cord sprang back, and the receiver clattered off the table, banging the floor.

Moving automatically, Leandra picked it up and placed it on the cradle. "Is it Hannah?" She seemed to hear her voice coming from some long, thin tunnel.

He shoved his hands viciously through his hair. "Katy."

Her knees wavered again and she sank down on the chair opposite him. "What?"

"Her jeep took a grenade yesterday." He ran his hand down his face. "They sent a chaplain to tell Sharon and Darian. But he—" His teeth clenched visibly. "Bastard wasn't even there with his wife. Jesus. Katy must have barely sent off her e-mail about her return before it happened."

Her eyes burned. She reached over and closed her hands over the fist he was pressing against the tabletop. "I'm so sorry," she whispered. Guilt—God, the familiar guilt that she'd tried to erase for so long, clawed at her. But this wasn't about her. It was about Evan. And his family. "What…what can I do?"

There were no vestiges of desire in his eyes now. "I have to find Darian."

"Let me call your parents. Maybe your dad can help find him."

"*Where* Darian is isn't the problem. He's probably with the woman he's currently screwing."

She flinched.

He stood, the chair skidding on the tile floor. "I need your car."

She rose, also. "I'll drive."

He gave her a hard look, one that nearly made her quail. But she hadn't been raised a Clay for nothing, and she kept her gaze steady on his. "*I'll* drive you, Evan."

He exhaled roughly. "Fine."

She swallowed, relieved that it hadn't come down to an argument. There was no question that he was significantly steadier on his feet than he had been when he'd been tapping on her bedroom window, but he'd also been dealt a heavy blow. "It'll take me just a minute to change."

She hurried to her room to do just that. She was buttoning her jeans when Sarah stuck her head in the door, her face sleep-creased. "What's wrong? I thought I heard the phone."

Leandra rapidly filled her in.

Sarah's expression fell, her hand pressing against her chest. "God. That's—" She shook her head, wordless.

"I'm going to drive Evan to Braden," she told her.

Sarah's eyebrows pulled together. "Are you sure you're up to that?" Her voice was cautious.

Leandra felt her eyes burning and resolutely blinked the tears back. "This isn't about Emi." Her voice broke a little. Hannah. That sweet, complicated child would never be reuniting with her mother.

Sarah just pulled Leandra into a swift hug. "Call me if you need me."

Leandra nodded and headed back out to Evan, Sarah trailing behind her. Her cousin didn't say a word. Just put her arms around his wide shoulders and pressed her cheek up against his. There were tears in her eyes when she stepped back to let them leave.

Behind the wheel of the car, Leandra looked at Evan. "Where to?"

He let out a low breath. "The Cozy," he said grimly, referring to a small, aging, out-of-the-way motel. "Darian's favorite home away from home."

She started the engine and silently drove through the dark, still town. When she reached the motel, Evan told her to pull up behind a dark-colored pickup truck.

"Darian's," he said.

She bit her lip. "I'll wait—"

But he shook his head. "Go home, Leandra."

"But—"

"I don't need you here."

The words might as well have been a slap.

She curled her hands tightly around the steering wheel, as if doing so would hold in the hurt.

She didn't say a word. Just nodded.

And when he climbed out of the car, she drove away.

Chapter Fourteen

The memorial service was two days later.

The church in Braden overflowed with family and friends and strangers, all who'd come to pay their respects to a young woman who'd died in service to her country. There was also a heavy media presence that worked Evan's last nerve down to a nub.

Bad enough that Sharon had insisted on Hannah attending. For any child such an event would be difficult. For Hannah, it was a nightmare.

Too many strangers. Too much activity. Too much confusion. She was in a constant state of terror, but nothing Evan said to her grandmother had any effect. There was no help from Darian's quarter, either. *He*'d spent nearly every minute since Evan had tracked him down at The Cozy in a whiskey-induced stupor.

For once, Evan didn't entirely blame the man.

As for him, he hadn't gone near a bottle since the night in Leandra's kitchen.

"Honey, we're heading back to the house." Evan's parents stopped next to him after the service, when he'd had to escape the cloying smell of too many flowers and haul some fresh air into his lungs. "We have a mountain of food to put out for the people who will be stopping by Sharon's to pay their respects," Jolie said. "Do you think I should take Hannah with us?"

"If you can pry her out of Sharon's grip." He could see them from where he stood outside the church. Sharon standing still and looking fragile, her hand seemingly fused to Hannah's tiny one. Darian had left the church the second the preacher stopped talking. "I haven't had any luck." Sharon had just gotten agitated when he'd tried. "But it's only a matter of time before one of those reporters gets close enough to put her and Hannah on air."

"Speaking of which…" Drew looked curiously over at Leandra, who was standing near her parents not far from them. "How did you keep Leandra's crew away from this?"

"I didn't have to." And Evan had been damned surprised about it, too, since he'd almost gotten used to those cameras following most every one of his moves. "She said they had enough footage for next week's show without intruding here."

His parents' gazes traveled over the news vans that were parked like soldiers shoulder to shoulder down the road. But if they thought it odd that Leandra would turn her crew away from a newsworthy event—painful though it was—they said nothing. "I'll go speak with Sharon," his mother said. "See what I can do."

"Thanks."

She just smiled sadly and patted his arm again before heading over to Sharon.

"Your mother's something, isn't she?" Drew tapped his black cowboy hat against the leg of his dark slacks.

"She doesn't hold Darian's actions against Sharon. They hadn't even met when he and Mom—"

Drew settled his hat on his head. "If it hadn't been for my brother, your mom and I wouldn't have found each other. We wouldn't have you. Or Tabby. Not a day goes by that I don't know that we came out on the high end of that particular stick." He clapped his hand over Evan's shoulder and squeezed. "Things like this happen, makes you even more grateful for what you have."

Someone called his name and he set off.

Evan watched his dad stride through the milling people. It wasn't the first time that Evan had to face the fact that Drew's forgiving nature hadn't rubbed off on him along the way. He wasn't feeling particularly grateful.

Anger? There was a helluva lot of that. Only there didn't seem any place to direct it. Guilt? There was plenty of that, too, and he knew right where to place that.

He was the one who'd encouraged Katy to join the service when she'd first talked about it. Her parents had been horrified and told her she was nuts.

She'd have been safer listening to *them*.

He watched Sharon, who was shaking her head as Jolie spoke with her, even as she was seeming to point Hannah into accepting a hug from one of the people working through the line.

His niece looked petrified.

He yanked at the tie strangling him and strode over to them. He bent down and scooped up Hannah. She felt as stiff as a poker, but her fingers clutched his tie like a life raft. "I'm taking her back to your place," he told Sharon, his voice even. He might have been wrong to encourage Katy, but he damn straight wasn't wrong where Katy's daughter was concerned. "The limo will wait here until you're ready to leave."

"But—"

"I'm taking her."

Sharon blinked. She looked nearly ready to collapse. An argument was clearly beyond her, finally. "All right."

He didn't wait around for her to change her mind; to want to pull Hannah forward to meet and greet every person who passed by them, the way she'd been doing. "See you at the house," he told his mom.

She nodded and he carried Hannah away from the melee, stopping only when Leandra cut across the grass to intercept them. "You heading back to Sharon's?"

"Yeah."

"I should probably go with you." She brushed her hand down the side of her simple black dress. "People keep asking me about the, um, the engagement."

Until she'd entered the church with her parents, he hadn't seen her in person since two nights before, when she'd dropped him at The Cozy. Had only talked to her once on the phone when he'd told her about the memorial service arrangements and she'd floored him by preempting his request that she keep her cameras away. But since he'd forced the pretense on her in the first place, he supposed she was right about keeping up appearances as an engaged couple.

"Fine. But all I have is the truck." She wore a black dress and high heels with an elegance that he'd somehow managed to forget she possessed, considering she was almost always in considerably more casual gear.

"Doesn't bother me." She waved slightly to her parents and they headed away from the church.

"Doctor Taggart!" A stiffly coiffed woman jogged across the street toward him. She held a microphone in her hand. "If you could just give us a few moments—"

He lifted his hand, giving her a hard look as he continued down the road. Beside him, Leandra's pace picked up, keeping even with him. Her heels clicked rapidly on the pavement.

"Your cousin died a hero." The reporter's voice followed after him. "Don't you have anything to say about that? What about your newfound celebrity status? Don't you think you owe it to the public to make a statement?"

He swore under his breath and lengthened his stride, grabbing Leandra's elbow with one hand. In his other arm, Hannah started squealing, a high-pitched sound that could have curled hair. "It's okay," he murmured to her.

She took no notice. Just kept up that high, keening sound.

Fifty yards and three more reporters approached before they practically tumbled into the cab of his truck. "Fasten her in," he told Leandra, and gunned the engine.

She was already doing so, and he shot down the street, watching the cameras turned in his direction through the rearview mirror.

Hannah let out a deep sigh and went silent.

He sighed, too. Brushed his hand down her sleek black hair. His gaze met Leandra's for a moment before she looked away.

What did he expect? He'd gotten her nearly naked in her cousin's kitchen, and then pushed her away when she'd only tried to help. He wasn't such a Neanderthal that he didn't realize his actions had been rough.

He *was* Neanderthal enough to have his eyes straying down her slender legs, smoothed in some slightly black nylons, to her ankles and those high, high heels.

Hannah reached past Leandra and opened his glove compartment, and he dragged his attention back where it belonged. He'd learned a long time ago to keep a few spare toy cars around for her, and she pulled out one of the red cars, then sat back again, her finger spinning the wheels.

When they reached Sharon's house, there was another phalanx of trucks waiting.

Hannah, looking out the window, saw, too. A low sound

came out of her pursed lips, growing increasingly loud and high. Her knuckles were white around the car she held clenched in her fist.

Leandra carefully touched the little girl's hand. "It's okay, peanut," she murmured. "Don't look at them."

Evan drove right on past the house. Ten minutes later, he was on the highway.

He drummed his thumb against the steering wheel. "You know, you see the news on television. In the papers. You know this happens. Katy knew it could happen when she enlisted. But—"

"But you don't think it will happen to you. To someone you know. Someone you care about." Her voice was soft.

He frowned. "I should have been there for Emi's funeral."

She was silent, absorbing the sudden announcement. "I don't remember her funeral," she admitted huskily. "Who was there. Who wasn't. It's a complete blur to me. Later, after, Jake tried making me go to a grief counselor with him."

"Why didn't you?"

She looked away. "I didn't want to feel better about losing her." Her voice was husky. "I didn't deserve to feel better. And for a while I hated Jake for not feeling the same way."

"It wasn't your fault, Leandra."

"If not mine, then whose?" She started when Hannah suddenly dumped her car in Leandra's hand and leaned her dark head against her side.

After a taut moment, she slipped her arm around the girl. Before she looked away again, Evan could see that her eyes were damp.

He reached out and turned on the radio, keeping the volume low. They weren't on the road ten minutes before Hannah began snoring softly.

The road hummed beneath the tires and for the first time

in days, Evan felt some of his tension ease. The inside of his truck felt quiet and intimate and…familial.

Did Leandra notice the same thing?

He stretched his arm out over the seat, settling a little more comfortably behind the wheel for the drive, and his fingers brushed the back of her head.

She didn't move away.

They finished the trek, with his niece asleep between them, and his fingertips buried in Leandra's soft blond hair.

He headed to his place, but they both noticed the news van parked in front of the clinic. "Dammit."

"Don't stop. We can go out to my parents' farm," Leandra suggested.

If he didn't have Hannah, there was no way he'd let a reporter run him off from his own home. But he did have Hannah to consider. "They might show up out there, too. You being my—"

"Fiancé?" she finished. "It's possible. But Howard can put a few hands at the gate. Nobody who shouldn't be there will make it past."

This wasn't a case of being inconvenienced by the attention from her show. "This isn't your problem," he said.

She looked pained. "You won't even let me act like a friend now? My parents would offer you the same thing and you know it. Consider it an invitation from them if you have to."

If he put his foot any deeper down his throat, he was going to suffocate on it. "Okay. But just until the attention dies down."

"That might not be as quick as you seem to think."

Leandra's warning turned out to be all too accurate.

If anything, the media attention seemed to increase. Particularly after that week's episode of *WITS* aired.

The footage of the memorial service had been from the news pool, not from Leandra's crew. But it had been part of the show, all the same.

By the next morning, he was getting calls from the major news networks, wanting him to make an appearance.

He tried to be polite as he declined.

The Clays put hands on all the entry points to the property—round the clock, turning away dozens of people each day. Evan stayed in one of the guest suites, and his mother came to stay with Hannah during the day while he breached the persistent looky-loos and reporters and tried to keep his practice from running into the ground.

He'd have been making trips to Braden to check on Sharon, too, but she and Darian had gone to Washington, D.C., for a service there. And though Evan rarely had much good to say about Darian, he was the one who'd convinced Sharon that Hannah should remain in Weaver with Evan.

Evan wished he could believe that Darian was really thinking of Hannah's welfare, but he was cynically aware that the man was happy enough not having to deal with Hannah on a good day.

These were not good days where Hannah was concerned. If anything, she'd withdrawn further into her isolated shell.

"Here." Leandra appeared on the porch beside him where he'd been watching the sun set. "Eat." She pushed a plate toward him. "Or be ready to face my mother's wrath. She saved this for you from dinner."

Her mother had been nothing but gracious.

"Hannah asleep?"

He nodded and took the plate laden with roasted chicken and vegetables even though he wasn't particularly hungry. "She asked about her mom today. Hasn't asked about Katy in months, but today she did."

Leandra sat down on the Adirondack chair beside his. "What did you tell her?"

"I told her she was in heaven."

"Do you think she understands that?"

"As much as she can understand some things."

They fell silent while he managed to make a dent in the food, and when he could stomach no more, he set aside the plate. "Talked to Jake today. Said he hadn't heard from you lately."

She tilted her head, looking at him. "Been sort of busy here."

"Not with filming the show." She'd kept the crew mostly at bay for several days now. He'd been perfectly happy about it, until he'd run into Ted that morning in town, and had learned just what it was costing Leandra.

She didn't reply.

"There was only one reporter at the gate today. So I'm going to take Hannah back home with me tomorrow. Think you can work without getting her on camera?"

"Yes." At that, she didn't hesitate. "Evan—have you thought about what you're going to do about her?"

It had been mostly all he'd thought about. If he wasn't thinking about Hannah, he was thinking about Leandra.

Both pretty impossible situations, as far as he was concerned. One he wanted, but knew her mother had never intended that. The other he wanted, but knew she'd been meant for someone else.

"She has special needs," he finally said. "Her autism is fairly mild, but she still needs special attention. If Katy hadn't—" He cleared his throat. "In North Carolina, there was a program designed for kids like Hannah right in town, where they'd have been living."

"The program that you were prepared to help pay for," she said. She reached over and closed her hand over his. "There's *nothing* in the area here?"

"Sure, if we went to Cheyenne. Gillette." Either option was several hours away. "She should be starting kindergarten next year. The school in Braden will take her, and do their best, but it's not the best for Hannah."

"We did a show once," Leandra said after a while. "On hippotherapy. Have you heard of it?"

"Occupational or physical therapy with horses. Yeah."

"It was geared toward children with varying degrees of autism. We followed one of the therapists for nearly six months. She was incredible with the children. The strides those children made in their daily lives just through the interaction with the therapist and the horse was amazing. This is a horse-filled community. Wouldn't you think something like that would be possible here?"

He'd seen the shows about it. Truth was, he'd watched every show that he'd known Leandra had been involved with. "Closest hippotherapy program is in Cheyenne. It's also too bad there's not a special ed teacher on staff at the school. In fact, there're a lot of things that are too bad." He pushed out of his chair, and Leandra's hand fell away.

"You'll figure it out, Evan."

He looked at her. "How do you know?"

She lifted her shoulders. "I just do."

Why she had faith in him when he didn't, he couldn't fathom. "You need an interview, don't you."

Her expression stilled. She moistened her lips. "No."

"Liar. I know Marian has been hounding you."

She turned her palms up in her lap. "What do you want me to say?"

"You're jeopardizing your job." She made no response and he leaned down, pressing his hands on the arms of her chair. "Why would you do that after you've worked so hard to get where you're at?"

She seemed to sink as far back into the chair as she could go. "Because I don't want to cause you any more grief, okay?"

Silence stretched out, thick and taut.

She moistened her lips.

"God, Leandra." His fingers brushed the nape of her neck.

Her lashes fluttered down. She tilted her head back into his hand. Her breath sighed out of her.

He shifted slightly, leaning closer. He brushed his thumb against her cheek and it felt as soft and smooth as Hannah's.

"Evan." His name was barely a movement on her lips. "This is getting too complicated. I don't do well with complicated."

"I'm not sure we have much of a choice on that, anymore." He brushed his lips over hers. It was enough to make the world tilt sideways. When he lifted his head, her lips followed his, seeming to cling for a breathtaking moment.

Then she leaned back in the chair again, her lips pressing together. Savoring the kiss, or trying to erase it?

"You can tape whatever you want tomorrow," he told her. "Ask whatever you need. But I have to go to Braden first and pick up some more of Hannah's stuff. Take care of a few things. It'll take me a few hours, probably."

She hesitated for a moment. "Okay."

"Can you stay with her?"

Her eyes widened, alarmed. "With Hannah? Your mom has been pulling that duty."

"She's got a school thing she can't miss with Tabby. Hannah likes you, Leandra. I wouldn't ask otherwise."

"And you can't take her with—" She broke off the question. "Never mind. Of course I—I'll stay with her." She smiled, but it looked forced. "What else are pretend fiancées for?"

Chapter Fifteen

It was raining the next morning when Leandra approached the house where she'd grown up, trying to talk herself out of the trepidation that was assailing her.

She could manage to care for one small girl for a few hours, couldn't she?

She entered through the rear door. She'd run into her father, already, on his way to the horse barn. He'd told her that Emily had her accountant hat on and was meeting with a client over breakfast in town. Aside from Evan and Hannah, the house was empty.

The guest room where Evan had been staying with Hannah was on the second floor, down the hall from Leandra's room when she'd been a child.

She headed up there, and still trying to talk herself out of the odd nervousness that plagued her, she knocked softly on the door.

But there was no answer. Nor to her second knock or when

she spoke his name. She cautiously pushed open the door, peering around it.

The room was spacious. The bed tumbled. "Evan?"

"Hey." He stepped into view and she gulped a little.

He wore nothing but a towel and remnants of steam.

She quickly looked down but his image was already seared in her brain. "I wasn't sure you were in here."

He stepped farther into the room from the connecting bathroom, holding the towel together at his waist. "Hannah's still sleeping."

"Right. Okay. Well, I'll just be downstairs then."

But he lifted his eyebrows a little when she continued standing there like she'd grown roots. "Did you want something else?"

You, she thought, and saw the flush that rose in her face in the mirror over the dresser.

As usual, her libido had disastrous timing.

"No," she assured him quickly, and backed out of the room, shutting the door after her, barely remembering to keep the thing from noisily slamming and waking Hannah.

With the door shut, she raked her fingers through her hair, pressed her palms to her temples and tried to squeeze sensibility back into her brain.

It was a futile effort.

Whether she had her eyes open or closed, she could still see Evan standing there, a minimal amount of white terry cloth barely providing some decency.

But even the vision of that wealth of long, roping muscular legs, a chest sprinkled with black hair and an abdomen the likes of which she'd only seen on the cover of fitness magazines wasn't what disturbed Leandra the most.

No, what disturbed her the most, what shook her right down to her soul, was the abrupt realization that she didn't just *want* her hometown friend.

She was falling in love with him.

"You trying to memorize the carpet pattern?"

She jerked, looking at Axel as if she'd never seen him before. "Dad didn't say you were still here. Where'd you come from?"

He grinned faintly and gestured with his thumb. "My room." She made a face and brushed past him, but he caught her arm. "What's wrong?"

"Nothing."

He snorted softly. "Yeah, and I'm destined to ride a desk my whole life. You having second thoughts about marrying him?"

How could she forget that not *everyone* knew the truth about that? Not even her own brother? "Sh-should I be?"

"Just figured he'd probably have Hannah with him a lot now."

And Axel assumed that would make a difference to her.

She moistened her lips. The truth was, a month earlier, it might have made a difference.

And now?

Now she was discussing an engagement that wasn't even real as if it *were*.

"Aren't you supposed to be at work or something?" She made a production of looking at her watch.

"Have a meeting."

"For CeeVid?"

"For work," he said, moving down the hall to the stairs. "Later."

She watched his departure. For work. Isn't that what she'd said?

Then she heard a noise behind Evan's bedroom door, and hurriedly escaped down the stairs, too.

She found fresh coffee in the kitchen and poured herself a mug, and within minutes, Evan appeared.

He was safely dressed.

No less distracting, though, in black trousers and a crew-necked ivory sweater. For Evan, the clothing was definitely not the norm.

"Hannah likes Cheerios for breakfast," he told her. "She'll probably sleep another hour, though."

She was plenty curious about his reason for being dressed up, but kept it to herself and just nodded.

He lifted the mug out of her hand and took a long sip, then placed it back in her hand. "Thanks for this."

The coffee? Or watching Hannah?

"Sure." She wriggled her tingling fingers around the mug.

He seemed ready to say something else, but didn't. He just checked his pockets and headed out the door. "I have my cell. Call if you need me."

"It's raining," she stated the obvious. "Drive carefully."

He nodded, and then he was gone.

She had no reason to feel bereft, yet she still did.

The house seemed to loom around her, silent and still except for the rhythmic tick of the grandfather clock standing in the front entry and the sound of raindrops beating against the windows.

She filled her mug to the top again and shut off the coffee maker, then climbed back up the stairs and cautiously looked in on Hannah.

The girl really was sound asleep, sprawled across the narrow bed, her little bow mouth parted softly.

Leandra closed the door and sank down on the hallway floor.

She tilted her head back against the wall behind her and stared blindly at the doorframe, behind which Hannah slept.

She *wasn't* in love with Evan.

How could she be? She'd known him forever and a day.

"Hello?"

She jolted at the completely unexpected voice, and scrambled over to the stairs. "Mom?"

Emily appeared at the bottom of them, looking up at her. "I saw your car parked outside. Come down and sit with me."

"Evan asked me to stay with Hannah while he ran to Braden and took care of some things. Don't worry, though," she added quickly as she descended. "She's sleeping. Safely. I just looked in on her."

"Well," her mother said after a moment, "that's quite a comment, Leandra. Do you actually think I would worry about Hannah being in your care?"

"*I* worry about it. Seems like everyone else should, too."

"Oh, darling." Emily plucked the coffee cup out of her hand and set it atop the wide square newel post. "You're so much like your father sometimes, it boggles the mind." She stood not one inch taller than Leandra, but she still put her hands around Leandra's face and had her looking up at her.

"You were a good mother." Emily's voice was firm, despite its huskiness. "Better than good. You were loving and kind and firm. And I was always, *always* proud of the mother that my own daughter was becoming. You were not careless and you were not thoughtless. Losing Emi was a terrible tragedy, and it broke all of our hearts. But tragedies are not alleviated by placing blame. They become part of us and we grieve and finally, we accept."

"You don't know." Leandra's voice went thick. "You don't know what it's like to bury your baby."

Emily closed her eyes. "I know what it's like to watch my baby bury hers," she said after a moment. "And know that there's nothing I can do to change that. I don't want to lose my daughter, too, Leandra." She let go and turned away, dashing a hand over her cheeks. "I know what it's like to lose family, darling. I was young, but I still remember when my parents died. I remember going to live with your grandfather, not feeling as if there were anyplace in the world that I belonged."

"Their accident wasn't at all your fault, though. So you don't know what it's like to blame yourself for someone's death." The admission felt raw.

Emily just sighed and shook her head. "I know what it is like to love someone who blames himself for someone else's death," she said quietly. "Leandra, you have to let it go. You have to let Emi go."

"Who are you talking about, because I know it can't have been Dad."

Emily's eyebrows rose a little. "Do you think you know every detail there is to know about your father and me, then? Yes, it is your father I'm talking about. And he'd have let everything that mattered in this life—including *his* life—slide into nothing because he couldn't let go of blaming himself."

"You're talking about my father. The guy who raises horses and used to be in the Peace Corps."

"It was hardly the Peace Corps," Emily said evenly, "but that's for your father to explain if he chooses. Suffice it to say that he felt responsible for an associate's death, just the same way you feel responsible for Emi's."

Leandra gnawed the inside of her cheek. "What changed?"

"He let me love him," Emily said simply.

Leandra's eyes burned.

"Where's my Evan?"

The tiny voice came from the stairwell and nearly made Leandra jump out of her skin. She looked up to see Hannah standing there. Three feet tall, sleep-creased ivory cheeks and lopsided black pigtails, she made Leandra feel like she was sitting on the north side of panic. "He had to go out for a little while and asked me to stay here with you." She looked to her mother, expecting rescue or something, but Emily just smiled calmly at them both.

She swallowed, hard, and faced the child. "Are you hungry?"

Hannah nodded and sat down on the stairs, scooting down the few remaining treads until she was sitting on the kitchen floor. Her pajamas had horses printed on them.

"Do you want some cereal?"

Hannah nodded. She ducked her head, but was clearly watching Emily.

"Well," Emily said. "I have things to attend to, so I'll leave you two ladies to it."

Leandra's lips parted. "You're not going to stay?"

"Nope." She gave Leandra a hug and kissed her cheek. "You'll be fine," she whispered. Then she turned to leave, only to stop short at the door.

Relief swept through Leandra. A reprieve.

"I completely forgot. Gloria called and she and Squire will be back in town tomorrow."

"How are we going to keep him from finding out about the party?"

"By avoiding the man, I suspect. Fortunately there is plenty to keep us all occupied until then." Her gaze went again to Hannah. "Hannah, after you eat, maybe you'd like Leandra to take you to see the horses?"

"I like horses," Hannah replied, looking at the wall beside her.

"There you go, then," Emily said, smiling faintly. "Breakfast, then horses. Plenty to keep you two busy." She opened the door.

"But, Mom—"

"You'll be fine, Leandra. You need to do this. Not just for Evan, but for yourself." She let herself out onto the rear porch and closed the door.

Feeling utterly deserted, Leandra stood there, looking at Hannah.

Hannah just looked back, blinking her beautifully silky black lashes. "Are you sad?"

Leandra started. "No. Are you?"

"I want juice."

Evidently Hannah wasn't sad, either. "Okay." She pulled open the refrigerator and found a bottle of apple juice. She lifted Hannah onto one of the bar stools at the counter and filled a cup for her, then found the cereal and placed it also before her. If she managed each small step, maybe they'd get through the morning without disaster.

Hannah ate quickly, with a minimum of fuss, her attention focused on the food. The moment she was finished, though, she slid off the high stool and faced Leandra. "Horse."

"You need to change out of your pajamas first."

Hannah nodded and held out her hand. "I need shoes."

Leandra stared at Hannah's small palm, extended with the full expectation that it be taken.

The child's mother was lost forever. Did Hannah really understand it? Or did age and autism blunt the painful reality of it?

She stepped forward and took Hannah's hand.

The child's little fingers curled trustingly around hers.

And they went upstairs to find the shoes.

It had been a complete bitch of a morning, as far as Evan was concerned. The only place he wanted to be was back home with Hannah and Leandra, but it seemed as if the world around him kept conspiring to make that task as difficult as possible.

By the time he pulled up at Clay Farm, considerably more than a few hours had passed. Nearly the entire day was gone. He let himself in through the kitchen, expecting Leandra to be at the end of her rope.

There was definitely a rope, he realized.

Only it was spread across the kitchen, one end tied to a table leg, and the other end tied to a barstool. And hanging over the middle portion of the rope was a large sheet, fashioned into a tent.

He shut the door behind him, and set the suitcase full of Hannah's clothes and toys, which he'd picked up in Braden, on the floor out of the way. "Hello?"

There was no answer, but that didn't concern him. Leandra's rental car was parked in plain sight outside.

They weren't in the living room, nor were they upstairs when we went up to check, though he could see that Leandra must have had her cleaning hat on, because the laundry piled on his floor was gone, the beds in both guest rooms were made and the paper that Hannah had methodically shredded into tiny pieces on the floor in her room had been vacuumed.

Frowning a little, he went back down to the kitchen and pulled aside one of the "tent" flaps. Two bed pillows were inside, plus an assortment of papers that had been drawn and colored on. He picked one up. Either Hannah's artistic skills had greatly changed, or Leandra had drawn the picture of his clinic and house.

He left the picture with the others and when he straightened again, he finally saw them. Through the window, outside, two colorful umbrellas bobbing as they headed toward the house.

He opened the door and waited for them. "Nice umbrella," he said when Hannah handed him her umbrella and slipped past him into the house. He shook it off, studying the cartoon dog-angels dancing around amid a bunch of clouds, and folded it.

"Where'd you find these?" He reached for Leandra's. Hers looked like an overinflated beach ball.

She pulled off the slicker that had been drowning her slender form and hung it on the peg next to where he hung Hannah's umbrella. "Dug them out of storage."

She seemed to avoid his eyes as she went over to Hannah, stopping her from climbing in the tent with her wet raincoat still on. "Let's take that off first," she said.

But Hannah shook her head. "I wanna wear it."

"Are you sure? You might get the stuff inside your tent wet and you worked very hard on the pictures you drew."

"I wanna wear it." Hannah looked adamant.

"Okay." Leandra backed away and looked at him. "I suppose the suitcase has more of Hannah's things?"

"Yeah. Looks like you two have been busy in here. Everything go okay?" His voice was careful.

Leandra folded her arms around her chest. "Yes. Actually, everything went fine. What about you? You were gone longer than you expected."

"I saw an attorney."

Her lips parted. She reached back and sat down on the bar stool, the one with the rope attached to its leg. "About?"

"Custody." He waited for her to look shocked, but she didn't. "You're not surprised."

"It makes perfect sense to me. But what about Sharon?"

"She's been hurt enough, I know. But she refuses to see that Katy has special needs. I don't want to take away her grandchild—or Darian's, for that matter. I just want to make sure Hannah has what she needs, too."

He let out a low breath. "I still feel like a bastard. It's not what Katy wanted."

"Katy expected to be coming home again. There's no way she wouldn't have wanted the very best for Hannah if she could have predicted this."

"I'm not sure I'm cut out to be a parent," he admitted gruffly.

Her expression softened. "Why on earth would you think that?"

"Genetics," he muttered.

Her eyebrows shot up. Then she gave a disbelieving laugh. "You're nothing like Darian, if that's what you're implying."

"Then why'd I show up at your house that night the way I did? The night we learned about Katy?"

A blush hovered over her cheeks. "Why *did* you?"

"Because I wanted you, but you're Jake's, and getting drunk gave me an excuse to pretend it didn't matter."

She hopped off the stool. "I'm *not* Jake's. I don't know why you'd think that even after all we've—" She broke off, flushing harder. "I belong to myself and that's all," she said finally. "Now, shall I call Ted and have him set up somewhere, or do you want to wait until tomorrow?"

He shoved his fingers through his damp hair. "Let's just get it over with."

She nodded. "All right. I'll go call him." Her cheeks still looking rosy, she left the room.

"Goodbye, Leandra." Hannah's soft voice was barely audible above the sound of the rain that had begun pounding harder on the roof.

Evan crouched down on the floor and peeked under the sheet. Hannah was adding her touches to the picture of his house and clinic. "Did you have fun with Leandra today?"

Hannah nodded and resumed her humming. She scratched at the picture with a dark blue crayon. He couldn't quite tell what it was she was drawing, though.

"Where'd you learn the song you're humming?"

The humming ceased. "Leandra." Hannah tucked her tongue between her teeth, added a final flourish to the picture, then dropped the crayon and didn't give the paper another glance. "It's Emi's song," she announced.

Surprise grabbed him. He sat right there on his butt alongside her and picked up the altered drawing. Hannah had added people. Completely out of proportion to the buildings that

Leandra had drawn, but they were definitely people. "Leandra told you about Emi?"

"The song is pretty. I want some juice."

"In a minute. Who are the people?" He pointed at the three figures she'd drawn.

"That's my Evan." She rubbed her thumb over the largest figure. The one that was taller than the house. "That's Leandra." She pointed at the middle-sized one. "That's Brandon." She pointed to the smallest figure.

"Who is Brandon?" He'd expected her to say it was *her*.

"Emi's brother."

"Emi didn't have a brother, honey."

"Not yet."

He almost asked what she'd meant by *not yet,* but caught himself. She was just being imaginative. That's what children did. Only Hannah rarely exhibited that kind of imagination. She saw things in extremely practical terms.

"What kind of juice?" he asked after a moment.

"Leandra's juice."

It was pretty clear to him that Hannah had definitely enjoyed Leandra's company.

Like uncle, like niece.

Chapter Sixteen.

The fifth episode aired and the following Monday morning, clips of it were being shown on both local and national talk shows.

Eduard called Leandra to tell her it was the best piece she'd ever done. Even Marian couldn't summon any criticism, though the serious tone of the episode—Katy's death and its effect on Evan and the rest of the town—was hardly her particular style.

Leandra ought to have felt like she'd won a battle.

Instead, she felt as if she were fighting something else entirely.

Her time in Weaver was coming to an end. She'd be staying only through the weekend—long enough to attend Squire's surprise party. The show would wrap several days before that, though, and the crew was scheduled to depart midweek.

They'd been following Evan around on rounds all morning; had gotten terrific footage of him in the muck and mire as he'd rescued a calf caught in barbed wire while a rain-swollen creek ran wildly at his feet.

He'd looked larger than life, and she'd known as she'd watched the tape that she'd found the final images for the last episode. If the series about Evan didn't inspire a whole new crop of wannabe veterinarians, she'd eat her hat.

Now, it was afternoon, and she'd sent the crew back to the motel to get dry. Evan was meeting in his living room with the attorney who'd come with a package of papers for him to sign, and Hannah was taking her nap.

Feeling restless, she put the pen down on the pad where she'd been drafting a brief, simple press release that would announce the breakup of her and Evan's engagement. She'd send it out in another month or so. She doubted that the news would make much of a headline, but it was an end that still needed to be tied.

Knowing it didn't seem to make her feel any better.

From the living room, she could hear the two men's voices, low and indistinct and she let herself out of the kitchen. She crossed to the clinic and punched in Evan's birthday code. The enormous door obediently rolled up.

She expected the dog they'd rescued to still be in one of the kennels where he'd been just a few days earlier. But he was loose, and the moment she stepped inside and the overhead lights began flicking on, he bounded toward her, all flopping ears and lolling tongue.

She crouched down, grabbing him around the ruff, and trying not to be drowned by dog kisses. She rubbed his silky coat, noticing that he wasn't exactly running free as she'd first thought. He did have a long chain on him, preventing him from exploring too much of the clinic's confines. She nearly fell over when he put his unsplinted paw on her shoulder.

"Ask a girl to dance first, buddy." She sat down and patted her thigh. He scooted down and tried to climb on her lap. She smiled faintly and let him do as he pleased. He finally settled half on, half off.

She was still sitting there, willingly pinned by the dog when she heard footsteps approaching. She looked up at Evan. He'd changed out of his muddy clothes into green scrubs before the attorney had arrived. "Everything with the attorney go okay?"

"Not exactly."

"What's wrong?"

But he just shook his head. "See you found your pal."

She lifted her chin away from the dog's tongue. "You give him a name yet?"

"Start naming animals and they start being your pets."

"That's the same reasoning my dad used with Axel and me when we were kids. We wanted to name this one turkey. He said we couldn't 'cause we wouldn't be wanting to eat him when Thanksgiving rolled around."

"What happened?"

"Mom named him Max and we had roast beef for Thanksgiving that year."

He crouched down beside her. "I've been calling him Fred." She bit back a smile.

"Owner still hasn't come forward," he continued.

"Are you going to keep him, then?"

"You haven't seen Hannah around dogs, have you? She'd be constantly upset."

"Yet she loves horses."

"Yup. The bigger the better where she's concerned. She *really* hates birds." He scratched Fred's head. "As long as she's living with me, Fred here's going to have to find another home."

She didn't doubt that Evan remembered her offer to take the dog. Nor did she believe he would have forgotten his response and her overreaction to it. She wasn't going to go down that path again. Defending her life's choices was becoming much too difficult. "So, is Hannah still napping?"

"Yeah."

"She'll be growing out of that pretty soon."

"Expect she will." He nudged the dog off her lap and straightened, holding out his hand to her. "Come on."

"Where?"

"No need to sound so suspicious." He beckoned her with his fingers. "Come on."

She exhaled and let him pull her to her feet.

But he didn't let go of her hand once she was standing. He kept hold, and led her out of the clinic, pushing the button to close the automatic door along the way. He led her back to the house, and her heart beat a little harder when he started up the stairs.

"What are we doing?" She kept her voice low, not wanting to disturb Hannah.

"I want to show you something."

She dug in her heels at the threshold to his bedroom. "What? Your etchings?"

He looked amused. "Maybe I was planning on talking you into playing doctor."

She flushed. "We were ten years old when we played doctor." And they really *had* played doctor, complete with tongue depressors and a stethoscope that Ryan had pinched from his mother's medical supplies.

"Maybe if we tried it now, we'd find it as interesting as it was supposed to have been back then." He pulled her farther into the bedroom.

She swallowed, more nervous than a cat. "Evan—"

"Shh." He leaned down and caught her lower lip between his teeth, lightly. Tantalizingly.

Shock and pleasure rooted her to the floor. "What are you doing?"

"What I've wanted to do for too damn long." His voice deepened.

"But Hannah—"

He closed his hand over hers and pulled her out into the hall again. Down a few doors, until he silently pushed one open. He waved at his niece.

She was sprawled on the narrow bed, tangled in the sheet, and hadn't so much as stirred when he'd opened the door.

"Told you," he said, closing the door once more.

Leandra trembled. He couldn't possibly know what had been running through her mind. Not unless—

"Jake told you, didn't he? What we were doing when… when Emi got out of the house."

He didn't have to answer. The truth was there in his vivid blue eyes.

Mortified, she turned on her heel, heading for the stairs, but Evan scooped his arm around her waist, hauling her back against him. "Don't run," he said. "Nothing's going to be solved by you always running."

Leandra squirmed out of his hold. "And what's going to be solved by *this?*"

"Maybe more than you think." His voice was low.

"Emi was taking a nap that day," she told him baldly. "She always slept at least an hour and a half every afternoon. And Jake—he was gone so much because of his practice. We hadn't—" She closed her arms around herself. "It had been a, um, a while."

He lowered his head, swearing softly. "You don't have to tell me this, Leandra."

Maybe it wasn't so much that he needed to hear it, but that she suddenly needed to say it. For once and for all. And then he'd understand.

And he would let her run as far and as fast as she wanted to run.

She gave Hannah's closed door a long look, then turned into Evan's bedroom, deliberately keeping her focus away from his rumpled bed. From the pillows that still held an indentation from his head.

"The only thing Jake and I hadn't done with the pool to safety-proof it was install an alarm. We'd done everything else. But Emi—" She shook her head, the memory sharp and painful. "Emi loved climbing. She tried climbing to the top of the refrigerator once. In the blink of an eye, she'd pulled out just the right combination of drawers and cupboard doors and was on top of the counter and looking for the bag of tortilla chips that were on top of the refrigerator. She wanted to play restaurant."

He sat down on the foot of the bed, his gaze hooded. "Resourceful."

"Yeah. When I was a girl, my favorite place to sneak off to was the swimming hole at the C. I guess it makes sense that Emi's favorite place to sneak off to was the pool. We gave her CPR. The fire department was there in record time. But she'd been without oxygen too long." She exhaled, looking at him through painfully dry eyes. "It wasn't planned, you know. Getting pregnant with Emi. Jake wasn't even finished with school. I was still trying to figure out what the heck I wanted to do with my life. But there was never a moment when I didn't want her. Never. And then, almost as quickly as she'd entered our life, she was gone again."

She looked away from Evan, her eyes finally glazing with tears. "It doesn't matter what anyone says. It was my fault."

"There were two of you in the house that day."

"Jake wanted to check on her and I told him she was sleeping. It *was* my fault. I stopped Jake and if I hadn't, Emi wouldn't have gotten out. My daughter died because I wanted to make love with her father."

"Your daughter died because she got past all the barriers protecting her from the pool. You could have been talking on the phone, or any number of other things, when it happened. And even if Jake had checked on her, what's to say she wouldn't have done exactly what she did ten minutes later?"

She shook her head. Why wouldn't he see the point? "Jake never touched me again. Is your friendship so great that he also told you *that?* It's because he blamed me, too."

"Do you think he still does?"

"When we signed the divorce papers, he told me he didn't."

"Did you believe him?"

"I needed to believe he'd forgiven me." She pressed her palms together, staring at her bare fingers. "Our…marriage wasn't working even before the accident. We both knew it, but there was Emi, and neither one of us was ready to do something about it. We never talked. We rarely touched. That afternoon was like a last-ditch effort to…recapture something together…and because of me, we lost the one perfect thing we'd ever done," she finished in a whisper.

He reached out, took her hands and when he pulled her down onto his lap, pressing her head against his shoulder, she didn't resist. "I was the only one who told Katy she was doing the right thing when she enlisted."

She drew in a shuddering breath. "Oh, Evan. Don't. Don't take that guilt on."

"You think you have a corner on it, then?"

She swallowed. "I can't do this. I'm leaving town next week."

"Can't? Or won't? You think by spending the rest of your

life without getting involved with someone else, you're going to feel better about what happened that afternoon?"

"Nothing can make me feel better. I don't *want* to feel better!"

"Don't you?" He tilted back her head, staring into her face. "Why the hell are you running around this country the way you do? You're not trying to feel better by watching other people live their lives, instead of living your *own?* You're trying to feel better, all right, you're just not using the right means."

"And you know what *that* might be." Her voice was tight.

He made an impatient sound, and covered her mouth with his.

Sensation exploded through her. Her hands opened and closed over his forearms.

He ripped his mouth away, pressing his forehead against hers. "I have wanted you for *years.*" His voice was grim, as if he weren't any too happy about the fact. "But right now, if you don't want this—if you're bent on convincing yourself you'd rather live like a nun out of some self-imposed punishment— then you'd better go. Because my patience has reached its end."

She shuddered and slid off his lap, yanking the filmy blouse she'd borrowed from Sarah firmly over her hips.

His jaw tightened and his hands closed in fists against his thighs. "Fair enough."

But what was fair?

Certainly not life.

It was full of too many twists and turns and tragedies. They both knew that. Had experienced it.

But when she turned to leave, her feet wouldn't move. Not when everything inside her heart implored her to stay. "Evan—"

He let out a deep breath and stood. "Don't worry. It's okay, Leandra. Everything will be okay."

She sucked in her lip for a second. "Why'd you turn me down that night when you rescued Fred?"

He went still. "It's not the first stupid thing I've done." His lips twisted. "Look how I agreed to do *WITS*."

She pressed her lips together. "You've been a good friend."

"If I was such a good friend I wouldn't have spent the last decade wanting my best friend's woman."

Her lips parted.

"Leave now, Leandra."

She swallowed. "I… No." The words were practically inaudible. Maybe if they finished what they'd started, she could finally, finally move on. She'd leave Weaver and—

Her mind simply refused to contemplate that thought any further.

His eyes closed for a moment and when they opened again, she felt scorched by the heat they contained.

"No," she said a little more clearly. A little more surely. "I don't want to leave."

His jaw shifted to one side. He stepped around her and with a nudge of his hand, pushed the door closed. He stepped closer to her, crowding into her personal space with a steady deliberation that was all the more heady for it.

Desire raced through her veins, doing its best to drown out caution, and she hovered there, tensely anticipating the race of his hands, the crush of his mouth.

But the rush of passion that had licked through them like a wildfire when he'd kissed her before was disconcertingly absent.

Instead, there was only the slow brush of his fingers as he touched her cheek. The glide of his hand down her spine as he closed the inches still between them.

He was slowly, deliberately intoxicating her.

She'd seen him with the animals. And with Hannah. Had experienced firsthand how gifted his long fingers were. But she'd never imagined the deliberate delicacy with which he would touch her.

It wasn't only his hands. It was his entire being.

From her cheekbones, slowly traced by his thumbs, to the point of her chin, slowly nipped by his lips. He found the inside of her wrists, slowly scratched his nails over the tender skin there, and she caught her breath as shivers danced down her spine.

She even felt his smile against her shoulder as he repeated the motion, causing another wave of gooseflesh.

"Like that?" His voice was low, and she had the fanciful wish that she could just swim for a while in that mesmerizing masculine voice.

"Yes." She breathed the word, equally afraid of breaking the spell he was weaving, and afraid she would never break it.

He grazed her arms back up to her shoulders, but not until he whispered for her to lift her arms did she realize he'd somehow pulled up her blouse, as well.

She lifted her arms, as obedient as a child, yet feeling anything but childlike. She ducked her head, letting him pull the top free. He let it go, and the filmy blue garment drifted to the ground.

She could hardly breathe as his gaze locked with hers and he reached for the hem of the thin blue camisole she'd worn beneath the blouse. Her skin felt snug and hot, and she knew her nipples were painfully obvious beneath the thin clinging fabric.

He was killing her by slow degrees.

She covered his hands with hers and pulled the camisole over her head. And while she was able to exhibit some mindless bravado, she got rid of her shoes and jeans, too, until she stood there before him, wearing nothing but her white lacy panties.

And still his gaze didn't waver from hers.

"Are you sure?"

He would have stopped if she weren't, she realized. Not because he harbored any uncertainty himself, but because he was just that kind of man.

She crouched down at his feet and touched the back of his calf. "Lift."

He lifted one foot then the other as she worked his tennis shoes off, setting them aside.

Then she rose, standing only inches away from him. She reached up and touched the collar of his shirt. Followed the V-neck down until she found the hem.

And doubly affirming her answer, she lifted the shirt and felt the long, slow breath he drew in when she did. A breath he released when he ducked low enough to let her pull it off his head.

He wore a T-shirt beneath and the fact that he wore more underclothes than she did made something inside her lighten.

She ran her hands down his chest, feeling the rigid points of his nipples beneath the soft white cotton, feeling the hard charging beat of his heart, and the way his muscles tightened when she pushed her hands beneath to that corrugated abdomen that had haunted her thoughts.

His breath hissed through his teeth and he grabbed her hands, pressing them flat against his belly. "Tease me next time," he muttered. "Right now, I don't have the patience."

Next time. The thought crowded in with the desire overflowing her veins, leaving her short on patience, herself. She tugged his T-shirt up, revealing more of his torso. Where dark hair swirled over even more hard muscles.

Her fingertips slowed, rubbing upward over the crispy-soft hair until it gave way again to smooth, warm skin stretched over the jut of his collarbone. He finally made a low sound and yanked the shirt off his head and threw it aside with none of the delicacy he'd shown her clothing. His arm slid around her back and he hauled her against him, up on her toes, his chest flush against hers, his mouth on hers.

She felt surrounded by him. His heat. His smell. His taste.

Her head spun and she realized he'd lifted her right off her toes. Was carrying her. He didn't stop until she felt the bed behind her calves, and she dragged in a lungful of air when he lifted his head and dropped her on the bed.

The mattress bounced. She automatically reached her arms out to steady herself.

His gaze no longer pinned hers to his. Instead, that deep blue focus slowly ran over her body, stretched out over the center of his bed.

She chewed her lip, feeling every nerve ending she possessed take notice of his silent perusal. He stood at the side of the bed, his legs planted as he loosened the tie holding the scrubs over his hips. The cotton rustled as he yanked them—and everything else—right off.

Leandra inhaled slowly, unable to pretend she wasn't affected by the sight of him. It was the last, slow breath she managed, for he closed his fingers over her ankles and slowly pulled her back toward him atop the mattress. Pulled steadily, inexorably, until she felt the tantalizing scrape of hair-roughened legs against her smooth ones.

She reached for his shoulders as he leaned over her, threaded her fingers through his thick hair, wanting to touch everywhere, but he gave her no such allowance as his mouth touched her stomach.

She nearly bowed off the bed. "Evan—"

His fingers hooked the narrow band of her panties and he slowly pulled them down her thighs, over her knees, past her calves, his mouth following in their path.

Her hands, bereft, clutched the nubby chenille bedspread as he tarried around her ankles, his breath warm and impossibly arousing. "Thought you said no teasing," she managed.

"No teasing *me*." He kissed her calf. Sliding his hands beneath her knees, bending them as he worked his way back up.

Her eyelids were too heavy. "Sounds unfair to me. Oh—" She pressed her head back into the mattress as he touched her. There.

His marauding fingers slid over her again, tantalizing, taunting and definitely teasing. "Are you complaining?"

She couldn't speak. Just shook her head, her hands twisting in the bedding as his fingers burned along her cleft, rediscovering every secret, every need. Learning just how much she *wasn't* protesting.

Her legs moved restlessly, and he caught them, his big hands holding her as he lowered his mouth and found her.

She cried out, the world shrinking down to exist only of them as she shattered. Abruptly. Completely. And just when she thought he could wring no more desire from her—when she thought her body could not possibly experience more— he kissed his way over her stomach. Reached her breasts and paid such exquisite attention to them that she cried out yet again. She could feel the rigid length of him against her thigh. "Evan." She reached for him and he shifted, finally, *finally* settling against the cradle of her hips.

But still he held back, until she was begging. "Please," she whispered, feeling broken.

His hand tilted her head and he kissed her softly. So softly she felt her heart fall open like a flower bathed in sunlight.

And when he filled her, when she heard him groan her name, when their world shrank even more until the only thing she knew anymore was Evan, so deeply a part of her that she no longer felt like a separate being, until she felt the tide pull them both under an ocean of exquisite perfection that had her gasping and crying out his name, she realized she wasn't broken after all.

She was whole.

Because of Evan.

Chapter Seventeen

Eventually, Leandra figured she had to move. She couldn't lie in Evan's bed all day long. Hannah would be waking eventually.

But every time she shifted, he closed his arm over her and pulled her back against him, and her willpower disintegrated on the thin beams of sunshine that were streaming through his window.

"Looks like it's stopped raining," she murmured.

"Mmm." He slowly ran his hand down her hip. Her thigh. She could lay there with him like that for the rest of her life.

The realization didn't come with any particular blinding clarity. It was simply there. And because she was deathly afraid the words would come out if she weren't careful, she made herself turn over on the bed and laugh a little. "You *did* want to show me your etchings."

His teeth flashed as he sat up. He pushed aside the tangled

bedding and climbed out of bed. "Actually, I was going for something else when you distracted me."

There was plenty there to distract her, too. Like the view of him.

He opened a bottom drawer on his dresser. When he straightened again, he held an oversized book in his hand. He returned to the bed. "Remember this?"

"It's our senior yearbook from high school." She took it when he held it out for her. "You really *are* feeling nostalgic."

He made a face and sat down beside her, pulling her back against his chest. "You said you wanted to make a difference in the world. Remember?"

Her fingers traced over the raised lettering on the cover of the dark blue book. "I don't think I have short-term memory loss. Yes, I remember. What's that got to do with the yearbook?"

"Do you remember what your senior statement was?"

She frowned. "No." She'd forgotten all about the form they'd filled out every year for the yearbook. "It was stupid stuff. Like how rich we wanted to be, how old we'd be before getting married, what ridiculously expensive car we'd drive."

He took the book back from her and flipped it open, paging through until he found what he wanted. "It wasn't all stupid." He handed it back to her, tapping the page.

Her hair had been long back then. Halfway down her back, in fact. Her back that now felt highly sensitized to the man's chest pressed against it. "What do you do? Pull this thing out and read when you're bored?"

"Haven't looked at it in years. I just happen to have an exceptional memory."

She snorted softly. "He who has to write reminder notes to himself that he needs toilet paper."

He covered her hands on the sides of the book, opening it wider and forcing it closer to her nose. "Read it."

She tugged the book out of his grasp. Beneath her senior picture, the statement was printed out in her own then-girlish handwriting. "I want every kid to have the great time growing up in Weaver that I've had." She gave a short laugh. "How incredibly earnest. I don't even remember writing that."

"I remember."

She shrugged, started to hand the book back, wanting just to forget that long-ago child she'd been, but stopped. "What about your statement?" She paged through to the *T*s and found Evan.

Lord, but he'd been a pretty boy. All long black lashes and hair, his eyes looking translucent in the black-and-white photo. No wonder he'd grown into such a striking man.

His handwriting hadn't changed as much as hers had. Even back then, it had been slashing, austere-looking and utterly practical. "One wife. Kids. Truck. Vet practice." She felt ridiculously touched, reading the bulletlike statement. "I'll bet if you looked back, your dad probably had a similar statement. Well, you've got the practice and the truck. And now Hannah. You're nearly there." She handed him back the book. "If you and Luce had gotten married—"

"Lucy and I would never have gotten married, even if she hadn't left for New York. She didn't want to marry me any more than I wanted to marry her."

"That's what Marian found out when she sent a crew to interview her. Otherwise, you would have seen Lucy on *WITS*, too."

"Marian." He closed the yearbook and tossed it to the foot of the bed, his disgust plain. "The woman's a tarantula."

"That may be, but she's also my boss." She climbed off the bed and pulled on the first thing her hand came to—his shirt. She'd always known that Evan had a low opinion of the show—but it had never hurt quite so badly before. "We have all the footage we need for the last episode," she admitted.

"I'm going to cancel the rest of the schedule for the week. No more cameras for you."

"Thank God."

She winced. "You've never really told me why you agreed to do it in the first place. You could have simply said no thanks and that would have been the end of it."

"And what would you have done? Gone back to Jake and worked on him some more until he gave in to you?" He rose from the opposite side of the bed.

"Jake wouldn't have given in. *He* had the decency to say no when he meant it."

"Too damn bad he doesn't have the decency to tell you the real reason he wouldn't do the show was because his new fiancée objected!"

"Excuse me?"

Evan swore. He turned away from her, propped his hands on his damnably lean hips and swore again. He snatched up his pants and yanked them over his hips. "Dammit. I *told* him to tell you."

"Jake is…engaged." She gingerly felt around the idea of it and realized it didn't hurt in the least. "Well, good grief. Why on earth didn't *he* tell me?

"I told you to talk to him. How many times has the guy called you lately?"

She felt a stab of guilt, thinking of the number of calls she'd ignored.

Mostly because she'd been too busy with Evan.

"I figured he was just checking up on me, as usual." Annoyance filled her. "And clearly *you've* known all along. Why didn't *you* say something?"

"It wasn't my news to tell." His voice was tight. "Yet here I am. Telling away." He swore again, yanking the tie at his waist.

She pushed her fingers through her hair, refusing to be distracted by the picture he made. "So…you agreed to do the show because you felt sorry for me."

He exhaled. "I didn't say that."

"You didn't have to when it's the only thing that finally makes sense." She turned away. Pity. Pity had motivated him all along.

And not with just the show.

"I've got to go."

"Dammit, wait—"

She kept moving, racing out of his bedroom, down the stairs and out the back door into the cold, his scrub shirt flapping around her bare legs. The gravel cut into her feet, but she still didn't slow as she tumbled into the car seat.

The keys were in the ignition where she'd left them and she gunned the engine, pulling away from the house, tires spinning over the gravel.

Her last sight of Evan was of him standing on the back porch, staring after her.

Before the week was out, her crew had packed up and flown back to California, where they'd take a break for a few weeks before they began shooting their next project.

They didn't know yet that Leandra wouldn't be part of the production team. That Eduard had come through with the promotion.

She would be getting her own show. She was scheduled to meet with him and the development team next week.

There was none of the satisfaction she should have felt, though. None of the anticipation for what lay ahead.

There was only the reality of the flight reservations she had for Monday.

When the rain returned again the day of Squire's party, it

suited her mood just fine, though it did make it more challenging for the party preparations.

It took at least half the family coming and going to the old barn at her parents' farm to ready it. Under the efficient eye of Leandra's mother, Axel and a handful of cousins erected the enormous white awning out on the lawn, and Leandra and the rest of her cousins spent the morning clearing the barn of any sign that animals had in fact lived there.

Their efforts definitely were not in vain. By that evening, the rain had calmed to an occasional drizzle and beneath the awning, a wooden dance floor gleamed in the light cast by about a million tiny white lights that had been painstakingly hung around the interior of the awning. There were even portable propane heaters that were guaranteed to keep the chill at bay.

Inside the barn were yet more lights, strung from every rafter. Enormous bunches of wheat stalks, tied with bright red ribbon, stood in the corners and decorated the long tables that were covered with red cloths.

"Think we're going to blow the power grid with all those lights burning?" Sarah stopped next to Leandra and put another tray of hors d'oeuvres on the table.

"It's a possibility. Can you believe we spent half the day sweeping a *dirt* floor?" She was going to be cheerful if it was the last thing she did.

Sarah looked down. "And yet, it still looks like dirt." She grinned. "So, you suppose Squire's still in the dark?"

"He sure didn't say a word to me this past week." The birthday boy was due to arrive in about an hour. She adjusted the edge of one of the tablecloths and repositioned a plastic-covered tray of crab puffs. "Pull that end of the cloth, would you? It's still crooked."

Sarah moved to the end of the long, narrow table and

tugged. Leandra readjusted the trays. "So, you want to tell me yet what's happened between you and Evan?"

"No."

"Must have been good," Sarah mused. "Seeing as how people have been talking for the past few days about how they saw you running half-naked around his house."

Leandra refused to be drawn. She hadn't been half-naked. She'd been wearing a shirt that came down to her knees. A shirt she'd pitched in the trash, only to go digging after it again.

Foolishly, she'd taken to sleeping in it.

Sarah just shook her head. "Well, at least tell me you're pleased about the show. The last episode airs tomorrow. Do you think you'll get the promotion you're after?"

"I already did."

Sarah went still. "What?"

Leandra shrugged. "Eduard called yesterday."

"Why didn't you say something?"

"I don't know," she said truthfully. She had a perfect view of the wide-open barn doors behind Sarah and she could see Evan approaching.

He wore black.

All black.

Black leather jacket. Black shirt. Black jeans. Black boots. And as he stepped into the light of the barn, and his gaze focused on Leandra, that sea of black made his blue eyes seem even more startlingly blue. And just looking at him made her catch her breath, even if she did tell herself that she was still furious with him.

She barely noticed the way Sarah did a double-take, looking behind her as if something in Leandra's expression had given her away.

Evan headed toward them, but Leandra turned away, hurrying out the other side of the barn.

He caught up to her before she could make it back to the house, though. "How long are you planning on running?"

She jerked her arm out of his grasp and yanked open the back door to the kitchen. "I have to help set out more food since *guests* are beginning to arrive. And where is Hannah, anyway?"

"Hannah's with my mother at my place. We need to talk about us."

"Us?" Her voice rose over the term. "There is no us, Evan Taggart. There never will be."

"Not while you're burning tracks under those heels of yours." His voice was tight.

Leandra stomped into the kitchen, nearly running smack dab into her aunt Maggie, who was carrying an enormous, empty, crystal punch bowl.

"Watch it there, honey," Maggie said, dancing around Leandra and Evan, and hurrying down the steps.

Her daughters, J.D. and Angeline, were hard on her heels, their own hands full, as well. They'd both arrived by plane the previous day. "Grab what you can," J.D. told her, grinning. "Reports have it that Squire's car is heading this way."

"ETA is about ten minutes," Angeline added.

"So much for the schedule." Leandra was grateful for the excuse to get away from Evan, and she grabbed the nearest tray of sandwiches that waited on the long countertop.

He picked up two more.

"What are you doing?"

"Finishing this crap so you can stop making excuses."

She turned on her heel, ignoring him, which was about as impossible a task as there ever had been and followed her cousins and aunt back to the barn, ducking her head against the fresh sprinkles that had begun falling.

She found a spot for her tray. Then, conscience nipping, she found a place for Evan's two, as well. The family was suddenly descending en masse on the barn, hurrying to get out of sight before Squire appeared.

Not that the man wouldn't know something was up when he saw the awning outside, but some things just couldn't be helped. You couldn't entertain half the town of Weaver without making some accommodations for the crowd.

Evan's hand closed over the back of her neck. She tried to shake him off, but his hold was relentless.

Gentle. But relentless.

He leaned down, his voice in her ear. "I'm not going to let you off the hook this easily, Leandra."

"I'm not stupid enough to get on the hook," she retorted. Someone she didn't recognize standing in front of her turned around and gave her a look. A moment later, the interior lights were doused.

"You might as well admit that you love me." Evan's voice warmed her ear again.

"Love!" She pinched his arm hard enough to make him curse under his breath. "Get over yourself. We both know what the other day was about and it didn't have *anything* to do with love."

"Shh-h!" The admonishment came from the woman blocking Leandra's view of the barn door.

"S-sorry." Leandra hissed the apology. There was enough rustling of bodies, quiet coughs and murmurs to alert an *unobservant* person, much less her highly observant grandfather.

"You sure about that?" His hand slid down her spine, curved around her waist.

His breath was warm on her neck. Her hands opened, closed, fighting the urge to touch him. To lean back even more against his tall body. "Don't." The command was much too weak, and she pushed his hand away from her hip with renewed vigor. "And I'm quite sure."

"What do you think it was about, then?"

"The same thing that prompted you to agree to do *WITS*. I don't need you feeling sorry for me!"

There was a sudden yell of "Surprise," and the light burst over them again.

His hand slid along her neck, curling around the back. "Jake getting hitched again is something I'm celebrating."

"So why didn't *you* tell me?" She turned and faced him, and the two of them stood there, squared off while all around them, party guests were making their way to the honoree. "Instead, you just kept asking if I'd talked to him!"

"What are you madder about, Leandra? That Jake's getting married again, or that you weren't the first one to know about it?"

Mad didn't begin to describe what she felt, knowing that what had really rocked her wasn't the fact that Jake was getting married again, but the fact that she'd found herself wishing that she were getting married again.

To Evan.

"I don't care if Jake told a hundred people before he told me! I care that *you* didn't tell me. It's the only reason you...we—" She broke off, flushing. "I should have known better. Friends don't just all of a sudden switch their stripes." It was a pitiful metaphor but no more pitiful than the situation.

She started to turn away, but he grabbed her arm.

She gasped, but it never had a chance to escape because his mouth covered hers and absorbed it.

It was deep. It was hot. It was about as perfect a kiss as she could ever have dreamed.

It was Evan.

He finally dragged his lips from hers. His breath was ragged. "I told you already. It is not *sudden*. It's been years. But once you met Jake, you only had eyes for him."

She felt wobbly. As if she'd sink into a puddle if not for his arms surrounding her. "Wait."

"I've been waiting years," he muttered, his mouth burning across her cheek toward her ear. "Dammit-to-hell, we're standing in the middle of your grandfather's birthday party."

She sprang back from him. What was wrong with her? She looked around, but the only people who seemed to have noticed their clinch was the pinch-lipped woman who'd shushed her and Leandra's father, who was watching them both with a narrow-eyed look.

She flushed. "I have responsibilities here. Mom's expecting my help."

"How long are you going to keep pushing everyone away, Leandra?"

"I don't push people away!"

He held out his arms to his sides. "Is that a fact?" He dropped his arms, took a step closer to her, and when she instinctively sidled an equal step away, he let out a short breath. "Yeah. That's what I thought."

"Just because you don't know how to take no for an answer is—"

He covered her mouth with his hand, muffling her voice. "Don't even go there, Leandra. It's small of you and my patience only goes so far." He pulled his hand away. "Tell your grandfather I'm sorry I didn't get a chance to wish him a happy birthday in person."

Turning on his heel, he strode through the crowd and out the back door.

She followed after him, wanting to stop him, but the words jammed in her throat, threatening to choke her. Which meant that she just stood there watching him disappear into the misty darkness beyond the lights of the awning.

Chapter Eighteen

"There you are." Sarah was cradling two bags of ice to her chest. "Here. Take one. You look frazzled. What have you and Evan been doing?" She headed toward the enormous barrel in the corner that housed a keg of beer.

"Do I really push people away?"

Sarah stopped in her tracks, but whatever quick comment had sprung to her lips went unsaid. "What's going on?"

"*Do* I?" She searched Sarah's expression. "Never mind. I can see the answer."

Sarah let out a short, puzzled laugh. "What brought this on? Did something happen with Evan? Where'd he go, anyway?"

Nothing was ever going to happen with Evan. Nothing permanent. Nothing lasting. No matter what she thought she felt, there simply was no future. She had her life and he had his. "No. Nothing happened."

Sarah watched her closely. "Is *that* what has you upset?"

"I'm *not* upset."

"Yeah, and I'm not freezing my chest with this bag of ice." She tore it open and dumped it into the barrel. "Do you remember how things used to be with us? I was the only one you told when Joey Rasmussen kissed you on the playground in the second grade. You were the only one I told when I was pregnant in college. We used to share everything. Do you really need me to tell you whether or not you push people away? Leandra, you've been pushing ever since Emi died. I just wish there was some way you'd let us get close enough to be your help!"

"This isn't about Emi!"

"Everything you've done for the past four years has been about Emi."

"Falling in love with Evan isn't." Leandra pressed her lips together, but the admission had already escaped.

Sarah's eyes widened and her lips rounded in a silent "oh."

"Look, it's just a crush. Forget I said anything." She handed her cousin the second bag and headed out of the barn.

"Wait a minute!" Sarah stepped directly in her path. "I can't forget this! How long have you felt this way? I can't believe it. Evan? I mean, I knew you guys had gotten a little cozy, but—"

"Hush! How many people do you want to hear?"

Sarah looked over her shoulder. The closest party guests were a good ten yards away, still trying to greet Squire in person. "I think you're safe," she whispered. "Most everyone here thinks you two are engaged, anyway."

"I'm glad you find this so amusing."

Sarah gave her a look. "Believe me, I'm not laughing. Actually, I sort of thought you were still in love with Jake. And you thought Evan was still hung up on Lucy."

"Half this town thought that," Leandra defended.

"Do you still?"

His voice echoed in her head. *I've been waiting years.*

She chewed her lip and shook her head.

"Then what's the problem? Where is he?"

"He left." She looked at the pile of ice inside the barrel. There was nowhere near enough to keep the keg cold. "We need more ice."

"It'll wait." Sarah stepped in her path again. "He left, and you're suddenly wanting to know whether or not you push people away."

"And you just confirmed that I do," Leandra's said flatly.

"Hey there, chickees. You know the beer will fill the glass faster if you actually use the tap." J.D. appeared beside them and studied the keg. "What's up?"

"Leandra realized she's in love with Evan."

"Sarah—" Leandra protested, but it was futile.

"Good thing since they're engaged," J.D. mused. "I'm just surprised it took so long."

Leandra did a double take, not at all certain she'd heard her cousin right. "What are you talking about?"

"The guy had it bad for you in college," J.D. said easily.

"The guy," Leandra countered, "was attached at the hip to Lucy, in case you've forgotten."

"Not in college he wasn't," J.D. drawled. "And then when you went off and fell for Jake, the *guy* was a basket case. Believe me. I saw what he was like."

Angeline joined them. "You know, the birthday boy is here." Her long brown hair was pulled back in a low ponytail and it swung over her shoulder as she picked up a cup from the stack alongside the keg.

"Leandra's jonesing for Evan," J.D. told her sister.

Leandra groaned. "So much for privacy."

Angeline shot her a sympathetic look. "What does he want to do, wait for the wedding night or something?"

Sarah muffled a laugh.

"That's not the problem," Leandra murmured, feeling her cheeks heat.

Angeline gave her a studied look. "Well, whatever's wrong, if you love him, don't let him go."

"Where are my granddaughters?" The commanding voice rang out, startling them all like they were still children. Leandra looked over to see Squire striding toward them, his arms wide. "Of course. Keeping company with the beer keg."

J.D. and Angeline reached him first, hugging his neck and kissing his cheeks. "Just waiting for you to have the first taste," J.D. assured him brightly. "And being glad that we don't have to hide out from you any longer since we arrived yesterday!"

Squire grinned. Like Evan, he had blue eyes. But beyond the name, there was no similarity in the actual color. While Evan's were as deep and vivid as a sapphire, Squire's were like a pale morning sky and just as piercing as they'd been when Leandra had been a girl. He'd always known when she was up to something, and even before he turned those eyes her way, she knew it was something else that hadn't changed. "Come here, girl," he bid. "You're not excused from hugging an old man, either. Been keeping secrets of your own, haven't you?"

Leandra reached up and hugged her grandfather. Sudden tears were clogging her head. "Happy birthday, Squire."

He squeezed her hard, practically lifting her off her toes.

Laughter from behind him announced his wife, Gloria's, presence. "Leave some stuffing inside Leandra, Squire," she ordered. "You'd think you hadn't spent the past few days fishing with the girl."

Squire let Leandra back down on her feet. He peered into her face. "You make up your mind about staying or going?"

She just shook her head, keeping her smile in place, though it took a lot of effort. And here she'd thought he was the only one who hadn't been wondering such things about her.

Fortunately, where the birthday boy went, the crowd followed, and Squire was soon distracted again by the rest of the family and the other guests. Leandra kept busy loading and unloading trays of food, freshening drinks and generally trying to hide out in the house as much as she could.

Finally, after what seemed hours, Squire had opened all of the presents that he'd protested receiving, the huge supply of food had amazingly been nearly depleted, the dance floor out under the awning had gotten well-scuffed by dancers despite the wet night, and the last of the guests who didn't have some familial connection to the name of Clay were heading down the highway back to their own homes.

Leandra's parents had departed for the house, along with her aunts and uncles, leaving only the "youngsters" as Squire referred to them, sprawled on a haphazard collection of chairs in the barn.

"You gonna edit together all the videotape Derek shot tonight for Squire?" Axel stretched his long legs out. He'd had an assortment of pretty girls on his arm all night, but for now, he seemed content to hang out with the family.

Leandra tucked the disks Derek had given her in the side pocket of her skirt. "That's the plan."

"Tell them about your promotion." Sarah pulled her feet out of her high-heeled boots and wiggled her toes.

They all looked at her. "What about your engagement?"

She felt her cheeks heat. "Evan and I will work it out." Her leaving would do that pretty effectively.

Running.

The truth of it sat heavily inside of her.

J.D. yawned. "How long do you suppose it'll be before the entire family is back in Weaver at one time again?"

"Entire family isn't here," Derek pointed out. "Lucy and Ry didn't make it."

"Last time was Leandra's wedding," Axel said. "Next time'll probably be another wedding."

Leandra pushed to her feet. She didn't want to think about weddings. "I'm going to head out. Sarah you want to come now, or catch a ride later?"

Her cousin kept rubbing her feet. "You go on ahead."

Leandra nodded. She made a tour of goodbyes and an hour later, she was sitting on the floor in Sarah's living room surrounded by four years' worth of high school yearbooks. Trust Sarah to have them all neatly in order on a bookshelf right there in the living room.

She flipped them all open, finding her picture and the accompanying statement. As a freshman, she'd still worn the braids that Evan had often tugged, and she'd wanted to be a movie star. Of course so had half the girls in her class, including Sarah. The second year of high school, the braids were gone and mascara had darkened her lashes. She still remembered the argument her father had given against the makeup and the way her mother had stood up for it. That year, she'd simply wanted to travel the world.

She flipped to the third annual. Mascara was there, still, along with shining lip gloss and a million curls down to her shoulders that had taken her and Sarah about two hours with a curling iron to put there. She'd wanted to be either president of the United States, or a psychiatrist. "Crazy," she murmured and pulled the senior book closer to her.

She opened it up, but didn't turn to her page. She turned to Evan's. That was the year that he and Lucy had broken up for a while. When he'd claimed his crush on Leandra. But by the time the senior prom had rolled around near the end of the school year, he and Lucy had once again seemed thick as thieves.

She brushed her fingertips over his image. Even then he'd known what he'd wanted.

She grabbed her cell phone and scrolled through the numbers stored in the memory and despite the ridiculous hour, she dialed. It rang several times before it was answered by a very sleepy, very female voice. "Luce? It's Leandra."

"What's wrong?" Lucy's voice was immediately more alert and alarmed.

"Nothing. Just wanted to hear your voice. Missed you at the party tonight."

She heard rustling, then a faint sigh. "You're calling at this hour because of that? I haven't heard from you since we talked last Christmas."

"I know. I'm sorry about that. And I'm fine. Or getting there, maybe. I'm sorry you had to put up with the *WITS* interview. I tried to stop it."

"Oh, that was nothing. How is Evan, anyway? I heard you two were engaged. Congratulations. He's a great guy. Always has been. Terrible about what happened with Katy, though."

Leandra closed her eyes, feeling like the biggest fraud of the year. "He's going to court to get custody of Hannah," she told her cousin.

Lucy made a soft sound. "Not surprising. Sounds like him. How…how do you feel about that? You going to be okay, I mean? Having a child to raise?"

Longing filled her, making her limbs heavy with it. "I'll be fine," she said huskily. "So, how's life with the ballet?"

"Well, I'm closing in on thirty years of age," Lucy said after a moment. "What do you think?" She let out a breath. "Don't tell anyone yet, because I haven't decided for sure, but I'm thinking about retiring from performing. Maybe open a dance school or something."

"Oh, Luce, that's great."

Her cousin laughed a little. "Yeah. There was a time when I dreamed of nothing but being on stage. But dreams change, don't they. Listen, tell everyone hello for me. I felt horrible not to make it for Squire's party, but we're debuting a new work in two weeks and things are pretty frantic here. If your wandering brings you this way, give me a shout, okay?"

"Will do." The call ended shortly after and Leandra sat there, her hand on the phone.

Wandering. Running.

Is that what her life had become?

She dialed again, this time aiming for the West Coast instead of the East, though Jake's voice was just as sleepy as Lucy's had sounded. "Hey," she greeted, feeling her throat grow a little tight. "Hear congratulations are in order."

"Lee. Yeah. I guess you heard. Evan, huh?" She heard a muffled voice in the background and guessed it was probably the future Mrs. Stallings.

"You could have told me, you know. About—what's her name?"

"Stephanie. She's one of the research lab techs. And I was trying."

She couldn't deny that fact. It had been she who'd been avoiding him. "So, when's the big date?"

"Next month. Lee, it's not just the wedding you need to know about."

She tightened her hand on the phone, something inside her already expecting the news. "Stephanie's pregnant."

"Yeah."

"Well." She let out a breath, expecting pain, but finding none. Just a sweet sadness for what they'd once had. "Congratulations again."

"I wanted to tell you—I just didn't know how. Are you okay?"

Surprisingly, amazingly, she was. "You don't have to worry about me, Jake. I'm going to be fine. I…am fine. Truly. Just…be happy, you know?"

"Yeah. You, too."

She hung up.

"Did you mean it?"

She turned with a jerk, the phone flying out of her hand, hitting the wall.

Evan was standing in the kitchen doorway.

"You scared the life out of me!"

"Kitchen door's always open," he reminded.

"Maybe I should tell Sarah to start locking it." She crossed her arms, ignoring the yearbook on the coffee table, still open to his photograph. "Where's Hannah?"

"Same place she was a few hours ago. Did you mean it? That *was* Jake, wasn't it?"

She looked at her phone that was now just pieces of black plastic littering the floor. "Yes."

"Yes…what?"

"Yes, it was Jake and yes I meant what I said. I suppose he also told you that he and Stephanie are having a baby?"

He looked startled. "No."

She supposed that was something. That he hadn't felt sorry for her over that fact, as well. "What are you doing here?"

"For some unfathomable reason, I can't seem to stay away from you."

"You don't look any too happy about it."

"Why would I be?" He stepped farther into the room, his gaze roving. "You come here for a few weeks, turn everything upside down and inside out, and will leave again as soon as you can."

She chewed the inside of her lip and nodded. "I…have a job."

"Jobs can be found anywhere, even here in Weaver."

"A career, then."

His lips twisted. No argument to that, she supposed. He nodded toward the yearbooks. "More reminiscing?"

Searching, more like. "Sort of." She pushed back her hair. "Evan, the show isn't turning out quite like I'd planned."

"Not as interesting as Jake would have been."

"There's no comparison." She held up her hand when his expression turned grim. "You're more interesting."

"Yeah." He looked disbelieving. "He deals with poodles owned by girls who are on the cover of gossip rags by day and is curing cancer by night, or something. I'm usually up to my ankles in horse droppings. You remember the weekend I brought Jake back to Weaver?"

The jump took her aback for a moment. "Spring break. We were all home from school."

"I wanted him to meet the girl I couldn't forget."

She looked away, pain spilling through her. "I didn't know. Didn't realize."

"And you never would have. If you'd been happy together, if you hadn't lost Emi, I would have gone on with life, Jake's friend, *your* friend, knowing you had what you wanted. But that didn't happen and I'm not going to keep my mouth shut this time."

"What do you want from me? Another romp in the hay?" She picked up the yearbook and pushed it at him. "I can't be what you want, Evan! I can't give you what you want!"

"You think I don't know that?" His voice rose, too. "You think I wouldn't choose just about anybody else if I *could?* My life is in Weaver, and you—you'd rather have a life anywhere but here. Hannah is a permanent part of my life no matter what happens with the custody suit."

"What do you mean by that? Is Sharon fighting you on it?"

"She hasn't decided." His jaw worked for a moment. "My attorney said I have a good chance of being awarded custody, though, since I'm supposedly getting married."

She stared. "I...see."

"I doubt it. And it doesn't matter because you're leaving Weaver, anyway."

"There you go, then." Her voice was thick. "We're better off as friends. Anything more is simply impossible. You can go find—" her voice broke "—find yourself a *real* fiancée."

He took the book out of her hand, and set it down. "You've been feeling pretty real these days. And it's only impossible if you believe it is." He caught her face between his hands and kissed her.

Her knees went weak. She caught his shoulders. But just when she would have told him anything he wanted to hear, agreed to anything he asked, he lifted his head again.

His eyes were damp. "I am in love with you, Leandra. I have been for years. But you have to decide for yourself what you want. I'm not going to beg and I'm not going to use Hannah as an excuse to try to persuade you to stay. With or without you, I'm going to do what's right for her. You were right. Seems I'm more like Drew than I thought.

"I'm finally ready to stop comparing myself to Darian— to stop expecting that I'll follow in his steps. Being like him is *not* what I want and I know it. If what you really want is *WITS* or a show of your own, then so be it. But if that all's just another way of running from the reality of Emi's death, then I hope to God you realize it before you spend the rest of your life missing out on the things that you really *do* want."

She opened her mouth, but no words would come.

And after what seemed an eternity, he finally let out a deep sigh. He pressed his lips to her forehead, then stepping over the pieces of broken phone, he walked out the front door.

He didn't look back.

Chapter Nineteen

"I wish you weren't leaving already." Emily smiled, but it was sad. "Seems like you barely just got here."

Leandra pushed her jacket into her tote, glancing at the big clock on the airport wall. She'd want the jacket for the flight back to California, since she generally froze whenever she flew anywhere. "Time flies and all that," she murmured. Truthfully, it felt as if her trip had lasted eons. Particularly the past two days, during which Evan hadn't so much as made one mention of that night after Squire's party.

It was as if he'd never visited her at Sarah's.

Never told her he loved her.

He couldn't have made things plainer. If anything were to change, it would have to be at her instigation.

"Do you think you'll make it home for Christmas this year?"

Christmas was months away, yet. "Maybe."

"Maybe. That's what you've said for the past four years. Hasn't come to pass, yet."

Her head throbbed. "Mom—"

"Oh, Leandra." Emily sighed and hugged her. "Don't mind me. I'm just missing you already."

Leandra hugged her back, trying not to cry. She hadn't expected leaving to be so difficult. Hadn't expected it to feel as if her heart was being ripped out of her. "I'm sorry I didn't spend more time with you at the farm. I should have."

Emily smoothed her hair, the same way she'd done when she was little. "Next time."

Leandra nodded. Who knew when that would be?

Her father reappeared with a bag of stuff he'd purchased at the small gift shop. "Here." He tucked it in her bulging tote, atop the jacket. "Just some chocolate and a few books."

"Thanks."

He shoved his hands in his pockets and paced the short aisle between the molded plastic seats where they sat. Leandra was aware of the look that kept passing between him and her mother.

She looked at the clock again. Soon she'd have to go through security.

Alone. Alone in life, alone in spirit. Because that was the choice she'd made.

"The stray that—" she had to force his name past her lips "—Evan saved? Fred?"

Her father lifted an eyebrow. "What about him?"

"He needs a home. Evan can't keep him because of Hannah."

"We don't exactly need another dog," Jefferson said dryly. "Given the way your mother keeps bringing them home."

Leandra looked to her mother. Who looked at her husband. "Jefferson?" That was it. That was all Emily said. Just his name.

Her dad smiled, as if that were all he'd been waiting for, and capitulated. "We'll pick him up on the way home."

If only everything were so easily solved.

She brushed her fingers through her hair. The haircut she'd needed a month ago was even more apparent now.

"When do you meet with Montrechet about your new show?" Her dad eyed her, but whatever he was thinking didn't show on his impassive face.

"Tomorrow."

Emily squeezed her hand. "You'll be wonderful, whatever you do."

"You don't look like you're celebrating the idea too much, kid."

"It's what I've been working toward for the past few years. Maybe I can really make a difference, then."

Again, a look passed between Jefferson and Emily. Leandra felt distinctly uneasy when her mother suddenly stood, murmuring something about needing a little walk. Then, even though they were surrounded by dozens of empty seats, her dad took the one that Emily had abandoned.

He stretched out his legs and sighed. "You know, it's okay sometimes to switch gears. Reevaluate what it is you want in this life. Dreams *can* change."

She started a little. Lucy had said the same thing.

"I spent a good part of my life chasing something I believed I wanted because it was easier than facing—and maybe losing—the thing I wanted even more. Are you sure you know what it is you want?"

Living up to her mother's reputation had never been particularly easy. Living up to her father's had been nigh impossible. "What I *want* is for Emi to be turning seven next year."

He sighed again and took her hand. "And that isn't going to happen, Leandra. No more than Emily wanting her parents to be back made it happen or Katy's parents wanting her back or Squire wanting my mother. But Emily found a home with Squire, and if she hadn't, you wouldn't exist. And Squire found

Gloria. If he hadn't, Belle and Nikki and all of theirs wouldn't be part of our family, too. And Evan will have Hannah. It doesn't mean we love the ones who are gone any less."

"I know, Dad. I *know.*" She pushed to her feet. "Knowing doesn't make it any easier."

Her father grimaced. "Anybody who says life is easy is full of crap. But easy or not, you just lift your chin and get to it. *That's* what makes a difference, Leandra. You don't have to go chasing down obscure documentaries the way you've been wanting in order to make a difference in this world. So if, like your mother claims, you're trying somehow to be like I used to be, then get over it. The years before I married your mother are not like *anything* I would want you involved in."

"But—"

"I'm not saying anything more about it. You want to make a difference?" He pushed to his feet, spotting Emily returning. "Make a difference in your own life. Start living it, again, instead of punishing yourself over things that can't be changed."

Her eyes burned. "I'm afraid of ruining it again."

He looked at her. "That's what makes you human, baby. What makes you a Clay—" he held out his hand toward his wife "—is going for it anyway. Seems strange for me to be the one to tell you this, since I know your mom and I have always told you to follow your dreams, but now I'm going to tell you to follow your heart."

Her eyes flooded. She'd never heard her father make an emotional statement like that. She looked at the clock. Less than five minutes to go. Get on the plane and go back to California and grab what she'd been working toward all this time. "What would I do if I stayed?"

"Whatever you want," Jefferson said simply. Then he looked beyond her. "*They* might have something to do with things if you'll let them."

Leandra turned. And there they stood.

Evan. And alongside him, looking just as wary as her uncle, was Hannah.

Leandra's fingers went loose on the tote. "Even if what I want is to use some of your horses," she murmured.

"For what? You want to get into breeding?"

She slowly shook her head, the idea so new and so obvious she wondered why it had taken her so long. "For kids like Hannah."

She missed the faint smile that touched her father's mouth. "Sounds good to me." He moved away with Emily, quietly making themselves scarce.

The tears blurring Leandra's vision didn't blind her to the way Evan held his jaw so tightly or the way Hannah clung to his leg when he started toward her.

"Hannah wanted to say goodbye," he said, his voice gruff when he stopped several feet away. "I wasn't sure we'd make it before your plane left."

Trying not to let disappointment swamp her at the reason for his presence, she crouched down and forced a smile for Hannah's benefit. "I'm glad you came, Hannah." She pointed at the sheet of paper the girl held. "Have you been drawing again?"

Hannah held the paper out. "It's for you."

Leandra's eyes burned even more. She took the paper and immediately recognized her own drawing from the day she'd watched Hannah for Evan. Only Hannah had definitely doctored it. "Thank you." The words were hoarse. "It's beautiful."

"Tell her who the people are, Hannah."

Leandra glanced up at Evan. He wasn't looking at his niece, though. He was watching her, his expression oddly intense.

"That's Evan," Hannah pointed at the picture, though she didn't let go of Evan's leg. "That's you. And that's baby Brandon."

Leandra lifted her eyebrows. "Who's Brandon?"

"The baby you gots to have with my Evan."

Not even a few weeks earlier and she would have winced at the painful idea. Now, she just felt suffocated by longing. She and Evan hadn't used any birth control when they'd made love, but she'd always been as regular as rain and the timing had been all wrong. She pressed her lips together for a moment, trying to make her tight throat work. "It's a very nice drawing, Hannah. Thank you." She stroked her hand down the little girl's head, feeling like she'd won a small victory when Hannah smiled.

Then she stood.

The clock over the gate told her it was time to leave.

She chewed the inside of her lip. Looked up at Evan. "I... Thank you for bringing her."

"I had another reason." Evan knelt down, and spoke to Hannah, clearly trying to extricate himself from her grip, but the girl had no intention of going anywhere.

He straightened again and faced Leandra. "Seems appropriate that she's attached herself," he murmured. "Since it's an indicator of the way it will be for years to come." He stepped forward, carefully moving Hannah right along with him, and the little girl giggled.

Leandra didn't have any laughter in her right then, though. "What other reason?" Her eyes searched his face, wanting to memorize every detail, knowing that no effort was really required there.

He was unforgettable.

He took her hands in his and she nearly started crying all over again at the way his warm hands shook a little. "I know you think you need to get on that plane. That you've worked hard for what's waiting for you at the other end. But I'm selfish. And I'm asking you not to go. I thought I could watch you walk away again, but I was wrong. And if I have to fight with every trick in every book, I'm going to find a way to make you stay. I want you as my wife, Leandra. I want you to have my children. But if all I can have for now is just you, in my life, then that's what I'll take." He dug in his pocket and pulled out a folded piece of paper. "I made a drawing, too."

She did laugh then, just a little, and speechless, she unfolded the paper. It was a mock-up like their yearbook page, she realized. He'd taped a snapshot of himself, which someone had taken during the shoot, onto the top of the paper. And beneath it, he'd written his statement.

I want to be with Leandra Clay.

She bit her lip. From the corner of her eye, she could see her parents standing with their arms around each other.

Nothing was impossible unless you believed it was.

She rummaged in the tote that had fallen open near her feet and found a pen. She flattened the paper on the seat of the chair behind her, wrote a line, then rose and handed it to Evan.

He looked down at it.

"She wants that, too." She whispered the words she'd written.

The page crumpled in his fist. "Are you sure? What about your promotion?"

"It doesn't mean as much as I thought it did." Her tears spilled over. "I'm not sure about a lot of things, actually. But that's not one of them. Not anymore." And for once, admitting it didn't seem so very hard after all.

Follow her dreams. Follow her heart.

How could she not have known until then that doing one meant doing the other?

She stepped toward him, closing the distance between them. And nearly lost her composure when Hannah's arm surrounded her leg just as tightly as it surrounded her uncle's. "I love you, Evan Taggart."

His gaze was fierce. "No more running?"

"Only toward you." She let out a shuddering breath. "You and whatever our life together brings us."

"Is that a proposal?"

She smiled, laughing a little, crying a little. "Aren't we already engaged?" She slid her arms around the man that she loved, the man who'd become so much more to her than a friend. "I don't want you to ever regret this," she whispered.

"Not in this lifetime," he assured her and closed his mouth over hers.

No, she thought, vaguely aware of Hannah squirming out from between them and of the cheers that were coming from the peanut gallery.

Not ever in this lifetime.

Not as long as they were together.

She cupped his face in her hands when he finally lifted his head. "Evan?"

Everything she ever wanted to see in his eyes was there. Naked and bare. "Yeah?"

"Take us home."

His smile was slow and sexy and warmed her right down to her soul. "Finally."

There was no way for anyone to ever truly know what the future would hold.

But she knew, thanks to Evan and Hannah, that she was no longer afraid to find out what *their* future would hold.

She smiled back at them both and held out her hand for Hannah. "Yes. Finally."

* * * * *

Be sure to look for Sarah's romance
as Allison Leigh continues her saga about
the next generation of the Clay family,
coming only to Silhouette Special Edition
in April 2007.

Happily ever after is just the beginning...

Turn the page for a sneak preview of
A HEARTBEAT AWAY
by
Eleanor Jones.

Harlequin Everlasting—
Every great love has a story to tell. ™
A brand-new series from Harlequin Books

S pecial? A prickle ran down my neck and my heart started to beat in my ears. Was today really special?

"Tuck in," he ordered.

I turned my attention to the feast that he had spread out on the ground. Thick, home-cooked ham sandwiches, sausage rolls fresh from the oven and a huge variety of mouthwatering scones and pastries. Hunger pangs took over, and I closed my eyes and bit into soft homemade bread.

When we were finally finished, I lay back against the blue-bells with a groan, clutching my stomach.

Daniel laughed. "Your eyes are bigger than your stomach," he told me.

I leaned across to deliver a punch to his arm, but he rolled away, and when my fist met fresh air I collapsed in a fit of giggles before relaxing on my back and staring up into the flawless blue sky. We lay like that for quite a while, Daniel and I, side by side in companionable silence until he stretched out his hand in an arc that encompassed the whole area.

"Don't you think that this is the most beautiful place in the entire world?"

His voice held a passion that echoed my own feelings, and I rose onto my elbow and picked a buttercup to hide the emotion that clogged my throat.

"Roll over onto your back," I urged, prodding him with my forefinger. He obliged with a broad grin, and I reached across to place the yellow flower beneath his chin.

"Now, let us see if you like butter."

When a yellow light shone on the tanned skin below his jaw, I laughed.

"There…you do."

For an instant our eyes met, and I had the strangest sense that I was drowning in those honey-brown depths. The scent of bluebells engulfed me. A roaring filled my ears, and then, unexpectedly, in one smooth movement Daniel rolled me onto my back and plucked a buttercup of his own.

"And do *you* like butter, Lucy McTavish?" he asked. When he placed the flower against my skin, time stood still.

His long lean body was suspended over mine, pinning me against the grass. Daniel…dear, comfortable, familiar Daniel was suddenly bringing out in me the strangest sensations.

"Do you, Lucy McTavish?" he asked again, his voice low and vibrant.

My eyes flickered toward his, the whisper of a sigh escaped my lips and although a strange lethargy had crept into my limbs, I somehow felt as if all my nerve endings were on fire. He felt it, too—I could see it in his warm brown eyes. And when he lowered his face to mine, it seemed to me the most natural thing in the world.

None of the kisses I had ever experienced could have even

begun to prepare me for the feel of Daniel's lips on mine. My entire body floated on a tide of ecstasy that shut out everything but his soft, warm mouth, and I knew that this was what I had been waiting for the whole of my life.

"Oh, Lucy." He pulled away to look into my eyes. "Why haven't we done this before?"

Holding his gaze, I gently touched his cheek, then I curled my fingers through the short thick hair at the base of his skull, overwhelmed by the longing to drown again in the sensations that flooded our bodies. And when his long tanned fingers crept across my tingling skin, I knew I could deny him nothing.

* * * * *

Be sure to look for
A HEARTBEAT AWAY,
available February 27, 2007.
And look, too, for
THE DEPTH OF LOVE
by Margot Early,
the story of a couple who must learn that
love comes in many guises—and in the end
it's the only thing that counts.

This February...

Catch NASCAR Superstar **Carl Edwards** *in*
SPEED DATING!

Kendall assesses risk for a living—
so she's the last person you'd
expect to see on the arm of a
race-car driver who thrives on the
unpredictable. But when a bizarre
turn of events—and NASCAR
hotshot Dylan Hargreave—inspire
her to trade in her ever-so-structured
existence for "life in the fast lane"
she starts to feel she might be
on to something!

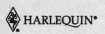
HARLEQUIN®

E V E R L A S T I N G L O V E™
Every great love has a story to tell™

Save $1.⁰⁰ off
the purchase of any Harlequin Everlasting Love novel

Coupon valid from January 1, 2007 until April 30, 2007.

Valid at retail outlets in the U.S. only. Limit one coupon per customer.

5 65373 00076 2 (8100) 0 11302

HEUSCPN0407

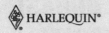

HARLEQUIN®

EVERLASTING LOVE™

Every great love has a story to tell™

Fall from Grace
Kristi Gold

Save $1.00 off

**the purchase of
any Harlequin
Everlasting Love novel**

Coupon valid from January 1, 2007
until April 30, 2007.

Valid at retail outlets in Canada only.
Limit one coupon per customer.

52607370

HECDNCPN0407

REQUEST YOUR FREE BOOKS!

2 FREE NOVELS PLUS 2 FREE GIFTS!

SPECIAL EDITION™

Life, Love and Family!

Silhouette®

COMING NEXT MONTH

#1813 MR. HALL TAKES A BRIDE—Marie Ferrarella
Logan's Legacy Revisited

Hotshot corporate attorney Jordan Hall had never worried about how the other half lived, until his sister asked him to sub for her at her legal aid clinic. He was touched by his new clients' plight—and by the clinic's steely supercompetent secretary Sarajane Gerrity. Would the charming playboy file a motion to stay…in Sarajane's heart?

#1814 THE BEST CATCH IN TEXAS—Stella Bagwell
Men of the West

Divorced physician's assistant Nicolette Saddler wasn't buying the office buzz about the new doctor from Houston. Then she caught her first glimpse of Dr. Ridge Garroway—good thing he was a cardiologist, because the younger man set her pulse racing! Alas, Ridge suffered the same condition when Nicolette was around. Now to find a cure…

#1815 MEDICINE MAN—Cheryl Reavis
For unhappy divorcée Arley Meehan, the healing began when she met captivating Navajo paratrooper Will Baron at her sister's wedding reception. But would their meddling families keep the couple from commitment?

#1816 FALLING FOR THE HEIRESS—Christine Flynn
The Kendricks of Camelot

Assigned to protect Tess Kendrick and her son, bodyguard Jeff Parker had no sympathy for the spoiled scion of American political royalty who'd ended her marriage on a whim. But when Jeff learned of her true sacrifice to save the family name from her blackmailing ex, he quickly became knight in shining armor to the heiress from Camelot, Virginia.

#1817 ONCE MORE, AT MIDNIGHT—Wendy Warren
Years ago, Lilah Owens had left for L.A. to find fame and fortune after her bad-boy boyfriend Gus Hoffman was busted. Back in town, broke and with a daughter in tow, Lilah was in for a surprise—Gus had gone from ex-con to *engaged* success story. That is, until old passions were reignited—and Gus learned that Lilah's daughter was his….

#1818 ROMANCING THE NANNY—Cindy Kirk
Widower Dan Major was Amy Logan's dream man. But falling for the boss was a no-no for the nanny, since Dan's systematic seduction seemed to be motivated by one thing only—his desire to have a loving stepmother for his daughter. His careful, by-the-book plan wasn't a substitute for true love, and Amy was holding out for exactly that….

SSECNM0207